ANDRÉ ALEXIS

WITH ILLUSTRATIONS BY LINDA WATSON

Days by Moon light

COACH HOUSE BOOKS, TORONTO

first edition

Published with the generous assistance of the Canada Council for the Arts and the Ontario Arts Council. Coach House Books also gratefully acknowledges the support of the Government of Canada, and the Government of Ontario through the Ontario Book Publishing Tax Credit and the Ontario Book Fund.

LIBRARY AND ARCHIVES CANADA CATALOGUING IN PUBLICATION

Title: Days by moonlight / André Alexis.
Name: Alexis, André, 1957- author.
Identifiers: Canadiana (print) 20189069295 | Canadiana (ebook) 20189069309 | ISBN 9781552453797 (softcover) | ISBN 9781770565791 (EPUB) | ISBN 9781770565807 (PDF)

Classification: LCC PS8551.L474 D39 2019 | DDC C813/.54—dc23

Days by Moonlight is available as an ebook: ISBN 978 1 77056 579 1 (EPUB), 978 1 77056 580 7 (PDF)

For Alana Wilcox

and it was all true in a way only the way kept changing

– W. S. Merwin, *The Folding Cliffs: A Narrative*

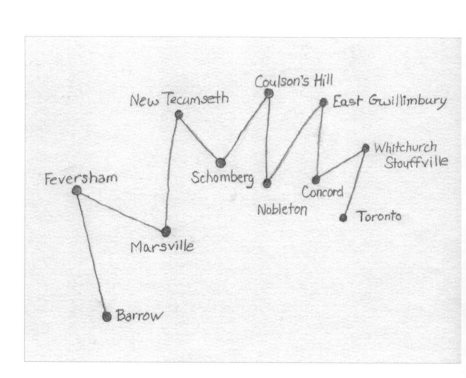

Coulson's Hill

New Tecumseth

East Gwillimbury

Whitchurch
Stouffville

Feversham

Schomberg

Concord

Nobleton

Toronto

Marsville

Barrow

August 20-27, 2017

1

TO EAST GWILLIMBURY

In August 2017, I was eating an egg and cress sandwich when Professor Bruno called to ask if I'd help him in his travels through Southern Ontario. I love watercress (*Nasturtium officinale*). It's delicious and it reminds me of my mother's garden. So, I was already in a fair mood.

Professor Bruno had been a friend of my father's. He was a kind man, one I'd known since I was a child. It would have been difficult to turn him down. The fact that his invitation came on the anniversary of my parents' death – a terrible accident on the

401 – made it doubly hard to refuse. I would take my yearly vacation from the lab and spend part of it with the professor, one of the many mourners who'd wished me well at my parents' funeral.

– I'm sure you find your parents' friends beyond boring, he'd said, but I hope you'll look in on me from time to time. It'd be lovely to keep in touch.

– Yes, I'd said.

And a year later, I was happy to show him that I'd meant it, that I was glad to keep in touch.

Professor Bruno proposed that we spend two or three days driving through the land on which the poet John Skennen had lived, the land about which Skennen had written, the land that had created the artist. The professor had spent years writing a 'literary account' of Skennen. He had all the basic facts, he said. He knew enough about the man's life to get a solid grip on the poetry. What he wanted from our trip were 'touches': a few colourful details, any anecdotes he might glean from people who'd known Skennen at different stages of his life.

– You never know, he said, where you'll find a detail, *the* detail, that'll illuminate a work.

– So, we're looking for light, I said, teasing him.

– Not just any light, my boy, he answered. We're looking for the *correct* light.

My duties: I'd carry the professor's bags, help him transcribe any interviews he did, and serve as his driver. In exchange, he insisted on paying my expenses – hotels, incidentals – and promised that I'd have time to do some botanical research. I wasn't happy about his paying my expenses. I make more than I can spend at Alpha Labs. Besides, he was doing me a favour, giving me an excuse to leave Toronto for a few days, a few days away from a city that was, at times, oppressive because I knew it too well.

But I could tell he was disappointed when I said I'd pay for myself. So, I relented.

– Thank you, I said. I'm grateful for the time away.

I was grateful for another reason, too: I'd recently heard about a plant called five fingers (*Oniaten grandiflora*) that was said to have fantastic medicinal properties – the ability to cure jaundice, for instance. Professor Bruno planned to visit Feversham, a town on the outskirts of which there was a field of *Oniaten*. So a friend of mine had heard tell anyway. I didn't believe that a plant with such qualities would be as little-known as *Oniaten* and I didn't quite believe my friend, a fellow lab tech with a strange sense of humour. But the professor's visit to Feversham would give me a chance to wander around outdoors – something that always makes me happy – while looking for a specimen of the plant.

Besides, I was sure Professor Bruno would be amusing company.

I'd be on vacation. I'd have an excuse to play at being the botanist I trained to be. I'd be distracted from my grief – my twin griefs – and we'd be visiting Southern Ontario, the countryside: the woods, fields, and farms I find calming and wonderful. If I worried about anything, it was that I didn't know the poet Professor Bruno was writing about, John Skennen. The professor didn't mind my ignorance, though.

– Alfie, he said, by the end of our trip you'll know as much about Skennen as anyone. He's a bit of a mystery.

– How so? I asked.

– Actually, Professor Bruno answered, it might be better to say he *was* a mystery. He stopped publishing twenty years ago. No one's seen him or heard from him since. Can you imagine? The talent of an angel. Gone! Like that!

As I'm sure he knew it would, his enthusiasm encouraged me from my torpor.

The professor was almost as tall as I am – six feet – but he stooped slightly. He had a full head of hair but his hair was like a contradiction: thick and youthful but white as cornstarch. He'd kept himself in good shape. He would walk for blocks – briskly, without stopping, despite his arthritis. And he looked debonair, always smiling. Not one of those big, broad smiles. A small smile, ironical. His smile made me feel as if we shared a secret. I'd felt this way about him since I was a child. His only flaw – and it wasn't so much a flaw as an occasionally misguided effort to be helpful – was that he would sometimes speak of things so learnèd my mind would fog up while listening to him. I'd never stop listening, but the professor's enthusiasm alone wasn't enough to help me with things like hermeneutics or the Freudian unconscious.

I had five days – from Wednesday to Sunday – to get ready. This was relatively short notice for work, but more than enough time to pack a few days' clothes. Not that anyone at the lab minded my going. In the year since my parents died and, yet more grief, the months since Anne decided we should not grow old together, I'd accumulated seven weeks' worth of overtime. Management at Alpha was probably relieved to grant me a few workdays along with my regular vacation. It was more difficult deciding what to do with the time before we left than it was getting days off.

In so far as I know myself, I'd say I'm cheerful and even-tempered. I like other people and I've always been sociable. The death of my parents certainly changed me. Though I knew their going would come – my father had often warned me that they would not be with me always – I felt as if I'd had no time to prepare for it. Anne's leaving had been almost as difficult, and it was more recent. I still turned to her side of the bed in the morning, anticipating her warmth, still found strands of her hair on my clothes.

The bewildering thing about grief, for me, is how difficult it makes the world to navigate. Home itself becomes foreign territory, though everything around you is familiar. For some time, none of the things I loved – trees, music, the novels of P. G. Wodehouse – had had any meaning, as if all of them had flaws through which darkness came. So, it really was a relief when Professor Bruno asked me to accompany him through Southern Ontario and a relief that I *wanted* to be around others again, *wanted* to see past my shrunken world.

We'd leave Toronto on the twentieth and in the days that followed the professor hoped to visit Whitchurch-Stouffville, Concord, Nobleton, Coulson's Hill, Feversham: places where he'd arranged to meet people who'd known John Skennen, places where John Skennen had been seen, places that were important to Skennen's poetry. I packed pants, shirts, underwear, and a mustard-coloured jacket. I thought of my mother, as I took the things she always reminded me to take: toothpaste, a toothbrush, and deodorant. I also brought my pencils, a sharpener, a kneaded eraser, and a sketchbook in which I planned to draw some of the plants I saw on our way.

Professor Bruno was surprised by my drawings.

– I had no idea you were a Leonardo, Alfie! I welcome the noble intrusions of Art!

– But I'm not an artist, I said.

It's something else that compels me to draw. I've been doing it since I was ten. Twenty-three years. I could not imagine a life without pencils, pens, inks, erasers, and sketches.

My mother used to say

– The world doesn't exist until you draw it, Alfie!

She was only teasing, but she was right, in a way. I feel as if the books I've filled with drawings are my journals. They hold my life and memories. The past rushes back whenever I open one of my sketchbooks. I remember where I was, the sensations I felt, the mood I was in – all at a glance. My first drawing was of a four-leaf clover I saw in the schoolyard at Davisville. The clover, which I'd heard brought good luck, was a kind of 'mixed signal.' I found it just before John Smith punched me in the face and I punched him back. Then again, John and I have been close friends since Grade 6, a year after I drew the clover. I'm not a mystical person, but I think of it this way: I'm drawn to flowers, herbs, and weeds, some of which I draw over and over. I feel a connection to them and, in drawing them, I allow them the place in my life they were meant to have. On the other hand, my love for plants is fairly straightforward, too. I'm attracted to their lines and curves, their structure and colour, their complex simplicity. These were the things that inspired my studies in botany, for which I've never had even a moment's regret.

Before we left, I bought the McClelland & Stewart edition of John Skennen's collected poems. I thought it might be helpful to Professor Bruno if I knew at least a little about Skennen's work. I was surprised by what I found. There were any number of love poems, some of them difficult for me to read without thinking about Anne. And there were more philosophical poems, some of which you could call light. But, overall, the poetry was gloomier than I'd expected. I couldn't see Professor Bruno in it. Of course, this could be because the first poem I read, the one that made the deepest impression, 'Rabbit and the Rabbits,' was from what the professor called Skennen's 'melancholy period,' just before he stopped publishing. In fact, it was the last poem in his final collection:

> Strange to see struggle but not what's struggled with –
> wire round your throat, head caught like a wintry
> birth. White as your mother's haunches, bloody specks
> when the rifle butt breaks your neck – a careless
> wind busy sweeping. Trees in rumpled linens.
> We who've killed you talk rosemary and onions
> while somewhere underground your family scarpers,
> running from the lumpish beings above.
> Scarpering still, they're carrying their jitters
> through my nights – along narrows, around dungeon
> corners – whiskering my dreams, their endless warrens,
> coming on like regret, vicious and remorseless –
> quick, quicker than memory in some respects.
> Caught but uncatchable, they rise unpredictably –
> digging up strange lands, hard soil, dark pitch.

The poem was well done, I guess, but I felt like I understood why he'd abandoned poetry: Skennen's talent hadn't brought him much happiness at all.

– Ah! said Professor Bruno. Now, there you're wrong, Alfie! To begin with, the object of poetry isn't the happiness or sadness of the poet. Artists do what they do because they're compelled. It's therapy that makes the patient feel much worse before it makes them feel better. If they ever manage to feel better at all! But the other thing to remember, Alfie, is that the psyche wants what it wants. You and I, untalented mortals as we are, live for sunshine. We live for the light! But the true Artist is different. For all we know, darkness may have been what Skennen needed. It may have been the very thing to bring him relief. Then again, it's damned hard to tell with poets. I've met my fair share, Alfie, and I wonder if any of them can distinguish between happy and unhappy.

The first town we visited was Whitchurch-Stouffville. We left early Monday morning, sun up and bright, the sky a light blue, the land its late-summer self: hot but forgiving. I've always loved driving in Southern Ontario, and as, that first day, we'd planned to visit two towns that are close to each other – Whitchurch-Stouffville and Concord – we were not pressed for time. I avoided the highways (the 400s) and drove instead along country roads (38, 29, etc.) that go up and down and take you past farm fields, villages, and towns.

So many things made our setting out pleasant: the smell of the land, the way cows or horses will sometimes stare at you as you pass, the farmhouses that look like broken old faces. Then, too, Professor Bruno seemed to know everything about every inch of countryside. As we drove, it was like the past and the present intertwined. He'd point out this place where, for instance, a farmer's cow had drowned in a pool of oil (1865) or that one where a bishop had taken a tumble down a hill (1903) which thereafter was known as Collar Bone Mound.

I loved the professor's stories, but then, I find it comforting to know that others have been somewhere before me. I'm not a Speke or a Bartram, not an intrepid explorer. But I do have a sense of adventure. I like to imagine I'm seeing things that those before me missed. I cherish little details. I've always been this way. My father, Doctor of Divinity as he was, liked to say that paying attention is a way of being devout. God had taken the trouble to put a spur on the ant's tibia. It was right to notice and admire His delicate work.

– Why, my mother used to say, are you giving your son excuses to be idle?

But we never considered attention idleness, my father and I, and it seemed to me, as I travelled with Professor Bruno, that the stories he told, coming as they did from paying attention – listening, not looking – were proof of devoutness, and I took great pleasure in them.

– I love hearing the old stories, I said.

– Yes, Professor Bruno said, it's good to remember that a place is more than earth and ground. It's all that earth and ground make possible! All the stories and imaginings. Goethe says: 'Wer den Dichter will verstehen muss in Dichters Lande gehen!' If you want to understand the poet, you've got to go to the poet's country. He's not wrong, not wrong at all! But I say if you want to understand a country, then you've got to go to the poets and artists, to the ones who refashion the world and make it live for their fellows. And where do these poets draw their inspiration? From earth, ground, stories, dreams, language, and history. That's what a place is, Alfie. It feeds off us while we feed off it. It's a bit of a paradox, you know, like context giving context to a context, but there you have it.

I'm sure the professor was right. But I remember his stories more than I do some of the towns and grounds we passed through, their buildings and streets. Whitchurch-Stouffville, for instance. By the time we got there, we were both happy to be out in the sun and away from the city. So, it's possible I was distracted. But the town itself, the Stouffville part, was like any number of towns in the area. It had a Chinese restaurant and a business of some sort housed behind a red-brick facade. That's about it. In trying to recall its streets, I find I'm not sure I haven't got it confused with Concord or Nobleton. In fact, there are buildings in my memory of Stouffville that, I'm almost certain, belong elsewhere.

We were there so Professor Bruno could talk to John Skennen's aunt, Moira Stephens, the last of Skennen's relatives who'd known him when he was young. Her house was at the bottom of a street that ended in a cul-de-sac. The house wasn't unusual — single storey, its front porch coming away, slightly, a few of the black tiles from its roof scattered on the front lawn — but it was painted light green. The colour shimmered and the smell of paint was strong. We were met at the door by a young woman whose hair was, in streaks, blue. She was tall and willowy. She didn't smile, exactly, but she politely said

— What do youse want?

— Ah, said Professor Bruno. We're here to speak to Mrs. Stephens about her nephew. I'm Professor Morgan Bruno and this is my travel companion, Alfred Homer.

— You're from the university? said the woman. Good to see youse! I don't think youse are going to get much out of Gram. She hasn't been herself lately, eh? But it's your own time youse are killing. Didn't you say something about a few bucks for the inconvenience?

— You must be Roberta, Professor Bruno said. I'm happy to make a contribution to your well-being.

He gave her a ten-dollar bill. She folded the bill, tucked it into her brassiere, and led us to a living room where there was a fuzzy yellow sofa whose cushions had worn down in places so that, here and there, hernias of white foam came through. There were two wooden chairs facing the sofa and, beside the entrance to the room, a faux-elephant-foot umbrella holder that held an umbrella and what seemed to be a walking stick. The room had an interesting smell, unexpectedly herbal. It smelled of basil. After a longish while, Roberta led poor Mrs. Stephens in. I say 'poor Mrs. Stephens' not to be unkind but because the woman looked tired and it didn't seem as if she wanted to be there. She was wearing a pink terry-cloth robe — strange, because it was almost as warm in the living room as it had been outside. Her grey hair, wet and sparse, must have been hastily done because you could still see the grooves the comb's teeth had left in it. She had white bedroom slippers on her feet.

— She just got up, said Roberta.

For a while, it didn't look like Mrs. Stephens would say anything. She frowned when Professor Bruno introduced himself. Then she stared at him when he asked questions about her nephew.

— When did you last see John? the professor asked. Did he ever talk to you about his poetry? Is it true that the last place anyone saw him was in Feversham?

Mrs. Stephens was provoked by the mention of Feversham. Her answer was almost a complaint.

— I don't know anything about that, she said. No one's supposed to know about that.

She moved her chair in Professor Bruno's direction.

— Why do you want to know about it? she asked.

Inspired by her sudden interest, Professor Bruno was suddenly exuberant.

— I love your nephew's work, he said. I've studied John's poems for years. I think he may be our greatest poet. Our secret Akhmatova! Our hidden Hölderlin! It was time someone wrote a literary biography — more about the work than the man, but still ... I'm looking for a few details from John's life. Things to illuminate the poetry. I'll leave the real biography to a real biographer.

Mrs. Stephens moved closer to him, her left shoulder raised to cushion her tilted head, but she didn't say anything. So, Professor Bruno went on.

— John's a wonderful poet, he said. I'm not saying he needs a biography so the poetry can be understood. His work's clear as Waterford Crystal. But I think my work brings out facets of the poetry and illuminates some of the obscurities. Not all of them! A poem needs its obscurities!

Mrs. Stephens moved her chair closer, little by little, as if she didn't have the strength to draw close at once. It seemed she wanted to hear Professor Bruno talk about her nephew. But then she inched her chair past him, pulled the umbrella (bright orange) out of the elephant's foot, and hit him with it. The blow was a surprise. Mrs. Stephens moved so quickly for an older woman. She caught Professor Bruno on the cheek with the umbrella's nib and drew blood. Before I could come to the professor's rescue — before he could defend himself — the umbrella opened on its own, an angry frilled lizard, and Mrs. Stephens started to cry. The sound of her crying was strange: the bleating of a kid but softer and more lilting and with long pauses as she drew breath.

When she could manage to speak, she cried out

— Don't you dare talk about him!

At these words, Roberta came in to see what was wrong. Finding her grandmother distraught, she tried to calm her. She wiped her grandmother's face with a tea towel and said

— There, there, Gram!

And added

— I'm sure there's nothing wrong with Uncle John.

— It's too much, said her grandmother. Don't you talk about him, either.

— I should of warned youse, said Roberta. Gram sometimes gets skittish.

She helped her quaking grandmother from the room, returning after a few minutes to say:

— She gets this way when she thinks about Uncle John, eh. Why don't youse come back tomorrow? She's not always like this. It's just sometimes she's sensitive about it, like no one's supposed to say Uncle John's name. She's got a heart of gold. Give you her last clean undies, most days. But she doesn't like to talk about certain things, poor Gram.

I thought it would be cruel to disturb Mrs. Stephens again, especially as she was sensitive about the one subject that interested Professor Bruno. But the professor, not wanting to disappoint Roberta, agreed to consider returning once we'd visited the other places on our itinerary. He held out a ten-dollar bill.

– Please take this for your troubles, he said.

Roberta refused.

– No, she said. We can't take more till you get your first money's worth. Come back when youse are done your rounds. Gram'll be feeling better by then.

Professor Bruno wanted to go on to our next town straight away. He'd found the episode with Mrs. Stephens embarrassing and wanted to put it out of mind. But I stopped at the walk-in clinic in Stouffville for a bandage and disinfectant. Mrs. Stephens hadn't done much damage, but there was blood on the professor's cheek and I'd have felt terrible if his cut got infected.

As it turned out, going to the clinic was, inadvertently, one of the most helpful things we did, not because the professor was in danger but because a sympathetic attendant at the clinic, Karen Kelly by name, unexpectedly pointed us to new details about Mr. Skennen.

– Mrs. Stephens doesn't know any more about John Skennen than I do, she said. I mean, maybe she did at one time, but the poor lady hasn't been right in the head for years. I'm not surprised she stabbed you with an umbrella. But if you want to find out about John Skennen, you should talk to my mom. She went out with him in high school.

Professor Bruno was warily enthusiastic.

– This is wonderful, he said. A real find. And to think we have an umbrella to thank for it!

Ms. Kelly's mother, Kathryn, was a surprising fount of information. She'd kept high school photos of John Skennen and seemed to remember every detail of their time together. And yet, there was little in what she remembered that you'd call remarkable. Mr. Skennen seemed to have been a normal young man, in the throes of first love – they would love each other forever, he wrote, and she was more beautiful than words could express, and he would spend his life making her happy. Except that he took poetry seriously, that he aspired to be a poet and actually became one, Skennen was not unusual.

It was strange to hear the love-elation I'd recently felt so nakedly expressed in the letters of a seventeen-year-old. It made me wonder if love, whenever it hits you, is always the same. Like the young Skennen, I couldn't help thinking about my 'beloved.' But, unlike him, I could no longer revel in the longing my thoughts of Anne brought.

Professor Bruno kept Mrs. Kelly talking for two hours and was rewarded by the discovery of a poem John Skennen had written as a seventeen-year-old. The poem was in one of the letters Mrs. Kelly had kept. She wouldn't tell us anything about its meaning, but she allowed me to transcribe it:

> Ticking tocks
> taking clocks
> before they
> hurt me,
>
> Train, unhinged,
> is what I bid
> toward me,
>
> Sheet of earth,
> I let you go
> above me

And limestone grey
is what I taught
to love me

Listening to Mrs. Kelly's memories also brought my parents to mind. What must it have been like for them, young and in love, both God-fearing, as they called it, both wanting to get out of Chatham, Ontario? They'd met in their teens, right around the same age as Kathryn Kelly and John Skennen, but their love had flourished and lived on to the end of their lives. How rare that seemed to me now.

Maybe because I had my parents in mind, it occurred to me that the young man in Mrs. Kelly's photos looked like Professor Bruno or that Professor Bruno looked like the young man: same thick hair, same strong chin, and, in one photo, the same complicit smile. The resemblance was so obvious that both Mrs. Kelly and the professor admitted it. It made me wonder if Mrs. Stephens had mistaken the professor for her nephew.

– But then why would she hit me? asked Professor Bruno. Wouldn't she be happy to see her nephew?

– You know, said Mrs. Kelly, I haven't spoken to John since we broke up, but there must be a reason he changed his name from Stephens.

– I suppose that's true, said the professor. And *Skennen* is the Ojibwe word for *peace*. I've always wondered if he ever found it.

– Oh, I don't think John ever found peace, said Mrs. Kelly. So few of us do, on this side of the lawn. Anyway, if his aunt didn't beat him with an umbrella, it would be one of the few things she didn't use. That generation liked to hit.

While we were in her home, Mrs. Kelly made sure we had lemonade – a clear lemonade with mint leaves crushed in it – and that we were comfortable and that the air conditioner was not too cold for us. Her kindness struck me. Though her living room was cool as a larder, it was still welcoming, because she was herself so generous.

Sometime later, Professor Bruno spoke of his admiration for Mrs. Kelly's beauty. I must have looked at him as if I weren't convinced. Mrs. Kelly was in her sixties, maternal in my eyes. The joints of her fingers were slightly knobby. She was thin but big-breasted so that her body looked weighed down. Her face had, I think, once been what's called 'beautiful,' but it was now gaunt and a little intimidating.

– Was she beautiful? I asked.

Professor Bruno was annoyed.

– No, she wasn't beautiful. She *is* beautiful. Her spirit is as warm as a sauna. And I mean a good sauna. Not one of those overheated contraptions where you can't breathe. I'm surprised at you, Alfie, observant as you are! You know spirit is as important to beauty as physical appearance, don't you? There's a difference between a leaf on a tree and one that's dead, isn't there?

– Yes, I said, but dead leaves are beautiful, too, aren't they?

Professor Bruno took a dark leather pouch out from somewhere in his suitcase. Our vicinity immediately smelled of moist and sweet tobacco, like tar, cinnamon, and oranges. He took out a brown pipe and, after he'd filled the pipe and lit his tobacco, he said

– I wonder what you mean by beautiful. Dead things aren't as beautiful as living ones. I mean, you can't be interested only in surfaces, can you? It'd be a great mistake if you were. I understand you artists and your *natures mortes*. You're fascinated by geometry. But all those still lifes with their skulls and flowers can't touch a well-done portrait or a vivid landscape. And do you know why? Because with still lifes you don't have to capture the spirit that animates a person or a place. It's an easier job, isn't it? I wonder if you know the story of Apelles, the Greek painter? He was drawing a horse, a running horse, and he'd got the painting's background and the horse itself perfectly. The work was going to be his greatest, except for one thing. The only detail he couldn't get right – a small detail – was the froth coming off the horse's mouth. For months, he tried everything – every brush, every way to apply paint. And despite all his skill, he couldn't get the froth right, and the fact that he couldn't get it right ruined the painting for him! His greatest painting! Ruined! Out of frustration, he took a sponge he'd been using and threw it at the canvas. It hit the painting at exactly the right place and got exactly the right effect: the froth on the mouth of the horse! I'm sure you've heard the story, Alfie, but people don't talk about the lesson in it. The living and spontaneous in the work of Art – the horse's froth – can only be caught by the living and spontaneous in the artist. True beauty, Alfie, perfection in Art, has spirit as its object and as its subject and as its substance. Do you see?

– But doesn't all Art have some of this spirit in it? I asked.

– Most works of Art, he answered, don't have enough of it to justify their existence!

– So then, are you mostly disappointed by Art, Professor?

– Oh no, he said, not at all. I live for a perfection I'll never find! That's the human condition in a nutshell, isn't it?

I wasn't sure what to say. I'm not any kind of artist. Far from it. And, where plants are concerned, I've always been happy with surfaces. The idea of perfection or even 'true beauty' had never occurred to me because I've always enjoyed what's there in front of me. I've never thought *that's a perfect lilac* or *here's the true beauty of celery*. In the same way, I wouldn't have said Mrs. Kelly was beautiful any more than I'd have said she was ugly. She was as I found her. In the end, I had no experience with separating the spirit from the thing. I wasn't even sure what the professor meant by 'spirit,' but I believed he was on to something, and it pleased me to think that one day I might understand what he was talking about.

We drove toward Concord along gravel roads. We were going to see one of John Skennen's childhood friends, Ron Brady. Mr. Brady lived on the outskirts of town on a farm, or what seemed once to have been a farm: a dilapidated barn, a stone farmhouse, fields overrun by weeds – Queen Anne's lace, mostly, the land smelling of sour carrots – the property delimited by fencing whose posts and struts were silverfish-grey.

We didn't see any dogs as we drove onto Mr. Brady's land, but his first words to us were

– Didn't the dogs greet you?

– Which dogs? asked Professor Bruno.

– My dogs, of course, he answered.

Mr. Brady was tall. His hair looked as if it had been dyed black. Recently dyed, I'd have said, because although he was in his sixties – his skin pale, the backs of his hands with faint spots on them – the hair on his head was an almost lustrous dark. In fact, Mr. Brady's hair had something defiant about it, as if it were a wig meant to challenge your conceptions of him, whatever they might be.

– It's nice to meet you, he said. Can I get you some tea?

Before we could say yes or no, he'd called his son into the room.

– Two teas, Dougal! he said.

Dougal didn't seem happy to be called away from what he'd been doing. He hesitated, then grumbled a few words I didn't quite hear. But Mr. Brady repeated

– Two teas for our guests, son.

And Dougal – a man in his forties, judging by the look of him – went from the room and came almost immediately back with two cups of tea, as if he'd made them in anticipation of the asking. This efficiency wasn't the most striking thing about him, though. Dougal was missing fingers on both of his hands. On one, half the thumb and the pinky were missing. On the other, the top of his ring finger was gone. Apropos of his son's missing fingers, Mr. Brady said

– That's what it means to live on a farm. It's a lazy man who still has all his fingers, is what I say.

He held up his own hands so we could see the places where fingers – or parts of them – had been.

– If the machines don't get you, the dogs will, he said.

Professor Bruno was impressed.

– That's nicely put, he said.

– I'm quoting Virgil, said Mr. Brady. A free translation I made of 'The Georgics.'

As well as being John Skennen's friend, Mr. Brady had been a poet in his own right.

– I didn't start out wanting to be a farmer, he said. That was my dad's business. Me and John, we wanted to be in a rock 'n' roll band when we were kids. Then he started writing words for songs and, next thing you know, we're reading Thomas Wyatt and all these guys who wrote madrigals. We were ... what? Eleven? Twelve? But I can still remember some of them – *Pastime with good company I love and shall until I die grudge who lust but none deny so God be pleased thus live will I ...*

– That's by Henry the Eighth! said Professor Bruno.

– Yeah, I guess it might be, Mr. Brady answered, but I don't remember the names as much as the poems. Strange, eh? For me, poems are like people's faces: I always remember faces even when I don't remember names.

— Was John always a good poet? asked Professor Bruno.

— Oh, yeah. Always. But maybe that isn't the way to put it. John could have been good at anything he wanted. But the poet thing came to him and he lived it from the moment it hit him. All his poems weren't good but they were always poems, you know what I mean? I wrote poems as bad as his and maybe a few just as good, but the mask never fit me. Not that being a farmer really fits me, either. But I'm okay with how it doesn't fit. You understand?

I think Professor Bruno understood. He nodded and said yes. But I didn't understand at all. Did John Skennen choose to be a poet or was he born a poet? I didn't want to get in the way of two men talking poetry, but I was curious. So, I asked Mr. Brady what he'd meant.

— It's a hard thing to explain, he answered. John liked to say poetry chose him, and I know what he meant. But it was more like playing at something you're good at. He was a natural.

— But you said he was good at a lot of things, didn't you?

— Nice to be around people who pay attention, said Mr. Brady. But I'm not sure I can say it any other way. It's got to do with destiny and if you believe certain people were made for certain things. John wasn't any happier being a poet than he would have been anything else. He was born unhappy. But he accepted poetry was his destiny, so all this talk about whether he was any good had nothing to do with it, as far as he was concerned. Even if he'd been a bad poet, he was destined to be a poet and he knew it the way you know where your hands are in the dark. Do you believe *you're* destined for something, son? If you do, I hope it's something you're good at.

He held up his hand with the missing fingers.

— Then again, he said, someone's got to be the farmer with missing fingers, a dead wife, and an ungrateful son.

From the kitchen, evidently listening, Dougal shouted

– I'm not ungrateful!

– It's a fascinating idea, said Professor Bruno. Did John believe in destiny?

– Yes, he did, said Mr. Brady. That he did, for sure. He used to say he knew how he was going to die as clearly as how he was going to live.

– You think he's dead? asked Professor Bruno. No one's ever told me for certain he was dead.

– Oh, said Mr. Brady. I know John's dead the same way you know when someone's left a room. You can't be as close as we were without there being some kind of connection. I'll tell you what, I even know the minute he died. It was in the days when my wife was still alive and she was in the kitchen cooking. And I was in the living room here, watching TV. I can even tell you what I was watching: *Kojak*, the show with buddy who's like a cue ball. And all of a sudden Marjory says, 'Answer the door!' Now why in the heck am I going to answer the door when there's no one there? I'm right near the door. She's all the way in the kitchen. There's no point me getting up. But she says it again – 'Answer the door!' – and I'm thinking, 'Well, maybe I was listening to *Kojak* a little too loud.' You understand? So, I get up and open the door. And it's like I thought, no one there. I was about to curse the old lady when I turn around and right where I was sitting – that's where John's sitting. I just assumed he and Marjory were playing a game on me. So, I start talking to him like it's no big deal. I haven't seen him for years, but I'm not going to be the one that cracks. But he doesn't say anything. He just sits there looking at me. And I'm getting kind of irritated, but at the same time I know something's wrong. Then he looks at me and points to his watch. And I can see it's nine-twenty. Makes the hairs on my arm stand up, just remembering.

Mr. Brady pulled up his sleeve and, from where I was sitting – a few feet away – I could see the hairs on his arm standing up on goosebumps.

– What happened then? Professor Bruno asked.

– I don't know, Mr. Brady answered. The dogs started barking. I must have looked away for a second. When I looked back, John wasn't there anymore.

– But how do you know that's the moment he died? the professor asked.

– Well, I'll tell you. When we were kids we were both a little obsessed with death – the way kids are – and we both swore that whoever died first, he'd come back and tell the other what death was like. I guess the dogs must have interrupted him, but I knew what John meant when he showed me the time. It wasn't something I could get wrong.

– But am I right, the professor asked, that he disappeared?

– You're very right, said Mr. Brady. But I hope you're not looking for him.

– Why?, I asked.

Mr. Brady smiled.

– It's bad luck, he said. Listen, people around here believe all sorts of things. When John died, he just disappeared. So, you can imagine the rumours. For a while there, it was so bad you couldn't read poetry in Simcoe County without someone making the sign of the cross if they heard you. To ward off the devil. It was mostly in fun, but John's become a bad omen.

– We're not looking for him, Professor Bruno said. Heavens, I don't know what I'd do if we found him. I'm interested in his poetry. I'm a critic, mostly. I only want a few biographical details. Enough for human interest. And it's more difficult to get those if the subject's around. So, no, we're not looking for him.

– John used some of his life in his poems, said Mr. Brady. A bio's not useless. But the important thing was always the poetry. Listen, I'm glad there's interest in his work. I thought poetry'd died out. The young don't know enough about it to keep the traditions alive.

These last words seemed to have been said pointedly. I thought Mr. Brady was talking about my generation when he mentioned the young. And I was about to say he was right, when I noticed Dougal had come into the room and it occurred to me that Mr. Brady's words – though they were directed at 'the young' – were likely meant for his son. Dougal must have thought so, too, because he said

– Stop saying that! Just because we write differently doesn't mean we don't know the traditions. You're so proud of your stupid stuff: *The cow, the old cow, she is dead; it sleeps well, the hornèd head!* To hell with that. I know as much about poetry as you!

– Oh? What poetry do you know? Mr. Brady asked. Teach me. Dougal sneered.

– Roses are red, violets are blue. You wretched bastard, fuck you!

– There, said Mr. Brady. You just proved my point. Your insult doesn't even scan.

Father and son were suddenly angry, both of them red-faced.

We had come at the wrong time, the professor and I. We'd interrupted an argument that now flared up again. Our visit was like the time between a match being struck and its cap catching fire. Professor Bruno must have thought so, too. We stood up at the same moment.

– You should apologize, Mr. Brady said to Dougal. You wouldn't want these people thinking you were raised in a barn.

– Why should I apologize for you being a bastard? Dougal answered.

I thought then that it would be polite to leave father and son to work things out. I couldn't imagine speaking to my father as Dougal had spoken to his, but neither could I imagine my father expressing such scorn for me. I excused myself and went out the front door. I assumed Professor Bruno was right behind me. But I was wrong.

As I stepped out the door, the sun was bright and the air was clear. It was warm, but I felt a cool breeze. Not a squamish but something like the opposite of a sirocco: a cool wind from the west. It was also quiet. So quiet that, as I walked to the car, I heard nothing. No wind, no call, no birdsong. Not even the three large white Argentine mastiffs that came up behind me.

How impressive they were! Their movements were so coordinated, it was as if the three dogs were one. That I heard them at all, in the end, was their doing. One of them growled, low and menacing. And when, frightened, I turned to face them, they growled in a more suggestive way. I had two impressions simultaneously: that the dogs were being cautious, lest Mr. Brady be alerted to their plans, and that I was being told to run. It was a strange moment, but I didn't have much time to think about its strangeness. I had a second to consider whether I should try to pet one of them.

Then the largest dog rushed me, biting my upper thigh so that, had I been even slightly better endowed, I'd have lost part of my penis. I was lucky in another way, too. Though the dog bit me and it hurt, the other dogs did not at first join the fray. They waited, I guess, to see the damage their companion could inflict. Also, I was bleeding but the dog had caught more of my pants than my flesh, so that a great swatch of fabric was torn away when it shook its head. I thought then that running was my best option. And despite my wounds, I did very well. I reached the car. If I'd had the keys to the car in my hand, I'm almost certain I'd have escaped further bites. I jumped onto the hood of the car, followed closely by the dog who'd bitten me, and there it bit me again, catching an expanse of my jacket before I slid off the hood and ran for the fences. This fired the other dogs up. All three now came after me and, in a manner of speaking, they lost their inhibitions, growling and snarling like they were out for blood. Which, to be fair, they got. One of them caught the leg of my pants, and I fell on ground covered by Queen Anne's lace, the smell of it like carrots, of course, along with something indefinable but poisonous and alive.

Maybe because I thought I was about to die, I felt quite cheerful. Not that I wanted to die, but that I had been given a last look at a world I loved: the countryside I'd visited with my parents when my father gave his guest sermons at churches in the area. Everything around me was wonderful, from the raw blue sky to the dark earth I'd disturbed in falling, from the snarls of the dogs to the sensation of their breath on my skin. I was bitten on the arms and legs a few more times before I heard Mr. Brady call, as if from far away:

— Laelaps! Chester! Melba! Leave it!

I take it the dogs were well-trained because, at the sound of their names, they eventually stopped biting me. One of them held on to my arm awhile, as if caught with food in its mouth and, ashamed to be seen eating, was unsure whether to spit out what it had or go on chewing. But they all retreated, running to Mr. Brady as if looking for some sort of reward.

My pants and jacket were badly torn and I was bleeding, but I didn't think I was in danger, reassured as I was by the reactions of the Bradys and Professor Bruno. None of them seemed at all concerned about my injuries. The first thing Dougal said as he helped me up from the ground was

— You're okay. It's not that bad.

And although I was in pain, I was grateful for his words. Mr. Brady then said

— I don't know what got into them. They've never done anything like this before.

As if seconding Mr. Brady's point, the three dogs sat up with their pink tongues lolling, looking amiable. Professor Bruno said

— I've seen worse wounds than these, Alfie, but I guess you'd better change your clothes.

— I think I should go to the hospital, I answered.

— Why? asked Mr. Brady. You've only got a few scratches!

I thought he might be worried that I was angry at him or his dogs, so I said it was only a precaution.

— I suppose caution's a good idea, said Mr. Brady, but you couldn't get me into one of the hospitals around here if I wasn't dying. I don't trust them.

I thanked him for the warning, but I clung to the idea of having my wounds tended. And, after hasty farewells, we were off, Professor Bruno and I, on one of the most uncertain rides I've ever taken.

I was uncomfortable in my wet clothes. In places, my shirt and pants clung to me like a second skin. I was in pain because some of the dogs' bites had been deep and burned when I moved, as if the saliva were a toxin. Then, too, I felt light-headed and I forgot to ask directions to the nearest hospital. I should not have been driving. But, maybe because I was in shock, I'd accepted the idea that I wasn't badly hurt and, besides, Professor Bruno could not drive. So, it was up to me, in any case.

Professor Bruno must have realized that I was not in a proper state of mind when I (unintentionally) ran through my first stop sign. It seems I ran through a number of them, and the professor was amused by this afterwards, but at the time it must have been harrowing. He sat beside me with a crooked smile on his face, his briefcase in his arms like a flotation device. Also, while trying to stay calm or trying to keep me calm, he began to tell me about Nature. It was mostly about shores and stars, but I admired his composure, his repeated efforts to keep me focused.

But then he got stuck on the difference between the Latin word *Natura* and the Greek word *Phusis*. The distinction was something he'd taken from a German theologian. Both words are translated as 'Nature' but, according to the theologian, the Greeks made no distinction between the human and the natural worlds, while the Romans viewed themselves as separate from Nature. I remember all this clearly, not because it was interesting but because (at least in my mind) Professor Bruno kept repeating the words *Natura* and *Phusis* as if they had some special force. He shouted the word *Natura*, for instance, as I drove through a stop sign and crossed the median.

Under normal circumstances, I doubt I'd have understood a thing. But, despite my light-headedness, the professor's words did reach me. They may even have kept me awake. Because, as I drove, I became convinced there really was no difference between myself and the world drifting by – ochre farm fields, greyish telephone poles, pale blue sky, trees in clumps of four or five, yellow signs showing where intersections were hidden.

At times, I felt such exhilaration that I imagined I could not die. And I drove on with little more than a vague feeling I was heading north, as we went past Strange, Happy Valley, Kettleby, and Ansnorveldt. I had never had such a strong sense that – as my father might have said – I was dust and my return to dust would be a great arrival as much as it would a departure. I felt indistinct from the ground on which we were driving.

It's a wonder we survived the half-hour drive.

Another wonder is how I ended up in an emergency ward in East Gwillimbury. I held on to consciousness just long enough to get us to a hospital. But I must have passed out as soon as we reached the parking lot of Our Lady of Mercy Health Centre. The professor later told me he thought we were lucky to reach the place. And I agreed. It would have been terrible if I'd passed out somewhere along the road. It felt, though, as if I had been guided to East Gwillimbury – an otherworldly feeling, a feeling made stranger by my coming to on a gurney, blood flowing into me from a sack suspended on a transfusion stand. I was more or less naked under a sheet. They'd left my socks on.

Our Lady of Mercy unnerved me. Because I have a fear of hospitals. Because, when I was a child, I spent months in Toronto Western watching my mother go through chemotherapy. Because the look and smell of hospitals remind me of being scalded by boiling water. I have no good memories of hospitals, and Our Lady of Mercy was not much different from others I've been in.

There were panels of white Styrofoam on the ceiling above me. In a gap among the panels were tubes of fluorescent lighting, darkened where their pins entered their holders. The light from the tubes was inconsistent – white, yellowish, blue. I had time to notice all this because I was on my own for quite a while. I didn't want to make a fuss but, after what felt like an hour, I finally called out.

– Can someone help me?
– Oh, a nurse answered, you're awake!
The woman had a freckled face with high cheekbones and her hair was red. She seemed so surprised, I wondered if my regaining consciousness was an unexpected turn of events.

– You lost a lot of blood, she said, and since you're here to have your tonsils out, we wanted to make sure your levels were good.

– Why are my tonsils being taken out? I asked.

– I guess there's something wrong with them, she said. People don't usually have them out otherwise.

I admitted this was true. But I expressed my reservations. I'd never been bothered by my tonsils.

– I think there's been a mistake, I said. My tonsils haven't given me trouble. I was bitten by dogs.

– Well, there you go, she answered. The dogs probably made your tonsils worse. That's how trauma works sometimes. But your gurney being in this place means you're ready for a tonsillectomy. We don't tend to make mistakes about these things, you know.

– But the dogs didn't get me by the throat, I said.
She said

– The doctors might have found you needed a tonsillectomy while they were treating your wounds. Wouldn't it be better to have your tonsils out now, while you're already a little injured?

– Could I see the doctor? I asked.

– I think it's better we don't disturb Dr. Flew while he's getting ready to take your tonsils out. Don't you agree?

She was polite, but I felt she'd been encouraged by my tone, maybe thinking I was unsure about my tonsils. We went back and forth like this, each of us expressing our side of the matter.

And, to my surprise, I was suddenly engaged in a pitched battle of politeness, those kindly – but ferocious – skirmishes that are so common in our country: each side trying to polite the other into submission. I prefer these sorties to the open arguments that happen in the United States. But I felt that, the battle being for my tonsils, it was important that I win. So, I asked again and again if she was certain I'd been left in the right place, seeing as I did not want an operation if it could be avoided.

Finally, she said

– Mistakes do happen. I'll look into it for you. Would you like that?

I was relieved and, thanks to the blood transfusion, I felt more or less myself again. The only things missing were my clothes or, at least, pyjamas so I could walk around. Without them, I was trapped on my gurney and, after a while, I fell asleep.

I woke when the nurses came for me. They were taking me to the operating room or, rather, to a place beside the operating room where the anesthesiologist would put me under.

– I don't need an operation, I said. I was bitten by dogs, that's all.

– You came in for a tonsillectomy, one of the nurses said. You can't just change your mind.

I insisted there'd been a mistake. I tried to get up from the gurney, but, in the end, what saved me from a tonsillectomy was chance. My gurney passed by a public waiting area on its way to the operating room and, despite my distraction, I saw Professor Bruno reading a book. I called his name as loudly as I could and he heard me.

The nurses were just as suspicious of the professor's words on behalf of my tonsils as they'd been of mine. But the weight of two testimonials must have instilled some doubt. So, they did a little digging around. They discovered then that my name was in fact Alfred Homer, as I'd repeatedly told them, not Arthur Helmers, and that they'd got my name wrong when I was admitted to the hospital. The other thing that saved me from a tonsillectomy was the discovery that Arthur Helmers had died from his infection.

– I told you it was serious, one of the nurses said.

For a moment, I wondered if they'd take my tonsils, anyway, as a precaution. But I was conveyed to a ward and, eventually, my suitcase was given to me.

I'd have liked to leave at once but there were papers to sign and apologies to be heard. At some point, I was famished because I hadn't eaten for hours. So, when one of the nurses gave me a pomegranate she'd brought for her own dinner, I was grateful. More than that, her kindness struck me as a good omen. I was reminded of my father's idea that the beginning of a trip casts its shadow forward, that it influences the trip itself. I remember thinking that, despite the small misunderstandings we'd encountered, the day had been a good one.

I could tell that Professor Bruno, who sat with me in the ward, was pleased I was out of danger.

– I hate to think what might have happened to you, dear boy, if we'd had an accident. I'm an old man. My death would have meant nothing. But you, Alfie, you still have your life in front of you. It would have been a tragedy.

His spirits were further lifted when I was discharged. He joked that the dogs we'd encountered were like Cerberus, the three-headed guardian of Hades, and thanked me for protecting him from them.

– The good news, he said, is that we've got past Cerberus. That's a rare feat, Alfie. Only Hercules and Orpheus have done it! The bad news is that, from now on, we'll be travelling through the underworld.

He smiled and patted my shoulder.

– God knows how we'll get out, he said, but at least we'll talk to the glorious dead!

I was on the edge of sleep again, the stress of nearly losing my tonsils having tired me out.

— We're going to Hell? I asked.

— No, no, no, he said. The underworld is the domain of Hades, the unseen. No punishment involved! Unless you count an eternity of talk as punishment. Which I do not!

I wasn't sure what to think about Hades or what to feel about it. I certainly wouldn't have minded talking to the dead, to my mother and father, above all. I had so many questions to ask them, so many things I would have liked to tell them.

I closed my eyes while listening to the professor's voice.

And I fell asleep while waiting for more paperwork, for the right paperwork to be brought to me. The hospital wanted official reassurance that I wasn't angry, I suppose. And I wasn't. I was grateful that nothing irreparable had been done to me. Despite my bites and bruises and the threat to my tonsils, the thing that had unnerved me most was Our Lady of Mercy, the hospital itself. Not just its clean surfaces and sceptic undertone but its banks of lights, long halls, and peach walls: endless passages to unpleasant rooms.

2

THE CITIES OF THE PLAIN:
NOBLETON AND COULSON'S HILL

It sounds crass, but I sometimes find my province difficult to understand. This was especially true on my travels with Professor Bruno. It was partly because our days were full of unexpected details, things I hadn't seen before, and partly because my fellow Ontarians, while kind, were peculiar beyond what I'd remembered of them.

In Nobleton and Coulson's Hill we spoke to two people who'd known John Skennen personally: Brigid Flynn, a writer, and Peter Henderson, one of Skennen's friends. Professor Bruno had corresponded with Ms. Flynn, an old friend of his, and as we were travelling in her vicinity, he wanted to spend a few hours with her. Mr. Henderson was a different story. The professor had neither met nor corresponded with the man. But he'd heard, through Ms. Flynn, that Henderson had been a friend of Skennen's. And, in fact, she had arranged a meeting between Mr. Henderson and the professor.

As we drove into Nobleton to speak with Ms. Flynn, we saw that the town was decked in red crepe, bright waves with troughs and peaks, stuck on the facades of the buildings. There were banners that hung across the main street, welcoming tourists and proclaiming the celebration of Pioneer Days.

I was glad we'd come when we had. I've always loved parades and public celebrations, the feeling you have of being among friends though you're with strangers. That said, Nobleton's festivities were unique. The townspeople – those we saw on the streets, anyway – carried the tools of the pioneers around with them. I mean, even those who weren't dressed as pioneers. And it was amusing to see men in business suits carrying staves or axes or, in one case, a briefcase and a rusty adze.

– What a lovely town, Professor Bruno said.

I agreed with him.

– Of course, I'm biased, he said. I grew up a few miles from here.

I hadn't known this about Professor Bruno. I'd always imagined him as coming from Toronto. It was there that I'd met him, there that he'd lived all my life. And the man was an academic, something I associate with universities and cities. Yet, for the professor, Nobleton was a homecoming of sorts. He knew the town well. And although it had changed in innumerable ways since he'd lived on its outskirts, the professor recognized a number of townspeople and understood Nobleton's traditions. It was he who explained to me the significance – the subtle details – of the house burning we would see that night. And he insisted we stay to watch it.

It was a pleasure seeing Professor Bruno in his 'original element,' as he called it. I could feel him relax. He was suddenly delighted by the world around us, the usual world: bakery, bank, schoolhouse, church. There was nothing we hadn't seen before, but, judging by the professor's high spirits, everything was new by virtue of being old. Knowing that John Skennen had come from a similar town, I thought I understood why the professor loved the man's work. When he read a poem like 'Johnson Grass,' which he'd memorized and often recited, he must have known the very fields Skennen wrote about. They were not as hypothetical for the professor as they were for me.

> When I was six, crick-side fields swayed on windless
> days, even. Johnson Grass, top-heavy, bowing
> while white elms let birds go in handfuls, like grain,
> and moths sewed their larvae up in birches –
> the fields and I, summer-long we shared our secrets.
> When I was eighteen, grasses stood up after
> hard rain – stern and dark from plunges in the mud.
> Not like grass at all – defiant, unbending –
> as shrews rose, wet and confused after the flood.
> I kept my own counsel then. Fields did not matter.
> Now I'm thirty-three. I have nothing to hide.
> I've worn out the wishes sung in churches
> and don't long for paradises to profane.
> I'm through at last with all kinds of knowing.
> The fields, close again, think of me less and less.

I enjoyed being in Professor Bruno's world. It gave me a more complete view of him. I couldn't help wondering, though, what had changed him from a farm boy to a literary scholar.

– Back then, he answered, I hated farms and cows. My dad was a dairy farmer, you know. We had to get up at five in the morning to milk the cows. I was thrilled the first time I read a book on my own. It was *Eagle of the Ninth*! I read that book so many times my mother burned it, because she assumed I was doing something unhealthy. But Roman Britain was as far away from milking cows as I could imagine. And after she burned my copy, I read everything I could get my hands on. I haven't looked back since.

– Were your parents disappointed? I asked.

— I never thought about it, he said. Not till these last few months, anyway. Now, I suppose, I'm the right age to think about farms and parents. That sort of thing. And this book about John Skennen lets me do just that. I go back to my childhood through literature. There's a lesson in that, Alfie: Londinium and Roma are never as far from Southern Ontario as you might think!

I took the professor's point, but his attitude brought up a tricky question: had he written this book to better understand Skennen's work or to revisit his own past? A little of both, no doubt, but as it would have been unkind to suggest his motives were unclear, I kept this question to myself.

Ms. Flynn was the most famous of the people I met through Professor Bruno. In fact, she was the only one I'd actually heard of. She and the professor had known each other since their twenties. 'Well, that's to be expected,' said the professor. Meaning: the two of them being around the same age and both being interested in literature, a thing that interested very few around Nobleton, it was natural that they should gravitate toward each other. Over the years, they'd flitted in and out of each other's lives, and this, our visit, was a way for him to reconnect with an old friend.

Before we entered her home, Professor Bruno warned me not to stare at Ms. Flynn's father. When I asked why, he reminded me what had happened to the family. Brigid Flynn had been a respected novelist — more literary prizes than you could shake a stick at, said the professor — when her agent advised her to write about the abuse she'd suffered as a child.

Ms. Flynn was destitute despite her literary renown. She was on the verge of abandoning writing. She was desperate. The problem was, she'd had a wonderful childhood and adored her parents, a situation that put her at a disadvantage where childhood abuse was concerned.

I thought the agent's suggestion was unscrupulous. But Professor Bruno wasn't so sure. He understood the agent's position.

— Look, Alfie, he said, it's what people wanted to read. In the early 2000s, the public was obsessed with all sorts of abuse. The worse the better. And they insisted it be real, too. Worse, they were hurt when it wasn't. Once Brigid agreed to write about the abuse she'd suffered, she had to pretend it was true. I admit the situation wasn't ideal, but when life refuses to hand you lemons, it's hard to make lemonade, you know.

Rather than abandon her profession, Ms. Flynn wrote a 'memoir' called *Take Me to the Water* that depicted the author's brutal childhood, a childhood during which the author was — beginning at age nine — physically and sexually abused by her 'dark-haired' and 'endlessly grimacing' father, abetted by a drunk and careless mother. It also depicted the author's recovery from her childhood. And it ended on a note of forgiveness and reconciliation at the deathbed of the now toothless dad.

Ms. Flynn published the book anonymously, but it was such a success that its fans obsessively sought the book's real author. And when they discovered that Brigid Flynn was the writer, many of them were unpleasantly surprised to find that her father — whose depravity had been so vividly described — was still alive, still able to hurt his daughter.

After that, it was Mr. Flynn who was surprised. He hadn't read *Take Me to the Water*. His daughter hadn't told him anything about it. She'd assumed her anonymity would protect them both. To make matters worse, Mr. Flynn's life grew slowly unpleasant, so that, after a while, he was sure he'd done something wrong but he couldn't decide when he'd done it, as when you pull a muscle that, days later, begins to hurt and hurt until the pain becomes difficult to bear. It seemed as if, without warning, people he knew well — had known for decades — greeted him coldly. Then churchgoers avoided him after mass. And the priest — Father Alanko — persisted in asking him if there were 'sins' he wanted to confess. By the time a neighbour knocked him down on Main Street, Mr. Flynn (now completely bewildered) was convinced he deserved punishment, though he'd have liked to know what it was for.

Mr. Flynn was such a loving father that, when he learned what his daughter had done, he blamed himself for taking the attacks on him too seriously. Above all, he was proud of Brigid, proud of her talent as a writer, a talent made obvious by the hatred some of his neighbours now felt for him. He would not let her confess publicly to what she'd done. He would not have his daughter face the humiliation.

Her father's love for her did nothing to ease Brigid's feelings of guilt. If anything, it made them worse. But his love and admiration did, at least, help Mr. Flynn deal with Nobleton. When strangers were aggressive with him, he felt as much pride as if he'd been the author of *Take Me to the Water* himself.

– Just think, he'd say, my daughter turned people against me who've known me for years!

The most striking thing about Mr. Flynn – aside from the fact that he himself told us his story with good humour – was the affection he showed us on first meeting. He was a slightly oversized man with bright red hair, though he was in his eighties, and green eyes. One of his eyes looked as though it had been recently punched, the area around it puffy and bruised. When we met him, he was wearing a black kimono on which bright red birds were sewn: a gift from his daughter, who'd recently returned from Japan. The kimono was too big but it suited him.

The Flynns' home had shag carpeting everywhere, bronze-coloured and thick. On the walls were framed paintings and sketches inspired by Irish legends. There were portraits of a pooka in ruffs, a banshee in a hooded cape, and a dullahan in a black tuxedo, his head held before him like a small wheel of cheese on which a mouth had been drawn in lipstick. There were also portraits of young red-haired women. In one, the young woman stood at the edge of a cliff and looked down on a moonlit valley of lakes, fields, and farmhouses. I assumed the painting was set in Ireland, but it was a faithful depiction of the Niagara Escarpment near Beamsville.

– People always forget how beautiful the land is, Ms. Flynn said.

– How beautiful and strange! said Professor Bruno.

Knowing what the Flynns had gone through with *Take Me to the Water*, I thought they'd be wary of others. But they were both lively and good-humoured to the point of being mysterious, the way people are when they've shared a joke they won't share with you. Ms. Flynn was like a younger, female version of her father. But she was more coarse than he was. When she greeted Professor Bruno, she said

– How you doing, Doc?

And she referred to her neighbour as 'the cunt from Belleville.' As in

– I see the cunt from Belleville is finally mowing his lawn!

Which is what she said after greeting us, pointing to a meek-seeming man in a checked shirt who was cutting the grass of the property beside the Flynns.

Professor Bruno seemed not to notice Ms. Flynn's language. I assumed this was because he knew her. But I was taken aback. I'd never heard a woman use the c-word so casually. And I found it surreal to be greeted that way. Then, too, I'd always been taught that it's the inarticulate who resort to bad language. That was my father's view. He felt a kind of pity for those who swore. But it would have been strange to call Ms. Flynn inarticulate. She was esteemed for her use of language. So, Ms. Flynn was a living contradiction to me. When I later mentioned my feelings to the professor, he was amused.

– She's been that way since she was eighteen, he said. I used to think she had Tourette's. But she doesn't always use profanity, you know. She just likes to shock people and this is the easiest way. But you have to remember, Alfie, that writers are obsessed with words, and there are some words whose roots bring earth up from the ground with them. Like pulling weeds from a garden.

That's something an American poet used to say about profanity. And I suppose he's right. Some words are satisfying to pull up.

This was an interesting explanation – maybe even true. Of course, I'd never really thought about words. If I'd had to compare them to anything, I suppose it would have been to cards played in a game I don't always understand. I prefer pictures and drawings to words. Whenever Ms. Flynn swore, I was startled despite myself, a reaction she seemed to find amusing. I'm sure she thought I was a hopeless prude but, despite that, she was kind to me. She was kind to both of us, generous with her time and considerate.

When Ms. Flynn and the professor had finished talking about people they knew and recent scandals troubling the literary community, they got on the subject of John Skennen. She hadn't known him well. They'd met at a Writers' Union general meeting – in Thunder Bay, was it? – both of them young. Well, John could only have been young, she said, since, as far as she knew, he never attended another AGM. He'd been nice to her and he'd been handsome. She hadn't slept with him, though.

– In my experience, she said, the most attractive men are always screwed up. Egos like ocean liners. And rampant Oedipal complexes.

Tongue in cheek, her father said

– That sounds like the last fellow you went out with.

– You mean the cunt from Belleville? she asked.

– I wish you wouldn't call him that, Brigid. It's vulgar.

– But, Daddy, that's what he calls himself!

Mr. Flynn changed the subject.

– I'll tell you one thing about John Skennen, he said. Everybody and his dog has a story about him. I can't count the number of times someone's told me they saw his ghost just after he died. And they all tell you the exact time he died, too. One woman – you remember Mrs. Lennon, Bridge – swore he died at seven-forty in the morning and she knew that for sure because he came to her while she was making sandwiches for her kids one Monday. She says he pointed to a clock and she couldn't tell if he was telling her about the kids needing to catch the bus or what. Then he started swinging around the kitchen like he was hanged, his feet off the floor and all, and she got the message.

– I've heard that story, too, said Ms. Flynn. I've heard it a hundred times from a hundred people, and it's never the same time of day when he shows up. Everyone who tells you about it believes it, too.

– Oh, said Mr. Flynn, I've only ever heard one Skennen story I believe. And I believe it because it happened to June and Jenny Wilson. You couldn't find two girls with their heads on straighter. Neither of them talks much. And when they told me what happened, it wasn't like they were trying to be interesting. We were talking about John Skennen and I asked if they'd heard any stories. June said, no, they hadn't heard anything. But they'd seen something. It was when they'd just got married, both of them, and they'd taken their honeymoon together in Sarnia, because they got a good deal on the hotel and they could all go out to some fancy restaurant across the river. So, the second afternoon they were there, the husbands went to Port Huron to do some gambling and the girls were taking an afternoon rest. June gets up before Jen and goes into her sister's room and what does she see? Well, sir, John Skennen is on top of her sister and they're doing what married women are meant to do with their husbands. And from the look of things, the two were awfully passionate. Skennen hadn't even had time to unbelt his pants. So, of course, June screams. And when she does, Skennen disappears and Jen wakes up. And that was that. For years, June thought she'd been seeing things because that's what Jen told her. But it's years later and Jen finally admits she'd been having a dream when June interrupted her. And in the dream, she was having sex with John Skennen. That's not the kind of thing you're going to tell anyone, even your sister, even if it was the most vivid dream you'd ever had. And the dream was so vivid she was sure she'd passed it on to her sister somehow. Maybe telecommunication.

— Telecommunication? said Ms. Flynn. You mean telepathy?

— Yes. But the reason Jen told her sister about it was that, after the things she'd experienced in her dream, she wasn't satisfied with her husband. She loved him, sure, but she felt she'd betrayed him. At the same time, she felt she was betraying herself by staying with him. She told June all this, so her sister could help her decide whether to stay with her husband or leave him for someone who could get her to feel what she'd felt with her dream version of John Skennen.

— That's an interesting story, said Ms. Flynn.

— Isn't it? her father answered. And Jen Wilson's the most no-nonsense woman you can imagine. Not the kind to leave her husband for something in a dream, you'd have said.

— Oh, Dad, said Ms. Flynn. No one knows anything about anyone else.

— So true, Professor Bruno said. But what did the woman decide to do?

— Who? asked Mr. Flynn. Jen Wilson? She stayed with her husband. She's still with him.

— Even if he is one of the most disgusting fornicators around, said Ms. Flynn. He'd cheat on her with a stoat, if you drugged it for him.

— Your bitterness is showing, said her father.

— Anyway, said Ms. Flynn, I never heard that story before, but it makes sense. No, not sense exactly. But I'll bet the hotel they stayed in was the old Venus Fly Trap on Christina.

— No, no, Mr. Flynn said. It was at Aphrodite's Arms.

— Oh, Dad, no one ever called it that. It was the kind of place you could rent a room for an hour, if you knew who to ask. It was a place to trap meat. Get it? Besides that, it had a reputation I've always wondered about. People used to say that if you rented a certain room on the second floor, sexual things would happen, whether you wanted them to or not. The hotel stopped renting the room to families or people who didn't know its reputation.

That only made the place *more* popular. I knew someone who rented the room every weekend for years, so she could feel pleasure. That's why it was burned down. I don't mean because of the person I mentioned. I mean because of its reputation, the Society for a Better Sarnia encouraged people to burn it down, for years, until some yahoos finally did. But the point I wanted to make was that the room on the second floor was supposed to be where John lost his virginity. So, if you stayed in the room, you felt the pleasure he felt, whoever you were. That's why Jen's story makes sense to me. You see what I mean?

Professor Bruno and the Flynns stopped talking for a moment. Their silence was the kind that follows an understanding or an appreciation of something complex. But I hadn't understood a number of things. I was baffled by the way we'd gone from talking about Mr. Skennen's biography to talking about places that were haunted by his pleasures. Part of what baffled me was the fact that I'd known so little about a man who seemed to have influenced all of Southern Ontario. How had I missed him? John Skennen was like an undertow that hadn't caught me until this trip with Professor Bruno.

Then again, I don't suppose any place reveals itself to you all at once. It comes at you in waves of associative detail. For instance, as I listened to Mr. Flynn's story, I happened to look out at the 'dog-strangling vine' – *Cynanchum rossicum* – at the edge of the Flynns' property, bordering the lawn of the man from Belleville. 'Dog strangling': such a vicious name for a weed that's made lovely when its tiny crimson flowers open. And yet, the name is right. *Cynanchum rossicum* is so invasive that, at its worst, it's easy to imagine its strands have a mind of their own, pulling dogs or cats into some lightless interior. At any rate, it made its way into my consciousness, so that it's bound with the Flynns, with Aphrodite's Arms, with the longing for one who is not there.

Out of curiosity – and respect for the wisdom of my companions – I asked why there should be such a fascination with John

Skennen, a poet, not an actor or pop musician or billionaire. And mentioned my surprise that the man's sexual doings should be commemorated.

– That's a good question, Ms. Flynn said. I've wondered about it myself.

– Well, said Professor Bruno, John was a fascinating man, by all accounts. He was what you'd call a 'local hero,' wasn't he?

– Oh, I don't think it's that, Ms. Flynn answered. I know any number of men and women who are just as fascinating as he was. I think it's more to do with poetry. We all know there's a connection between words and death. And there's a connection between death and sex. So, there you go.

Mr. Flynn said

– I'd have had a drink if I'd known this is the conversation we're going to have.

– I'm not saying poets are good in bed, Dad! I can't count the number of writers I've slept with who couldn't tell a clitoris from a bottle of mouthwash. I'm talking about something else: the place words come from is the same place death comes from.

Professor Bruno was impressed.

– It takes one poet to understand another, he said.

But Mr. Flynn rose from his chair and shook his head.

— No, he said, this is exactly the kind of crap that drives men to drink. Young John Skennen was what my parents called a scamp or a scallywag. And scamps give people something to talk about. Also, the man had children with dozens of women. That and the fact nobody knows how he died or even *if* he died. That's why people around here talk about him.

To me, he said

— Don't pay any attention to these two, young man.

— Daddy, said Ms. Flynn, you are so simple-minded! It's a good thing you're lovable.

As Mr. Flynn shuffled a short distance away, his kimono moved like a billowing piece of night, its painted birds chuffed and slimmed as if they were preening before sleep. From a glass-fronted credenza he took a bottle of greenish liquor. To me, he said

— It's asparagus wine. My own invention. Something to drink when academics come by.

— Don't drink it, said Ms. Flynn. It's foul.

— Foul but bracing, said her father.

It was both of those things. It tasted as if asparagus had been recovered from a septic tank and soaked in grape juice. It was potent, too. After I'd politely drunk a second offering, I didn't quite feel the nausea I'd felt on first tasting it. And, to be fair to Mr. Flynn — who was pleased I'd agreed to a second draught — it did help the time pass. I remember very little about the discussions that followed. Ms. Flynn and Professor Bruno went on talking about John Skennen, with Ms. Flynn agreeing that the professor's portrait of Skennen — the one in his manuscript — was almost certainly accurate. Naturally, this made the professor happy.

— What are you going to call the book? Ms. Flynn asked.

— I was thinking *Persephone's Beau, or, John Skennen in His Own Work.* Do you like it?

They then went on about the difficulty of titles. But the next thing I really remember is being woken by Professor Bruno, who was anxious that I hear the conversation about Pioneer Days.

Though Ms. Flynn described the festival as 'typically Canadian,' judging by her account, it sounded unique. From what I got, the town of Nobleton decided sometime in the 1950s to celebrate the 'pioneering spirit,' the current that had passed through the men and women – Europeans, mostly – who'd founded the town in the 1800s, carving it out of the scrub, shrub, and rock. The people of Nobleton decided that, during the third week of August, every summer, the citizens of Nobleton would hold a competition to see which group could build a house fastest, using only the means available to the earliest pioneers.

The town was divided in two. Those to the east of King Street competed against those to the west. The winner received bragging rights and the Nobleton Cup, a trophy that was kept in Bill's Barber Shop (if won by the east) or Mona's Hair Salon (if won by the west). That said, the biggest reward was the considerable amount – around $25,000 – won by whoever had bet on the winning team while coming closest to the actual time it had taken to build the house. And, of course, every year before the competition began, the previous year's houses were burned to the ground in a spectacular bonfire.

A change to the competition came in the late 1960s, when it was deemed wasteful to burn the houses down. There were, after all, any number of poor families in Bolton County who could benefit from free housing for a year. And so, in an inspired moment, a raffle was created, the winners of which would occupy the houses built during Pioneer Days. At the end of a year, the houses were set afire as usual and other tenants were chosen for the following year.

An ethical wrinkle in the proceedings formed in the late 1980s, when it occurred to the organizers of Pioneer Days that the down-on-their-luck families who'd won occupancy of the houses might come to feel attachment to their abodes. This was especially the case with families who had young children – children being inclined to treasure their homes. So, in another moment of inspiration, the committee decided to allow families to save their raffle-won homes from burning, if they were able, using whatever means they could.

At a stroke, this decision resolved tensions and increased the house burnings' popularity. To begin with, the buildings and burnings were moved to a dale just outside Nobleton in which two wells were dug. The wells, generous and deep, gave the families a fighting chance to douse the flames. And then: those who felt it was wrong to give unfortunate people homes they hadn't earned (Conservatives, mostly) were appeased when they saw that few of the poor families had the wherewithal to actually save their houses. This failure created the kind of amused pity (in those who believed in self-reliance) that tempers resentment. As well: the sight of log houses burning while families tried to save them was a close approximation of true pioneering distress. So, the spectacle provided onlookers with a living lesson in history, the past and present intimately touching. Finally: when, in the 1990s, families began to take up the challenge and practised dousing big fires during the year — some of them becoming expert — the people of Nobleton began to wager on the time it took to build the houses as well as whether or not a family might or might not save their home.

The house burning was now the centrepiece of Pioneer Days. Aside from the spectacle of unfortunate families trying to save their homes, there was the increasingly more generous prize money for the individual who guessed, first, how quickly the houses would be built (if they had to be built), then if the house (or houses) would survive, and, finally, how long it would take to save the house(s) or, alternatively, how long it would take the house(s) to burn down.

— Has anyone been hurt? I asked.

— Quite a few, said Mr. Flynn. It's barbaric, but everyone's got such good intentions that no one minds.

— That's not true, his daughter answered. Four or five deaths in all these years. And the ones who died weren't poor. They were drunk and trying to influence the outcome. The whole thing's part of life's rich pageant. And at least it's not as stupid as Coulson's Hill's Indigenous Parade!

– It's barbaric, Mr. Flynn repeated. It's a Hell created by town council. Good intentions gone nuclear.

– Oh, Daddy, you're just being fashionably pessimistic, said Ms. Flynn. Good intentions are at the heart of love, too, you know.

– Yes, said Mr. Flynn, but love done by town council is not anything I'd want to experience.

– He's got you there, Bridge, said Professor Bruno.

Despite Brigid Flynn's enthusiasm, the idea of watching houses burn was unappealing to me. And although I don't like to disappoint the people around me, I would have preferred to remain in the Flynns' guest room, transcribing Professor Bruno's conversation with Ms. Flynn. But Professor Bruno himself asked me to come.

– Do you know, he said, I haven't been to Pioneer Days since I was a teenager. My family loved going to them. I admit I used to hate house burnings, but I suppose this'll be the last one I see, and I'd prefer to see it through the eyes of someone who's never been.

On hearing this, I agreed to go with him, my respect for the professor bringing an obligation, despite my feeling that our journey was being waylaid.

It was five o'clock when we set out. The sun was bright but the world had already committed to evening: lengthening shadows, a hint of orange to the light, a satisfying coolness to the breeze. From somewhere, we caught the smell of lamb cooking on a barbecue. We drove through Nobleton – Ms. Flynn driving with the windows down – past pedestrians who were all heading in the same direction we were. There were so many people that Professor Bruno wondered if we'd find a good place to sit. I only understood his anxiety when we got to Kiiskinen's Dale, a gentle expanse about a half-mile across, surrounded by grassy hills, as if it were the bottom of an almost perfectly formed bowl. It wasn't so much that there were bad vantages from which to watch the houses burn. With binoculars, one could see clearly from any of the hillsides. It was rather that, depending on wind direction, this or that declivity could be hospitable or unaccommodating or momentarily either. It was best to be where you could quickly move away from wind-blown smoke. With wind direction in mind, people made for this or that hillside.

Wind direction was naturally a concern for the participants – the poor families – as well. Though the dale was protected from major winds by the hills around it, currents of air sometimes swept through, fanning a fire and driving the bucket-carrying hopeful away from their burning homes. The only ones unperturbed by the winds were those who bet on the event. Wind currents added a further element of chance, making the outcome even more difficult to predict, making it more difficult to cheat, and making things tricky for the firemen who kept the spectators at bay while themselves being prepared to intervene, should there be any danger to human life.

This year's house burning had a heightened local angle to it. A Nobleton family – the McGregors – had managed to save their burning home for three years straight. No other family had ever gone beyond two. Their home had suffered great damage, of course. A quarter of it was not much more than ashen pillars that would not fall. The whole of it had been blackened and charred. But the McGregors, struggling tenaciously and with a modesty that made them crowd favourites, lived in a single room, bereft of most of their possessions. This unprecedented display of heroism and dignity had already brought about a change in the house burning's rules. It was decided that, should the McGregors save their home a fourth time, they would have a new house built for them so that, in the year to come, they would not have to live among the ashes, should they choose to remain in Kiiskinen's Dale.

You could see the crowd had real affection for the McGregors. A microphone was set up and, before the burning began, there was an interview with the family members — mother, father, three sons, two daughters. The spectators cheered their every response, especially those of the father — Malcolm McGregor, an unemployed cook — who spoke, humourously, in a bad Scottish accent.

— Och! he said, we're after doing what we done these past few years. Ye can't keep a Scotsman down!

His words done and the cheering stopped, the two families — McGregors and Ainsleys (the novices) — were taken a distance from the homes they'd lived in for a year while flammable things were put at strategic points inside and outside their houses and then set alight.

This, as far as I could tell, was the end of reason. There was a prolonged, almost soundless moment as the McGregors (seven of them, from ages twelve to fifty) and the Ainsleys (eight of them, from ages six to thirty-five) were held back until their homes caught proper fire. Nor did it take long before the fire was frightening. It was so frightening that I felt a late-blooming admiration for the McGregors. It seemed incredible that they should have willingly endured this terror for four years running. All to save their home and the meagre belongings they'd gathered in its blackened room.

Although I felt that reason had gone, there was still order. The McGregors, the more experienced, ran to their home. Father and sons began by shovelling sand on the outside of their house, suffocating the flames with help from the buckets of water brought by the mother and daughters. They were impressively efficient, breaking their windows to let the smoke out before entering their burning home to put out the flames. After only fifteen minutes, it seemed certain the McGregors would have their new home. But then, a bit of bad luck changed their fortune.

The Ainsleys, inexperienced as they were, did not really know how to go about it. They went to their well as individuals, rather than forming a chain to carry the buckets. They depended solely on water to douse the flames. Also, though there were eight

Ainsleys in total, their three youngest – aged nine, seven, and six – were too young to participate. That left them with five: two willowy girls (eleven and twelve), a thin young man (fifteen), and their malnourished, exhausted parents. After fifteen minutes, it was clear that they would lose their house and whatever belongings had been left inside. This must have been clear to their six-year-old girl, too. Breaking away from the crowd, unseen by the firemen – who were naturally absorbed by the conflagration – she ran to what had been her house and disappeared inside.

Now there was real alarm, the plight of children being of some concern to most Canadians. A number of people streamed forward along with the firemen. All had only the safety of the Ainsleys' six-year-old in mind, though, from where I stood, it seemed impossible that she should survive.

(Here, I passed one of the most unpleasant moments in my life. I rose to my feet, ready to intervene. But then it was as if I couldn't move. I felt bound by circumstances. I was part of a ritual I did not understand, so, naturally, neither did I understand my place. Was it up to me to save the child or were there others there to save her? Would I get in their way if I acted? I was helpless, and this helplessness brought me back to my early childhood, to myself and my mother watching my father speak before a congregation that rose and fell at his words, as if my father controlled the tides, while I could do nothing but struggle with the desire to be elsewhere, to escape my own passivity.)

What saved the girl – and the doll she had gone to rescue – was the McGregor family. The sons of Malcolm McGregor, seeing the girl run into the burning house, ran in after her. The rest of the McGregors and the Ainsleys, seeing the young men run into the house, devoted all their attention to the Ainsleys' home. They shovelled dirt on it. They brought buckets of water. For the minutes – it seemed like hours – the girl was inside, the minutes – it seemed to take forever – before the firemen came rushing from the hills, the McGregors' home was allowed to burn away. More: by the time the sons of Malcolm McGregor carried the Ainsleys' youngest from her burning home – the girl's Barbie doll smoking like a censer – there was little of their own house left to salvage. The last portion of the McGregors' home burned brightly on its square of ground.

From this point, the spectators collectively exhaling as girl and doll were rescued, everything passed as if time were elastic, some actions happening as if in slow motion, others too fleeting to catch. The McGregors, seeing their home lost, now helped to save the Ainsleys'. The crowd cheered the final collapse of the McGregors' home, as if a matador had delivered a coup de grâce. Or were they cheering the rescue of the Ainsleys' home? Either way, at the end of the proceedings, the general mood changed. Once it was certain the Ainsleys were safe, a chorus of boos came from all around.

– What's happened? I asked Professor Bruno.

– The McGregors lost their home, Ms. Flynn answered. Everybody's disappointed.

She said this as if she were stating the obvious, but it wasn't any more obvious to me than it had been to Professor Bruno. I'd felt relief at the young girl's rescue and I was sure I wasn't alone. But then I sensed the crowd's mood and, for a moment, I was a stranger amongst my contemporaries. Were they really more disappointed in the McGregors' loss than they were happy at the young girl's rescue?

As we walked away from Kiiskinen's Dale, we were met by the Flynns' neighbour, the man from Belleville, still in the checked shirt he'd worn to mow his lawn. He seemed such a polite and unassuming man, I was shocked when Ms. Flynn called him the rude word to his face.

– This is my neighbour, she said, the cunt from Belleville. And then

– Cunty, this is Morgan Bruno and his assistant, Alfred.

– Pleased to meet you, he said. But, you know, many people call me Alby. The other is only my nickname.

— How did you get such a strange nickname? asked Professor Bruno.

— The nickname is strange, he said, but the story behind it is banal, I'm afraid. I was born in Germany, yeah? My family is from the nobility. My name is Wilhelm Alberich Baldur Peter, Graf von Neuenahr Ahrweiler. My parents are proud of our heritage. So, they used to insist people call me Graf von Neuenahr Ahrweiler. That's even when we moved to Belleville. Which is where my mother went to practise medicine. When I was in Grade 8, I made the mistake of telling someone that *Graf* means *Count* and that meant I was a *Count* from Belleville. The rest you can imagine. I've been called *the cunt from Belleville* so often, it feels like my real name. And, you know, I don't think about it anymore, unless someone asks me where it comes from.

— Don't you find it inconvenient? asked the professor.

— Not exactly, Alby answered. When I was young, I liked it, because it made my parents furious. These days I like trying to guess who'll use it and who's horrified. I thought Brigid would be horrified, but I was wrong. I don't think there's anyone who's happier to call me *cunt*.

— But I'm not calling you that! said Ms Flynn. *Cunt from Belleville* is an honorific.

— Well, almost, said Alby. But I'm not sure it matters, anyway. A rose by any other name ...

Rather than drive us back to her home, Ms. Flynn insisted we eat at the Wolf and Pendulum, a place that reminded me of taverns I've been in throughout the province – television behind the bar, Canadian flag above the shelves of hard liquor, a number of booths and a number of tables, the place full of people who'd been to the house burning or seemed to have been, all the audible talk being about McGregors and Ainsleys.

When we'd got a table, Ms. Flynn ordered food (shepherd's pie and tourtière), and a round of Old V (for all but me), plus a Nobleton Hard Pear Cider (for me). Count Neuenahr Ahrweiler said

– This makes the second house burning I've seen. I think I'm going to wait a few years before I see another.

– Why's that? Ms. Flynn asked.

But before the count could answer, a number of people – three or four, I think, though the number changed whenever I looked up – moved their chairs to our table and joined the conversation.

– The cunt from Belleville's right, said someone. The house burning is too much. People can't give the poor anything, without they burn it down, too.

– The fuckers giveth and they taketh away.

– But at least we're not Coulson's Hill.

– You look up *stupid* in the dictionary, you'll see a picture of the Indigenous Parade.

With that done – everyone having acknowledged the problems of the house burning while ridiculing Coulson's Hill – the conversation turned to what was uppermost on people's minds: the treatment of the McGregors. There was general agreement that an injustice had been done. The McGregors had lost their home while rescuing a six-year-old child. It wasn't up to them to look after the Ainsleys' children. That was the committee's duty! The whole thing amounted to taking from the innocent – the McGregors – for doing good. Even the Ainsleys thought so. They'd volunteered to surrender their home to the McGregors. But the committee wouldn't hear of it. They refused to take circumstances into account. It didn't matter to them *why* the McGregors' home burned down. The fact of it was all that mattered. And what was their reason?

A short, red-faced man who'd been getting more and more agitated spoke up.

– There's no reason! They're damned unreasonable!

He was shushed by another short, red-faced man. No, no. The committee *did* have a reason. Just not a very good one. It seemed, as far as the committee was concerned, that one had to remember the whole purpose of the house burning. The purpose was to celebrate the past through understanding. In the past, fate made no exceptions. Fire came. Houses burned. Lives went on, differently. Had their house burned two hundred years previously, the McGregors would have been left as they were now. That was the point. For the legions that had come from Europe and pushed the Indigenous off the land, calamity was irrevocable.

A third short and red-faced man – a cousin to the others – said

– But this isn't the past! It's 2017! Why shouldn't we be humane when we have the luxury?

– Exactly! said his short, red-faced cousin. What Bobby said! We should be building a home for the McGregors!

Though I didn't drink anything after the pear cider, I couldn't make out the time on the clock behind the bar. But it must have been late when the serious arguments started. Because although I appreciated the passion my companions brought to the subject of the McGregors, I lost the thread of the argument. I was left with impressions: grey hair recently grooved by a comb, white T-shirts stretched taut over bulging stomachs, ruddy skin, yellowed teeth, missing teeth, phrases that struck me ('My chickens were inebriated,' 'You can poach rhubarb, eh'), the smell of beer, the smell of whisky on someone's breath, the smell of french fries and just-microwaved chuckwagons: slices of ham and slices of bright-orange cheese carelessly tucked into a wrinkled hamburger bun.

Beneath these small impressions, there was something deeper. I could feel the flow of that particularly Canadian thing: passion brought on by outrage. Outrage seeped into the Wolf and Pendulum and permeated the place: an outrage that turned, at times, to aggression, an aggression that few of those in the pub would have permitted themselves unless prompted by their sense of political imbalance – the fate of the poor, petty rules running roughshod over good people, distant committees dictating to those who lived in Nobleton. In the Wolf and Pendulum, I recognized what you could call a 'Canadian instinct' or, if you were being unkind, a Canadian addiction: moral reproach.

Now the house burning made a kind of sense to me. In the past, I've often been dismayed by how desperately my compatriots crave the feeling of moral superiority. No opportunity for finger-pointing goes untaken, while the finger-pointing itself leads nowhere but to more finger-pointing. On this night, however, the cries of 'Shame!' or 'Fuck the committee!' were reassuring, because the emotions expressed were so typical of Canadian life, of my life.

This feeling of familiarity – of reassurance – lasted until I went to sleep.

The following morning, after a quiet breakfast with Brigid's father, we left for Coulson's Hill.

The first time I saw five flower (*Monotropa cinqueflora*), a variation of the ghost plant, was as we drove along Highway 27, the old Simcoe County Road between Nobleton and Schomberg.

Professor Bruno was not feeling well. He (and Brigid) had drunk too much the night before. Just past Schomberg, he asked me to stop the car a moment so he could let his stomach settle. While he sat in the front with the windows down, I walked in a ditch by the side of the road. The sun was somewhere above, burning through a thin curtain of cloud, the blue sky visible in scarlike stretches. There was wind – the trees shook and dry stubble in a field sounded like a rattle.

I thought at first that the five flower was a tall mushroom or an unusual fungus. It had white flowers and a white stalk, as *Monotropa* does, but it was growing out of the rotting trunk of a fallen elm. Then I saw that it was 'four-headed' – four bell-like flowers growing from one stalk – and recognized it for what it was. I was surprised – *cinqueflora* is usually found in old-growth forests – and pleased. I was also hopeful of finding a fully developed flower, one with five heads. I examined quite a length of ditch and, although I didn't find one, I came away feeling grateful that I'd finally seen a flower I'd often heard about, most recently from Professor Binama, a former teacher of mine.

When Professor Bruno's stomach had settled – he'd spit up in the weeds and felt better – we went on to Coulson's Hill. The farms we passed smelled of their own greenery – corn, canola, cilantro – and of the greenery around them: Johnson grass, Queen Anne's lace, buttercups, chicory, maple trees, elms, the occasional clump of evergreens, sticking out as if there by some mysterious design.

According to Professor Bruno, Coulson's Hill was named for George Coulson, a cobbler from Brighton who, in 1840, had a dream that he was destined to find a fortune somewhere in North America, that his family was destined for great wealth. A few years later, he was on his way across Canada, heading to California, when he fell ill near what became Coulson's Hill. Feverish and near death, George Coulson dreamed of a seam of gold directly beneath the grass on which his burning body lay, a great seam that would make him rich. And when he'd recovered, he dug up the land beneath him and found pure gold, a brilliant vein in a long stretch of quartz. It was enough gold to make him a wealthy man, but not rich. Faithful to his dream, convinced he'd find more, Coulson spent his money digging up the land around the spot where he'd found gold. He dug systematically, for twenty years, until he'd excavated every bit of ground within a square mile, save for a kind of hillock, a raised circle whose diameter was twenty-five feet.

By the time he was fifty-seven, Coulson had spent most of his gold searching for more of it. Yet, neither age nor lack of funds put an end to his digging. This did: the hillock, derisively known as 'Coulson's Hill' by his neighbours, was all that was left to him of his dream. If he dug it up and found nothing, his twenty-year search would have to be called a delusion. To have found another modest seam of gold would have been almost as bad, scarcely worth the decades he'd devoted to it. He was at an impasse.

George Coulson died in his seventies, having neither excavated the hill nor permitted anyone to do the digging for him. After his death, no one was interested in his plot of land. No one believed he'd been much more than a fanatic. So, Coulson's Hill, which now serves as the name of a village – a crossroads, really – became something of a synonym for broken dreams, hesitation, and futility. Professor Bruno could not think of Coulson's Hill without feeling both pity and scorn.

My own feelings were harder to pin down. I agreed it was a pity George Coulson had never learned for certain if he was meant to find more gold. But I also felt – maybe because I'd just seen my first *cinqueflora* – that Coulson, by refusing to dig, had kept alive the possibility of finding something precious. Despite the professor's view, the name Coulson's Hill struck me as hopeful, maybe even forever hopeful.

– No, not really, said Professor Bruno. The hill was dug up long ago. It's buried under the 27 somewhere. No one ever found anything there but shale.

I must have looked puzzled because he added

– The fact you believe in a dream doesn't make it real, Alfie.

A thought that's difficult to deny. But it occurred to me, as Professor Bruno spoke the words, that being awake is no proof that what you see is real any more than being asleep is proof that it's not. The realms – sleeping and waking – are different, but you have to be attentive in both. Not that my dreams are as hazardous as reality. They're strange and sometimes frightening, but there's a consistency to them as well. The memorable ones, the ones that recur, almost always begin with me going on a long trip – as I did when I was a child, travelling to churches with my parents. They often end similarly, too, with some variant of us (me, my mother, my father) driving home along the curve of the lakeshore, the CN Tower in the distance.

Mr. Henderson, the friend of Skennen's who'd been recommended by Ms. Flynn, lived just off the 11th Line. He was a tall man. At a guess, I'd say he was six feet five and looked as if he weighed at least three hundred pounds. He was intimidating. As was his voice. It was a loud whisper. He'd got it – the raucous whisper – when, as a younger man, he'd been hit in the throat by a bar stool. The stool hadn't hurt him all that much. It had been wielded by his younger brother, Henry, when they'd both been drunk, after winning a number of bets as to where on Mr. Henderson's person hard objects could be broken.

– I don't do that kind of thing anymore, he said.

There was no bitterness in his voice. If anything, there was nostalgia for the days when he'd had brooms, plates, chairs, and beer steins broken on his head, shoulder, chin, and elbow. He spoke affectionately of his brother, Henry, the 'icy crook,' who'd recently passed away.

– Ah, he said, Henry could steal your shorts while you were wearing them.

I found the idea of stolen underwear amusing, partly because I'm finicky about my undershorts and partly because I've rarely 'gone commando,' disliking as I do the flops you get when you don't wear briefs. Mostly, though, I was amused because I was suddenly reminded of Anne, who disliked my farting if I was naked, because flatulence was somehow worse to her when done 'without a barrier.'

As if the world were of the same mind as me, these thoughts were accompanied by a terrible odour, like gusts from a summer outhouse. I'm not certain anyone else noticed. In fact, I wondered if I were the cause of the smell. Had I farted without knowing? Or was it Mr. Henderson? The odour didn't stop the conversation, but my thoughts and self-consciousness negatively influenced my first impressions of Mr. Henderson.

To be fair, this mild anxiety about flatulence came from my parents. Not farting *in public* is part of the civility they taught me, a civility they expected from me. But they were inconsistent. My farting in public was taken as something that tarnished their reputation. At home, I could fart almost without consequence. They didn't like it, but neither of them objected too much if accidents happened. (I don't believe I ever heard my mother fart. My father I only heard once and that was while he was delivering a sermon at St. Andrew's, poor man.) But my parents considered it impolite to notice when others were flatulent. And there was the contradiction: if it was polite for me to ignore the flatulence of others, why should others not ignore *my* flatulence? Now that I'm older, I realize that this is, more or less, how it works. People fart and you politely ignore them while holding your breath. As a child, though, I wondered why my parents didn't simply allow me to fart and then allow convention – the tacit agreement that we not acknowledge the public flatulence of others – to take over. The other thing that puzzled my nine-year-old self was my first inkling of how tricky society can be. Since farting at home seemed less grave, I began to wonder if the farts of strangers were harder to tolerate than those of our intimates. I eventually put it down to cuisine. Strangers did not eat as we did, so perhaps their flatulence was more noxious to us. When I put this idea to my father, he was surprised that I'd spent so much time thinking about it. But he made things worse by asking me what would happen if we started eating the cuisines of others. Would we come to accept, say, Macedonian farting? I now know the answer to his question is no. After all, I sometimes find it difficult to bear my own gas, let alone that unleashed by others. But I spent quite a bit of time puzzling his question through.

By further coincidence, no sooner had I recalled this conversation with my father than Mr. Henderson himself farted, brutishly and at length.

– Christ! he said. That was a good one.

That, you'd have thought, would confirm my negative impression of the man. But it didn't. Tall and heavyset though he was, there was something delicate and fine about him. It wasn't just that he whispered, either. (Though this did make everything he said sound intimate.) His hair – greying along the sides, black elsewhere – stuck up in spots, so there was something untamed and vulnerable about him. Besides which, Mr. Henderson was as generous and attentive as Mrs. Kelly or the Flynns had been, making certain we had what we wanted to eat and drink. The more I knew him, the more I came to feel as if, on first impression, I'd mistaken a dancing bear for a marauding one.

When the air had cleared, Professor Bruno turned to the matter that interested him.

– What do you remember about John Skennen? he asked.

– What do you want to know? answered Mr. Henderson.

– Why don't we start with his disappearance? said the professor. Do you know anything about it?

– Whose disappearance? asked Mr. Henderson. John's? I don't know why people think he disappeared or died or whatever. He's around here all the time.

Professor Bruno's left hand made what looked like an involuntary movement, twitching as if he meant to grab a glass that wasn't there. Keeping his excitement – if it was excitement – in check, he said

– When was the last time you saw him?

– Day before last, I think, said Mr. Henderson. He's around from time to time. Of course, you won't see him today. John hates the Indigenous Parade. He can't stand the crowds or the stupidity.

Having heard so much about the parade – so much that made it seem a bad thing – I was curious to hear how someone from Coulson's Hill might describe it.

– What, I asked, is the Indigenous Parade?

And Mr. Henderson was kind enough to answer my question.

As with so many things in our beautiful country, the Indigenous Parade was the product of a committee. It was also the product of an era and a longing. Like most Canadians, the people of Coulson's Hill sometimes noticed that the Indigenous populations of Canada had been mistreated in any number of ways and for quite some time. Most felt it was not enough to simply notice this. Justice demanded restitution, even if only a symbolic one. So, when Councillor Bergin put forward the idea of an 'amusing but serious' form of symbolic restitution, the rest of the town council were receptive. 'What if,' the councillor asked, 'we had a parade and allowed Indigenous people to throw tomatoes – or any soft fruit – at the country's founding fathers?' When Bergin added that there is a Spanish town that holds yearly tomato fights, the rest of the council gave their enthusiastic consent, it being common knowledge that European traditions are generally prestigious.

For the first Indigenous Parade, various townsfolk dressed as the 'Fathers of Confederation' – John A. Macdonald, Adams George Archibald, et al. – and their families. These hundred or so people were distributed over twelve flatbed trucks and driven up and down the main road while the rest of the town's population – and some who'd come from as far away as Markham – dressed in 'Indigenous costumes' – eagle-feather headdresses, ceremonial beads, moccasins, etc. – and threw tomatoes (largely) and rotten plums at 'George Brown,' 'Alexander Campbell,' and all the rest of those who'd betrayed the Indigenous population of Canada.

The parade was, economically speaking, a great success.

To begin with, it attracted tourists. It attracted so many that they taxed the town's modest resources. A number of visitors had to go to Nobleton, Schomberg, or East Gwillimbury to find accommodations. For three days, there were lineups to get into Coulson's Hill's greasy spoon (Frank's Charbroiled Grill) and its one pub (the Rebarbative Moose). There were lineups to use public washrooms. And stores sold out of Coulson's Hill memorabilia – in particular, a T-shirt with a picture of a highway intersection in the middle of nowhere, beneath which were the words 'Coulson's Hill, the Possibilities Are Endless.'

In other ways, of course, the parade was a disaster. The use of sacred native symbols was roundly condemned by Indigenous people from around the country – or, at least, by the few who actually heard about the parade. But so was the idea that Indigenous people should be the only ones allowed to throw tomatoes at the Fathers of Confederation. Where, for instance, was the restitution for the Chinese who'd died building the railroad across the country? Or the Japanese who'd been driven from their homes? And how could Coulson's Hill, the town, say they 'stood with the Indigenous' while enjoying the privileges that had come from Confederation? Then, too, there was the uncomfortable – and entirely unforeseen – fact that the French Fathers – George-Étienne Cartier, Jean-Charles Chapais, Hector-Louis Langevin, Étienne-Paschal Taché – and their families were more vigorously pelted with tomatoes than were the English Fathers.

Politically, the first Indigenous Parade was a debacle.

But a committee with an altruistic and *profitable* idea is like a pit bull with a cloth mouse. The Coulson's Hill town council chose to reform its parade rather than cancel it. So, during the second parade, no ceremonial headdresses or symbols sacred to Indigenous people were permitted. Those who threw tomatoes wore buckskin britches and moccasins. Their tops were a variety of shirts and blouses. Space was made for those who represented other groups with legitimate grievances. Some wore blackface, there being so few Black people in the area. And those representing 'other grievances' showed this by throwing rotten fruit or cooked bok choy. More: those townsfolk who dressed as the French Fathers were not distinguished from the English Fathers. That is, there were no fleurs-de-lys on any of the trucks. And, finally, the consumption of alcohol was discouraged, the parade being about justice – even if it was only symbolic – not drink.

This second parade was also a mercantile boon, bringing in as many tourists and as much money as the first. And, like the first, it earned the town serious criticism, at least some of which might have been anticipated. For instance, any number of Indigenous people were insulted by the idea that they would stoop to such childish violence or that throwing tomatoes at men, women, and children dressed in nineteenth-century costume was any kind of restitution. On the other hand, a dozen or so young men from the Curve Lake and Alderville First Nations *did* participate. Being Indigenous, they did not dress in any special way. And they seemed to enjoy throwing tomatoes at the costumed Fathers. This caused real anger among the white people dressed as the Indigenous. Though the idea of Indigenous people throwing tomatoes at the Fathers of Confederation was appealing, the fact of it, the reality of actual Indigenous men throwing real tomatoes at representations of the Fathers, was offensive to many in Coulson's Hill. As the attack was no longer altogether symbolic, it brought out passionate – not to say violent – argument and passionate defence of the underappreciated Caucasians who'd done so much to make the country what it is. The Fathers of Confederation, when you thought about it, had made their own (posthumous) humiliation possible. And that – the constitutional possibility of humiliation – was something worth defending.

The least you could say about the Coulson's Hill's town council (largely Liberal) is that its members were persistent. Over the years, they tweaked or changed the rules to accommodate the criticism they'd got. For the third parade, for instance, signs were put up forbidding the participation of Indigenous people in the Indigenous Parade, unless they wished to dress as Fathers of Confederation. This led, a few years later, to the 'baffling' seventh parade in which a number of Indigenous elders, dressed in ceremonial costume, defiantly stood on the trucks meant for the Fathers of Confederation while citizens representing the Indigenous apprehensively threw tomatoes at them.

Many thought this seventh parade would bury the whole thing beneath its avalanche of meanings. But it didn't. Coulson's Hill's town council persisted, and the parade we saw – the eleventh – was yet another refinement of the original idea.

It was a beautiful afternoon. The sky was a consistent and unperturbed blue, looking like a postcard of sky. At the entrance to town, we were asked if we had tomatoes of our own or if we wished to buy some. We were politely frisked to ensure we had no Indigenous artifacts on us – moccasins, for instance. Mr. Henderson generously paid for a bag of rotten tomatoes and then we were given blue sheets with which to cover ourselves, blue being a sacred colour. The sheets, which descended to our ankles, had eye and mouth holes cut in them and they were held in place by bolo ties whose clasps were red plastic circles.

Maybe it was the day – almost quiet enough to hear crickets – but I found the Eleventh Annual Indigenous Parade peculiar. At least, it was not what I expected. All along the main street, on both sides, men, women, and children – each covered by their own blue sheet – lined up on the sidewalk in front of the town's stores and small businesses. I thought the spectators were unusually silent, until I realized that their words were muffled and their

73

hearing partially impeded by the sheets they wore. Most of them held paper bags in front of them, filled, I assumed, with tomatoes or rotten fruit.

There was a kind of excitement as the trucks came into view. The flatbeds were identical – fifty feet long, eight feet wide – with white aprons. On each of the twelve flatbeds: six tall figures in blue sheets, six short figures in blue sheets. Those on the flatbeds were meant to represent the thirty-six Fathers of Confederation, their wives, and their children. Not all the Fathers had had two children. Most had had more. But, in parades past, the crowds had thrown more tomatoes at the families with greater numbers of children, on the understanding that the French had had larger families than the English in the old days.

The spectators, beneath their blue sheets, enthusiastically threw tomatoes at the blue-sheeted people on the flatbeds. The tomatoes – a local variety known as Medicine Heart – left their bright red pulp in a kind of low wave along the hems of their sheets, few of the tomatoes hitting anyone on the trucks above the knees. Then, the trucks turned around and passed through town a second time and, once again, the blue-sheeted figures were pelted with tomatoes by blue-sheeted celebrants.

And that was the Eleventh Annual Indigenous Parade done.

After we'd sat down in the Rebarbative Moose, we were told that this was the best parade the town had ever held. More than that, most of those in the pub were convinced that this parade proved them morally superior to the people of Nobleton who, for entertainment, endangered women and children. I myself had a difficult time judging the relative moral densities of Nobleton and Coulson's Hill. Was it virtuous to burn down poor people's homes, having given them homes in the first place? Was it noble to wear blue sheets and throw tomatoes at people who also wore blue sheets? Both events – the parade and the house burning – were founded in notions of justice, but both seemed perverse.

– John would agree with you, said Mr. Henderson. He calls both of them displays of power, not goodwill.

The Rebarbative Moose was done up in the faux-English or faux-Irish style of pubs across the province. The bar was stained wood, as were the bar stools and most of the tables. Behind the bar, there was a picture of Prince Charles and his consort, Camilla. Beside the picture was a clock that looked like an owl with its eyes wide open. The pub's name was meant to suggest England. At least, it sounded English to its owner, a Flemish immigrant who was convinced the word *rebarbative* was Shakespearean.

We – Mr. Henderson, Professor Bruno, and I – sat at a table near the centre of the Moose. All around us, men and women drank a local cider known as 'amber mole' – so named because, according to the waitress, 'if you drink too much of it, you won't care what hole you're in.' Her words brought cheers from the tables around us. Mr. Henderson paid for our pints. But when the cider came, Professor Bruno pushed his glass toward me.

– I'm sorry, he said, but I'm not allowed alcohol. My kidneys are giving me trouble. Alfie's young. He'll be happy to drink mine.

He smiled at me, and, in that moment, I understood that it wasn't the alcohol that troubled him but, rather, the cider itself. The professor had evidently tasted it before. And after my first mouthful I understood why he didn't want to repeat the experience. The cider tasted as if apple juice had been strained through dirty socks.

– How do you like it? Mr. Henderson asked.

– That's hard to say, I answered.

– Well, drink up, he said. I can't stand drinking alone. It reminds me of my ex-wife.

I couldn't decide how to drink the cider. The faster I drank, the faster I'd get over the unpleasantness. But when I drink quickly, I tend to get drunk, which makes it harder to turn down more. The thing is, I didn't want to get drunk, because the Moose had an unpleasant atmosphere. It felt as if all the pub's patrons were aware of our presence and weren't happy about it. I drank slowly, though this meant, with every sip, I was haunted by the thought of someone rubbing their socks in my face.

As it turned out, our presence was irritating to the Moose's patrons. Professor Bruno resembled a person who was disliked in Coulson's Hill: Bob Grenville, a man from Nobleton who'd seduced and impregnated a number of young women in the town. The seduction and impregnation were not what people held against him. What they couldn't forgive was that Grenville had, in a drunken rage, burned down the town's post office – a nineteenth-century wooden manse that had been lovingly preserved – because he resented that the constant demands for child support he received inevitably bore the stamp of the Coulson's Hill post office.

Still, all went more or less well until, after drinking a few pints of cider, Mr. Henderson went off to the washroom. As soon as he'd gone, a man approached our table.

– The hell you doing here? he asked.

The pub was quiet.

The man, who wore a red baseball cap that said *Massey Ferguson*, swore at the professor.

– You piece-a-shit building burner, he said. Go back to Nobleton.

– I'm from around Nobleton, said Professor Bruno, but I've never burned anything.

– Shut up, said Massey Ferguson, nobody's asking you. We know what you did.

– I think you've got the wrong person, I said. This is Professor Bruno from the University of Toronto.

– Oh, said Massey Ferguson, that changes everything. He's from Toronto!

Mr. Ferguson, tall and muscular, lunged at Professor Bruno and tried to pull him up by the lapels. I got up at once, reached behind me for my chair, and tried to bring it down on Mr.

Ferguson's back. I'd never been in a bar fight. My reaction, desperate and almost instinctive, was inspired by movies I'd seen, movies in which chairs shatter on people's backs. In the movies, it's fluidly and easily done. So, one can imagine how astonished I was when I realized I hadn't grabbed a chair, as I'd meant to, but, rather, a large and very unhappy owl.

It's understating it to say I found this moment astonishing.

A number of things had to happen for me to grasp the bird. To begin with: when we came into the Moose, I mistook the owl at the bar for a clock. It was, in fact, a real owl perched *beside* a clock. My misapprehension had been a trick of the mind. But then, it's so unusual to find birds indoors, my first thought would naturally have been that the thing was a statue or a stuffed specimen. As a result, I was not on the lookout for an owl.

Then, while reaching for the back of my chair, I somehow managed to grasp the bird without looking at it.

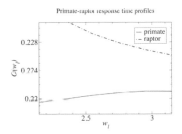

Moreover, I caught the bird's legs at the exact moment it had extended them in order to land on the back of my chair!

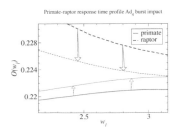

The bird was almost certainly at ease with human beings, being the pub's mascot. But I think it must have been as stunned as I was by the turn of events. It began to screech as soon as I caught it and flapped its wings about wildly. Incongruously, in the midst of its screeching and struggle, the expression on the owl's face was not of panic but quizzical dismay: eyes wide open, furiously blinking. as if it were trying to understand what I was doing.

I froze for a moment, holding the owl away from me as if it were a child having a temper tantrum. Then I let go and the owl flew up, its green siftings falling as it flew back to its place at the bar: near the picture of Charles and Camilla, beside the clock. There it preened, ruffling and unruffling its feathers, as if trying to recover its dignity.

You'd have thought the Moose's patrons would be offended and angry, having seen their mascot manhandled by a stranger. And, for a moment, they did seem to collectively consider how to react. The place was so quiet that the only words I heard were those sung by Gordon Lightfoot, the *Canadian Railroad Trilogy* playing for an nth time on an old jukebox.

Massey Ferguson still had a grip on the professor's lapel with one hand. His other hand had been raised to fend off the owl. But then Mr. Henderson returned from the washroom and the atmosphere changed again. Mr. Henderson struck the young man's head, as if slapping salmon from a stream. And, hands now up to protect his hat, Massey Ferguson meekly apologized: to Mr. Henderson, to Professor Bruno, to me, to everyone in the Moose.

Mr. Henderson glared at the man but let him walk away.

– Knob Grenville died last year! someone shouted.

And all around us there was mumbling, the sound like a pack of feral mothers soothing a child. Without any of us asking for them, several pints of cider came to our table, and the Moose's mood was once again light, the main topic of conversation being, once again, the moral superiority of Coulson's Hill over Nobleton.

Feeling obliged to drink the cider that had been bought for us, I was soon light-headed. One of the last things I remember clearly was a friend of Mr. Henderson's telling us about the origins of Coulson's Hill. The man told us the same story I'd heard. But he added a detail. Though the town's founder, George Coulson, had refused to excavate the last bit of ground on his property, George's son, Edward, had dug up the hill as soon as his father died. So, it was Edward Coulson who discovered a seam of gold that brought him great wealth. In fact, the seam ran deep, through all the property of present-day Coulson's Hill. Though they wore baseball caps and dressed like unsuccessful farmers, everyone with property in Coulson's Hill was, according to Mr. Henderson's friend, immensely wealthy.

– I thought, said Professor Bruno, that the hill had been dug up and there was nothing there.

– You're from Nobleton, aren't you? asked Mr. Henderson's friend.

– Near there, said Professor Bruno.

– Well, there you go, said Mr. Henderson's friend.

After a bit more banter, Mr. Henderson and Professor Bruno finally began to talk about the subject they'd met to speak of: John Skennen. I heard fragments of their conversation, but by then I'd drunk too much and the last thing I remember before passing out was Professor Bruno admitting that, in the end, the place he'd come from, this dull patch of Ontario, was more mysterious and threatening than he'd remembered.

3

THREE HAMLETS: SCHOMBERG, NEW TECUMSETH, MARSVILLE

Though I brushed my teeth a number of times, I couldn't lose the taste of brass. I'm almost certain this was down to the cider I'd drunk the night before. All morning, I was reminded of 'amber mole.'

My mother and Anne were on my mind, too. I couldn't think why, until I remembered that I'd heard Gordon Lightfoot's voice: the voice of my mother's favourite singer. ('Black Day in July' is the first song I remember hearing.) It had been a surprise to discover, when we first moved in together, that Anne, too, loved Lightfoot's songs.

— Why not listen to something modern? I'd say. I hear Glenn Miller just dropped some hot wax!

Which had been my way of teasing her and which, on reflection, I regret. How uncivil I was, in those days when I took her for granted.

I seemed to be the only one suffering from our time at the Moose. Professor Bruno hadn't drunk alcohol, of course. But Mr.

Henderson, who'd drunk more than I did, was in a good mood at breakfast. He boiled eggs for the three of us – the sulphuric aroma unfortunately reminding me of his flatulence – along with thick slices of a dark rye as dense as polished felt.

An unhappy coincidence: as he made breakfast, Mr. Henderson suddenly started singing 'Summer Side of Life.' He hoarsely whispered the words, which I recognized immediately. The song – more Lightfoot – was Anne's favourite and, as if a curtain had been drawn aside, my feelings for her flooded in, so it was all I could do to eat breakfast and listen to the professor and Mr. Henderson talk.

The two men had grown close. They now spoke as if they'd been intimates for years, as opposed to the acquaintances they'd seemed the day before. Mr. Henderson was in his bathrobe, on which white clouds were depicted against a light grey background. His hair was neatly combed but he'd parted it down the middle and it made him look like a muskox. Professor Bruno was in a clean pair of pyjamas: white cotton with a single breast pocket over which there was a crest from the University of Toronto. As they ate, they talked about small towns. They went on about Stephen Leacock. They rhapsodized about Algonquin Park 'in the seventies.' They recalled the devastation of Hurricane Hazel. They spoke of so many old things, I began to wonder if we'd make Feversham, an hour or so away, before nightfall.

The professor must have caught my impatience, but he picked up on my sadness as well.

– Do you know, he said, I think Alfie's unhappy. What is it, son?

I thought about hiding my feelings, not wanting to trouble their good spirits with my heartbreak. But Mr. Henderson said

– The young man's in love, Morgan.

Struck by his sensitivity, I thought it would have been dishonourable to lie. So, I said yes and told them how difficult it had been for me to be left by a woman I loved. I told them my story as plainly as I could, so we wouldn't have to dwell on it.

— Ah, said Professor Bruno, we've all been there, son. I couldn't eat for a year when my wife left me. These things are painful, but they help us live, if we survive them. I'm only sorry you've had to go through this now. We've had such wonderful weather, if you know what I mean.

I knew what the professor meant and I understood his reaction. Mr. Henderson, though ...

As I spoke about my heartbreak, Mr. Henderson held his teacup immobile before him, the porcelain vessel like a dollhouse cup between his thick thumb and index finger. When I finished speaking, he was overcome by emotion. He began to cry. It made for an odd sight: a muskox in pyjamas, sitting quietly as his tears fell, riveted by his own emotions.

Thinking himself responsible for his friend's distress, Professor Bruno apologized.

— I shouldn't have brought my heartbreak up, he said. I'm sorry to have upset you!

— No, no, said Mr. Henderson, it's got nothing to do with you, Morgan. I can usually talk about heartbreak without a fuss. But you two made me think about John, and then Alfred made me think about John and Carson. It's the damnedest thing crying about other people's affairs, but I can't help myself.

There was a moment of silence before Professor Bruno's curiosity got the better of him.

— You don't have to talk about this if you'd rather not, Henny. But did you say 'Carson'? Is that a friend of John's?

— You could say that, answered Mr. Henderson. She was the love of his life. But, you know, it's not their story that gets me. It's the witch's.

— Which witches? asked Professor Bruno.

Mr. Henderson sighed.

— It's a long story, he said, but John's in it, so you might be interested.

John Skennen had had a hand in the burning of Coulson's

Hill's post office. He, like his friend Bob Grenville, had been involved with women from Coulson's Hill. In fact, he'd fallen in love with a woman named Carson Michaels, herself a poet and, reputedly, the most beautiful woman in Southern Ontario. Not that Coulson's Hill could entirely claim her. Michaels had been born in Schomberg, that most mysterious of towns. But she'd come to Coulson's Hill, an already lovely twenty-one-year-old, dark-skinned, of Antiguan descent.

Also by reputation: Carson was modest and kind, but she was not a pushover. She suffered fools politely, but not for long. And she was extremely private. Though Carson had never been married, people thought of her as a Penelope waiting to meet Odysseus. In any case, she had a number of suitors, young men who congregated around the till at Lee's Garage, where she worked.

So, for practical reasons (the crowding around the till was bad for business) and for personal ones (she was exhausted by the consideration she felt obliged to show the people interested in her), Carson Michaels devised a question to ask of every suitor: what is the only object that makes me cry? She would ask the question three times. If a man or woman could not answer it by the third ask, they would find themself banished from Lee's Garage.

This was an efficient way to deal with the obviously smitten. The herd was quickly thinned out, with space at the cash register left for customers or for those who, not interested in Carson themselves, were amused by the fate of those who were. There may have been men and women discreetly attracted to Carson. If so, these were people who, by their discretion, saved themselves from the attentions of Lee. Because Lee – who owned the gas station, garage, and general store – had been Carson's father's closest friend and he took this banishing business seriously. Once banished, a suitor was fair game for Lee's pit bulls – Frick and Frack – who were vicious at the best of times. Not to mention that Lee himself, a giant man with a temper as bad as that of his dogs, took a sadistic pleasure in throwing people out of his establishment. He didn't care if they resisted or complied. What mattered was that the suitor – male or female – be thrown out and that they never return.

As far as anyone could remember, there had only been one fatality. A man from Napanee had died of a heart attack while running away from Frick and Frack. He'd been older than the usual run of suitors and, though no one knew it, he'd had a deathly fear of dogs. That is, unforeseen circumstances combined to overburden his heart. His death, marked by a crucifix near one of the gas pumps, was spoken of in hushed tones by suitors, and it served as a warning.

Whether the banished suitors were good people or not, worthy or not, Carson Michaels never allowed herself to learn. It wasn't that she had no interest in them. She was a compassionate woman, but she couldn't really understand their interest in her. None of them knew anything about her. They had no idea who she was. She was nothing more than an object of attention. That being so, Carson was satisfied that any suitor who could answer her question, any who could tell her what it was that made her weep, was worthy of her time, having devoted time to thinking about her – about who she was, about the things that had made her herself.

News of a beautiful woman and her smitten (or dog-bitten) suitors quickly spread throughout Southern Ontario. John Skennen first heard about Carson Michaels while sitting in a bar in Sutton. A man at the table beside his began to cry, though he didn't seem drunk: no slurred words, no spittle, no red face. What the man had were fresh stitches on his right hand and a crown of stitches above his left ankle. The stitches were the result of an encounter with Frick and Frack. It wasn't the physical injuries that had moved him to tears – though, of course, he hoped feeling would eventually return to his right hand. No, it was his regret at not finding out what it was that made Carson

Michaels cry. His guesses had been: a lost teddy bear, a cup once used by her now-dead father, her first tube of lipstick.

— You'd be surprised, he said, wiping his tears, how many people guessed those same things.

How did he know this?

Because Carson Michaels's suitors, men and women, shared their stories and their guesses. This was in the days before subreddit categories or easy internet access. There was, instead, a typed and handwritten list that, by the time it was copied for John Skennen, was fifty-five pages long. It was dauntingly (or obsessively) well-organized. Guesses at what made Carson Michaels weep were alphabetically ordered from *Adder* (skin shed by) to *Zest* (of yuzu fruit).

It seemed to the weeper in Sutton that this list — which he'd got only *after* he'd been chased from Lee's — was both devastating and tantalizing. Tantalizing because the list was long and potentially helpful in what it eliminated. Devastating because there were so many things in the world, and each thing had, at very least, the potential to sadden Carson Michaels. The suitors could fill an encyclopedia with guesses and not scratch the surface. How could one not despair at the thought?

On hearing of this 'Venus from Coulson's Hill,' John Skennen was fascinated, but his fascination took the form of outrage. His sense of justice was offended. He resented the assumption that men could not resist a desirable woman. And, allowing his outrage to overtake his common sense, Skennen resolved to 'deal with' the woman from Coulson's Hill. He did not allow for the possibility that he would himself fall in love with Carson Michaels. But fall in love he did, walking into the store at Lee's Garage like walking into a well-known ambush.

What is it like to fall in love at first sight?

Skennen had never felt anything like it. His outrage vanished at the sight of Carson's face. It didn't seem to him a 'beautiful' face, though he understood why some might call it that. To him, her beauty was beside the point, overcome as he was by her face's rightness. No other face, seen at the moment he first saw hers, could have had the same effect on him. His sense of justice was appeased and expanded. It wasn't that Truth was Beauty or Beauty Truth. It was that both 'truth' and 'beauty' were avatars of Justice, both manifestations of rectitude. In fact, you could have called this love at first sight a kind of crossed wiring in which all the higher ideals – Truth, Beauty, Love, Honour – seemed to be avatars of Justice.

Somehow – was it because desire for her had afflicted so many that she immediately recognized the signs or was it that he radiated longing? – she knew at once what his feelings meant. He approached the till, bringing with him a bag of Lay's Potato Chips. He did not look directly at her, until she asked for his payment. He was careful to say nothing to betray the fact – the impulse, the instinct – that he loved her. His first words to her – as he stared at Wilfrid Laurier's receding hairline and pursed lips on the five-dollar bill he gave her – were

– There you go.

He would have welcomed any words she spoke, but her first words struck him as elegant.

– Thank you, she said.

But she added, as he stood there trying to figure out where to put his change

– There's a thing that makes me sad. Do you know what it is?

Skennen allowed himself then to look directly at the woman he loved and almost lost himself in contemplation. No particular aspect of her struck him as inescapable. He had seen eyes as lovely (but where?), lips as appealing (not possible!), a brow as noble, hair as lustrous. But he'd never been as affected by these things. He'd never felt as he did and, really, it would have been difficult for her *not* to recognize his state.

– I'm sorry, he answered. I'm afraid I don't know you at all.

– No need to apologize, she said. Would you like to guess?

Skennen said the first word that came to him.

– Portulaca?

To one side of the till, there were four or five men – locals all, from the look of them – standing around, quietly watching. At Skennen's mention of the word *portulaca*, they snorted in unison. But Carson was kind.

– I've never heard that before, she said. It's a flower, isn't it?

– It is, he said, but I was thinking of a poem.

One of the locals – pink face above a blue-and-green plaid shirt – said

– You phony bastard!

Ignoring him, Skennen quoted Dennis Lee.

– 'Lovers by the score come sporting fantasies like we had, strolling bright-eyed past the portulaca ...'

– That's lovely, said Carson, but, no, portulaca doesn't make me sad. Neither does poetry.

Skennen felt dismissed. There were customers behind him waiting to pay.

– I'll be back when I know the answer, he said.

– I'd like that, said Carson Michaels.

She sounded polite, nothing more. Lee, on the other hand, was cheerful as he met Skennen on the way out. Warm and friendly, if you went by the man's smile. But he radiated menace. It wasn't only that the man was six feet nine inches tall and three hundred pounds. It was that, even standing still, he seemed like a vicious dog straining to break a metal link chain.

– That's one guess, he said. When you come back it'll be two. You get three in all, then I feed you to Frick and Frack.

Skennen considered pleading ignorance or expressing doubt that he'd be back at all. But there'd have been no point. In the same way that Carson Michaels had known he was smitten, Lee knew that Skennen would be back. They all knew, even the men who were probably still snickering by the till.

Surrendering to his fate — his fate being love for Carson Michaels — Skennen took this task seriously. Where was one to begin when trying to discover what made a woman weep? Difficult question. And the first thing he discovered was just how particular his difficulties would be. To begin with, it was next to impossible to see Carson on her own. Not only did she work in the general store attached to Lee's Garage but she lived above Lee's as well. She was not sequestered, exactly, nor did she live the life of a hermit. But she was inevitably accompanied by Lee or Lee's sons, wherever she went. She was chaperoned — or, as rumour had it, jealously guarded by Lee's eldest son.

Skennen's next idea was to petition her family and friends for help. They were bound to have at least some idea of what made Carson cry. This thought was obvious and, among the suitors, common. But Michaels, her family, and her close friends were all from Schomberg, one of the most unnerving towns in Southern Ontario. Schombergians were secretive at the best of times, but Carson Michaels's suitors had driven her family and friends to a pugnacious silence. Skennen did not find a single acquaintance of Carson's who would speak to him, and, as far as he could tell, her family had disappeared entirely.

His third — and final — idea was to talk to Carson's old suitors, the ones who'd failed and were now bitter enough to co-operate with anyone who might win her, bitter enough to wish her 'defeated.' There were quite a number of banished suitors, enough of them to fill a modest-sized town: bigger than Napanee, say, but smaller than Quinte West. Skennen met these people singly or when they assembled in support groups. And though they were of every race, height, gender, and size, Michaels's former suitors shared a greyness of soul. Each had his or her own tale of despair. And none had any information to help him.

Or, rather, almost none.

One evening, Skennen met a man named Glenn Baillie in much the same way as he'd met the weeping man in Sutton. Baillie was sitting alone in the Pig's Ear Tavern, in Peterborough. The man was young – in his late twenties, say – and he was extremely fit. This, he said, had to do with his diet. He claimed to eat only vegetables, fruit, fish, nuts, and yogourt. He was a fanatic about his health, he said. The strange thing was that he made these claims aloud, though he was by himself. More: his concern for his health was contradicted by the seven shot glasses of whisky that stood in a straight line before him.

It was this seeming contradiction and the fact the man spoke so blithely to himself that interested Skennen. After watching him awhile, he approached Baillie's table and politely asked why, if he was concerned for his health, he would drink so much in one go.

– I haven't drunk anything, Baillie answered. I'm waiting to see *if* I drink them.

There being no answer to that, Skennen nodded and was about to turn away when, unprompted, Baillie asked

– Do you know Carson Michaels?

The question caught Skennen completely by surprise. He hadn't been thinking of Carson. He turned to look at Baillie again: young in appearance, his hair falling into his eyes, medium build, slightly shorter than Skennen, pale with a hopeful expression on his face.

– I know about her, Skennen answered.

Baillie's expression changed from one of hope to one of concern.

– Do you love her? Baillie asked.

– Yes, said Skennen, but I don't see how that's your business.

– I love her, too, said Baillie. I've never loved anyone half as much, but I know for certain she'll never love me. Even if I could answer her question.

Despite himself, Skennen offered his sympathy.

– No one knows the future, he said.

Baillie looked at him, then, with unconcealed dislike.

– I have to tell you a story, he said, one that might concern you.

Glenn Baillie, born in Liège, had moved with his parents to Petrolia at the age of five. Ashamed yet proud of his 'foreign accent,' he deliberately spoke English – a language he'd easily mastered – with an exaggerated French accent. He couldn't always maintain it, though. From time to time, an English-Canadian accent or even a Flemish one would come through.

He'd been an unhappy child. Though he was the third of five children, he grew up lonely, close to no one in his family, close to no one around him. Canada itself struck him as miserable: uncultured, bland, hypocritical, and quietly cruel. So, at eighteen, he returned to Europe and, for a time, drifted through its countries working on farms. He ended up in a small village in Normandy, penniless and desperate for work. More exactly, he was in a tavern near Clasville. The place was sullen and poorly lit, and when he entered, all conversation stopped.

About five minutes after him, an older woman came into the tavern – 'older' to him, though she was all of thirty-five. At her entrance, it was as if the silence itself had gone silent – an absolute zero of conviviality. There was something about the woman that made him wary, but he was young, defiant, and, although usually shy, he asked if she would like a drink.

Without hesitation, she said

– Thank you. I don't drink what they serve here. But maybe I could offer you something. I'm looking for someone to help around the farm. It's apple season. My trees need picking. You look like you could use a little money.

– I could, he said. I was looking for a job.

And just like that, the woman hired him.

There were signs – there always are in retrospect – that Madame Madeg was not what she seemed. First, the tavern's barkeep gave Baillie a strangely charitable look when it was clear he'd be working for the woman. This look was followed by a refusal to take money from him. Then there were the strange looks he and Madame Madeg got from pedestrians, some of whom made the sign of the cross as her car passed. In his innocence, Glenn Baillie took these things as expressions of concern for Madame Madeg's car, a 1957 Citroën that rattled its way to her farm.

Further signs: there were bats nailed to the doors of her house and barn.

— Just ignore them, she said.

But they were not the kind of things he could ignore. The poor creatures were nailed through their hearts, their bodies and wings curling around fixed points like drying leaves curled around their midribs.

— But why do you do this? he asked.

Madame Madeg shook her head.

— I don't do it, she said. The neighbours do it to intimidate me. If I take them down, they replace them. So, I've got used to them. It's not so bad. The creatures only stink for a day or two once they start to rot.

He never got used to them. It was easier to close his eyes as he approached the doors.

Madame Madeg had hired him to cull the apples from her orchard — about a hundred Gros-Hôpital trees, their apples a kind of dirty green with, here or there, an outbreak of red. The trees were ready for culling but there seemed to be little urgency about it. He was the only one she hired and she didn't appear the least interested in the number of barrows he emptied into the ancient wooden crates in the barn.

Nor did he know what she did while he was picking apples. He rarely saw her during the day. What he saw, now and then, were the women who came to see her. Were they friends? Business associates? Clients? It was impossible for him to tell. Those who happened to see him never returned his greetings. Some seemed frightened. Others gave him defiant looks. But none ever spoke to him.

His evenings were another matter. The farmhouse was simple, spacious, well-lit, and clean. Its kitchen was large and almost intimidating with its supply of pots, pans, and the paraphernalia of preparation. (Preparation for what, though?) On one shelf, there were alembics of various sizes and test tubes. The dining room was more inviting. Its large oak table was pleasing as only wood can be, having accommodated countless diners, their many touches.

Despite the warmth of the room, it was sometimes awkward to sit alone with Madame Madeg. On those occasions, he was spared discomfort by a framed reproduction of *La Kermesse* by Pieter Balten. The painting – which hung on a wall – was one of those in which the artist had depicted countless scenes from the daily life of his own time. It was one of those 'life's rich pageant' things – like something from Hieronymus Bosch – and it was diverting when neither he nor Madame Madeg had anything to say.

From the beginning, Baillie understood that Madame Madeg wanted something from him. But, young as he was, seeing nothing valuable in himself, he could not guess what that might be. Nor did Madame Madeg help him guess, or not directly. She was considerate. She fed him well. She made sure there was enough for him to drink. But then, every once in a while, she alluded to his appearance – his brown eyes, his muscular shoulders. So that, from time to time, he had the distinct impression that she desired him. But here, too, his inexperience got in the way. Madame Madeg was, to his mind, like a friend of his parents.

And yet ...

Those were the days when his own sexual longing was oppressive. He went to bed at night with an erection and woke in the morning with another. His mind and glands conspired to keep him aroused. A wind that blew sand on his neck, a warm touch on his wrist, the sight of Madame Madeg's feathery brown hair, a glimpse of her breasts, pale white where the sun had not reached, the smell of her perspiration mingled with the lavender of her soap ... almost anything could call pleasure to his mind and body.

So, it should not have been a surprise when, one evening when he'd drunk more wine than usual and Madame Madeg had left her hand on his upper thigh as she praised him for his work around the farm, he'd felt longing. But it *was* a surprise. The immediacy of his arousal – every atom of him suddenly, humiliatingly filled with longing for Madame Madeg. And then: how easily and expertly she touched him! In those hours between their kiss at the dining room table and the bluish dawn light that finally revealed her body to him, Baillie learned that what he'd previously taken for pleasure – the quick satisfactions he'd given himself when desire was overwhelming – was to real pleasure like a pond is to the ocean. Now aware that Madame Madeg put his body to better use than he could, he'd have done anything for her.

They spent the next months copulating, wearing clothes only when it was unavoidable, Madame Madeg as enraptured with him as he now was with her. That is to say, Baillie spent the winter making love with the most accomplished and, to some, most terrifying witch in Normandy.

Not that Baillie knew Madame Madeg was a witch. Not that winter. No, the world they created was meant for lovers – a dense garden, a bed smooth as a wafer of sunlight. And although women (mostly) and men (ashamedly) still came to see Madame Madeg, Baillie never thought to ask why they'd come. That winter, he couldn't wait for them to leave. But then, as spring approached, he sometimes went into Clasville with Madame Madeg, so as not to be away from her. It was on these excursions that he first became curious about her work. For one thing, the people in Clasville inevitably nodded at him in silent greeting. Few talked to him. There weren't many occasions when they could. But when they did they were pointedly circumspect, as if worried about the impressions they'd make.

When he asked her about this, Madame Madeg said

– I always forget how little you know,

teasing him before unbuttoning his shirt and running her hand over his chest, down to where the hair started beneath his navel. It seemed to him then that arousing him – which she did easily – was her way of changing the subject. He began to resent it a little, despite the pleasure.

So, he persisted with his questions about her. From time to time, when he was bored or spent from pleasure, he asked about what she did or asked about her life. And, at last, when spring arrived and the land smelled of loam, she told him.

– I was born, she said, in Caen.

(Here, Mr. Henderson stopped a moment and sighed. It was only then that I noticed he'd been crying, the tears on his left cheek creating a sheen. When he noticed me looking at him, he sniffled.

– How sharper than a serpent's tooth it is to love, he said.

Professor Bruno reached across to pat his shoulder.

– It's all right, Henny, he said. Go on. It's a terrific story. I'm intrigued by the witch.

– Thank you, Morgan, said Mr. Henderson. Thank you. I always cry at this part.)

Marthe Madeg was born just off Boulevard Maréchal Lyautey in a quartier called la Grâce de Dieu. Nor was she born to be a witch. Au contraire, from her earliest days, she had a deep love for God – a love that she still possessed, though her notions of 'God' had changed. If anything, it was her natural piety – her instinctive absorption in prayer, her attention to the natural world – that her parents found disturbing. They were themselves believers but only just this side of atheism. To 'loosen her up,' they sent her to spend summers with her aunt Mireille in Clasville.

The first summer she spent in Clasville, Marthe was twelve and ostentatiously pious, proud of the love she had for God. In retrospect, she thought she must have been insufferable. That said, it seemed to Marthe that her aunt was at least as devout as she was. For one thing, there were crucifixes in every room, along with what she took to be paintings of female saints in agony. It did seem odd that the crucifixes were all hung upside down. But Mireille made the sign of the cross whenever she herself entered or left the house – the house in which Glenn Baillie now sat – and that was enough to reassure young Marthe that the crucifixes had been hung that way in error.

Mind you, there was something sly about the way Mireille made the sign of the cross. Marthe sometimes had the feeling she was being mocked. And then, too, the portraits of the saints were not as saintly as she'd first thought them. The paintings were dark, save for the women at their centres. At the edges, there were men with antlers or wild animals – wolves, mostly: sculpted shadows with white eyes and yellowish teeth. They seemed surreptitious and terrifying, and one felt sympathy for the women in the paintings. And yet, these saints in white dresses or robes had the most ambiguous looks. Were they crying in pain and terror or was it something else that drove them to roll their eyes back, to clutch at their breasts or middles? And why did they wear no underclothes – pale haunches in view so there was little left to the imagination?

That first summer, there were so many things just beyond her ken. But one thing was clear: her aunt adored her. Not for a moment did Mireille treat her like a child. From the start, it was as if they were sisters, though Mireille, then in her forties, was clearly the one with things to teach. What did Marthe learn? Flowers, herbs, roots, and stems: the taste and smell of them, the uses of lemon balm and mugwort, foxglove, and lavender. In fact, for the first three summers, Marthe did little else but study roots, stems, and leaves, learning to draw them so well that she made her own 150-plant herbarium from memory. It was only then, when Marthe was fifteen, that her aunt began to teach her about spells, charms, tonics, potions, and, most intriguing, augury.

The summer she was fifteen was significant for another reason: Marthe began to understand what the portraits of the 'saints' signified. They were like stations of the cross devoted to sexual pleasure.

Mireille was sensitive to her niece's disapproval and aware of her discomfort. One morning, in an effort to explain herself, Mireille spoke to her niece about the 'facts of life.' She told Marthe about her own fifteenth summer, the summer when a talented witch had read *her* future. The woman had informed her that she (Mireille) would never fall in love and, that being the case, it was best if she became intimate with her body's wants and desires. Mireille had taken the woman's words as fact. From her fifteenth year, she had been open to all the pleasures of the body.

Though Mireille did not want to influence her niece in matters of sentiment, she admitted that, for her, the idea of 'romantic love' was an encumbrance that men and women took on for different but equally bad reasons. In fact, it was far from clear to Mireille that romantic love existed at all. Or, if it did, that it was in any way superior to the love she had for her family and friends. Really, she had no regrets.

(Here, it was Professor Bruno who interrupted the story.

– I don't think I could choose pleasure over love, he said.

– It is a drastic choice, said Mr. Henderson. But I wonder if more men or women would choose pleasure over love.

– Younger men, maybe, said Professor Bruno. The search for pleasure gets a little tiresome, after a certain age. But I'm not sure this is a male or female question, Henny. It's a question of libido, surely. Don't you think?

– I'm with you part of the way, Morgan, said Mr. Henderson. I don't think the difference between men and women is absolute. But I don't know for certain what it means for a woman to have sexual pleasure. So, I've never quite known what to make of Madame Madeg's aunt. Maybe she was fortunate.

– But she had no choice, I said. What could she do if being loveless was her fate?

– You've found the right question! said Mr. Henderson. What's a life, if physical pleasure is the best it has to offer?)

Having heard her aunt's story, did Marthe wish to know her own fate?

Yes, she did.

So, Mireille cut open one of the pigeons she kept for haruspication, poking around in the bird's entrails after Marthe had breathed on its innards. And she read her niece's future.

– My poor Marthe, she said after thinking about it, you're luckier than me and less fortunate, too.

What she meant was that Marthe had a choice where her romantic future was concerned. She could choose a life of pleasure, as her aunt had. In which case, like her aunt, she would know the heights of pleasure but not of love. Or Marthe could abstain from lovemaking until her beloved came to her.

And who would this beloved be? That Mireille could not say.

And would he or she love her? That Mireille could not say.

When would her beloved come? No one could tell her that, sadly.

But would this love endure? It would endure within her, yes, to her dying day. But her beloved would not stay with her long. Nor would she ever love again.

It was impossible to say what she might choose now, but Madame Madeg's fifteen-year-old self chose without hesitation. Bewitched by ideas like 'god' and 'purity,' she chose to forego pleasures of the flesh for the possibility of true love. And though, in the twenty years that followed her decision, she often wondered if she'd made a mistake, her soul would not allow her to sleep with any of those who desired her.

That's not to say that Marthe spent twenty years pining for her beloved. Far from it. She devoted herself to the dark arts her aunt had mastered. She learned the subtleties of spell casting, the precision of potion blending, the various grammars found in the innards of pigeons, bats, and certain fish. In fact, by the time Mireille died in her arms, Marthe had long been accepted as a worthy successor to her aunt, accepted as a 'bride of the devil,' one who was, in some areas, superior to her aunt. Her love potions, for instance, were much more effective.

And then, on a day when her only thought was apples, when she entered the tavern in Clasville looking for workers to cull her orchard, she heard his — that is, Baillie's — voice and knew at once that love had come. It was nice that he'd spoken to her, but that hadn't changed a thing. She'd have known him if he'd sighed or coughed or stayed silent. She knew him by what she felt at the sight of him: like the door to a forgotten but thrilling room being pushed open before her. And how strange to recognize someone you don't know! But she did recognize him and that's why she hired him on the spot. It was also why she hired him alone. Knowing what she knew — that this slightly awkward, fawnlike twenty-year-old was her destiny — she wanted no one else around, no one to share him with, no one to distract them.

The days before they made love had been almost unendurable. She had never felt such fascination for another. The very smell of him even — as he walked near her, as she put his bedclothes in the wash — was intoxicating. Nor could she have anticipated such longing, desire so strong she was constantly distracted by thoughts of him. And how humiliating! It felt as if anyone might have known her most private feelings by a glance at her face, as if anyone could have seen how much she wanted to touch him. And yet, she was defiant. Let them read her!

Baillie had thought her expert in bed. But, of course, she'd had no experience at all. She'd been, rather, so virulently innocent that she'd seemed jaded. More: knowing that this relationship would not last — but not knowing when it would end — every moment with him was miraculous.

There: now he knew what she did for a living and, to an extent, who she was.

In revealing herself to him, Marthe had been generous, open, and vulnerable. The older Glenn Baillie, the one who told his story to John Skennen, understood that fully. And he found it humiliating to admit that it was as Madame Madeg confessed her love for him that a coldness had invaded him. He was suddenly aware that he felt nothing like this 'once-in-a-lifetime love' for her. Well, after all, he was twenty at the time. For him, physical pleasure was a transaction, a mechanical operation. He had no inkling that, when one loves, the word *pleasure* hides a set of desires and expectations that are not easily met by just anyone. Hearing her speak of the 'miraculous,' he began to suspect that although *he* may have been meant for her, *she* was not meant for him. The days that followed confirmed his suspicion.

Did she realize something in him had changed?

Oh, yes. She knew at once. It was like turning a green leaf over to find a dark line of aphids. More: his doubts infected every aspect of their life together, effectively ending what had been six months of glorious, almost irresponsible pleasure.

Did she wait for his feelings for her to disappear entirely?

Yes. Because she hoped he'd return to her. And yes, because having waited so long for love, she wanted to know all of it, right down to its dregs, however bitter. She willingly accepted the bewilderment and the suffering at their broken bond. Baillie, for his part, was happy to carry on fucking until his feelings for her were so distant that physical pleasure became a chore. Not capable of understanding Marthe's feelings, he was done with her a month or so after her confession.

There were a number of things Baillie regretted about his last days with Marthe. With each retelling of their story, he felt greater or lesser humiliation at the thought of this moment or that one. As he spoke to Skennen, for instance, he was mortified at the memory of the awkward silence that followed his excuse for going away – 'My parents need me back home.' Marthe had smiled at his words.

– But she let you go? asked Skennen.

She'd done more than let him go. She'd cooked a simple but lovely meal for his departure, a feast for two, though he didn't actually see her eat the dark meats and bitter greens she'd prepared. Nor did she drink any of what she called 'Ego Fata Domini Tui,' a concoction that looked like a tequila sunrise: sweet orange juice in which a layer of what he thought was grenadine – but which tasted herbal, like dandelion wine, and salty, like blood – lay at the bottom.

– Ego fata domini tui, said Skennen. I'm master of your fate? Why would you drink that?

– Is that what it means? asked Baillie. She told me if I drank it I'd have control over my fate.

And for ten years, he had no reason to think he'd been wrong because, for ten years, there were no consequences to his behaviour. His time near Clasville became a distant, erotic memory.

Then he fell in love with Carson Michaels.

You'd expect a man who'd never been in love to change when love found him, and Glenn Baillie *did* change. He changed in all the usual ways: his heart raced at the thought of Carson, his thoughts all strayed to her, his days were filled with longing and hope. He lived in fear that his feelings might not be returned.

All of this naturally reminded him of Madame Madeg, of her feelings for him, but now he found his memories of Clasville painful. There was more to it than that, though. The moment he fell in love, Baillie was overcome by a compulsion to tell the story of his and Marthe Madeg's relationship, compelled to tell it to those who were also in love with Carson Michaels. Nor could he avoid Carson's would-be lovers, because along with the compulsion to tell came an unerring ability to find those who loved her.

Did the need to tell his and Marthe's story lessen after he'd failed to answer Carson's question?

On the contrary, it was then that the compulsion to tell became oppressive, almost taking over his life. It was as if he had some neural disorder that manifested as storytelling. That or he'd been cursed.

No sooner did the word *curse* occur to him than Baillie was sure Madame Madeg had had a hand in the torment he was living through. Desperate for peace of mind, he returned to the outskirts of Clasville – to Marthe's farmhouse – for the first time since he'd fled. There, all of his doubts were quelled at once. Though he'd told no one where he was going and had arrived without warning, it seemed Marthe had expected him. She stepped from her farmhouse at the very moment he got out of the car he'd rented in Rouen.

– So, she said, you're finally in love.

There being no doubt that she knew, he told her the truth.

– And you're suffering? she asked.

– Yes, he said. Please help me.

– That I won't do, she answered. I *want* you to suffer.

Nor was that the worst thing she told him. Her curse had a harsher sting in it. Not only was Baillie doomed to love someone who could not return his affection, but the story of his and Marthe's relationship – the one he was compelled to tell – had something in it that would allow someone (but not him) to win the love of the one he loved. So, not only was he forced to tell the story of his thoughtlessness, but that very story would help another person win his beloved.

Baillie pleaded for forgiveness. But Marthe would not give it.

– When the woman you love loves someone else, you'll be set free, she said.

Those were her last words to Baillie and they were Baillie's penultimate words to John Skennen. Having come to the end of his story, Baillie drank the seven whiskies he'd ordered. He drank them quickly, one shot after the other. Immediately after drinking but before the alcohol hit him, Baillie, obviously distraught, told Skennen to leave him alone.

Which, to spare him further pain, Skennen did.

If the encounter with Skennen was devastating for Baillie, it was something else entirely for Skennen. Having heard Baillie's story – knowing that it contained a clue for the suitors of Carson Michaels – he was astonished to find he now had a very good idea about what made Carson weep. He wasn't certain, of course, because any reasonably long story is a wilderness of signs. The thing that made Carson cry might be a bat, a pigeon, blood, apples, a Citroën ...

And yet, while listening to Baillie speak, Skennen had had the impression that someone else was speaking to him – someone behind Baillie, speaking through Baillie, as if Baillie were a ventriloquist's dummy. When *La Kermesse* was mentioned, it was as if a bell sounded inside him. *La Kermesse* was one of the very few paintings Skennen knew intimately. He'd lived with a reproduction of it that had hung in the library in Petrolia, the town where he'd spent much of his childhood. And although the painting was as detailed as a Hieronymus Bosch, a specific part of it had come vividly to Skennen's mind the instant Baillie mentioned it: from the painting's right side, about halfway up, the depiction of a woman with a reddish top and white apron carrying a porcelain jug up from a cellar. It was the way she holds the jug: up before her, both hands beneath it, as if it were being presented to someone no longer there. The instant the white porcelain jug came to him, Skennen knew that Baillie's story had been meant for him, that a porcelain jug was the thing that made Carson Michaels cry.

The following day, he made his way to Coulson's Hill and Lee's Garage. He waited until his turn came at the till. As before, Carson smiled politely and asked if he knew what made her cry.

– Yes, answered Skennen, a white porcelain jug.

There was a moment as Carson Michaels took this in. Then, as if to prove his words right, she began to cry. No, she wept, overwhelmed that a suitor had discovered her secret. On hearing her weep, Lee came over and grabbed Skennen by the throat. He'd have done more damage, too, had Carson not prevented him.

– He answered my question, she said.

Carson's tone, Lee's dismay, the sudden quiet in the store ... It occurred to John Skennen that Carson Michaels had not expected anyone to answer her question. Perhaps she'd had some sort of agreement with Lee. Perhaps the rumours had been true: Carson had been promised to one of Lee's sons. Whatever the case, when she recovered her poise, Carson Michaels said

– I get off at five. I'll see you then.

Lee let go of Skennen's lapels, which – after surrendering his hold on Skennen's throat – he'd been holding on to as if he thought John Skennen needed help to stay upright.

– Hmm, he said.

Carson Michaels did not immediately love John Skennen. As far as she was concerned, 'love' – whatever it was – had not been part of the compact. She had only promised to pay attention to one who'd paid attention to her. Then again, what is love if not a particular kind of attention? She liked the way Skennen smiled. She found his hands – graceful as a pianist's – beautiful. It was pleasing to listen to his voice, a pleasure doubled by the fact that he had interesting things to say.

And, of course, there was poetry. He read to her from the work of Rimbaud and they translated *The Drunken Boat* together. But she introduced him to the work of Anna Akhmatova, a gift he carried with him thereafter: memorizing the translations, moved by Carson's love of Russian poetry, grateful to have discovered such precious work in Coulson's Hill.

All of which is to say that, after five months of seeing each other, alone and with others, Carson Michaels loved John Skennen – however one wishes to define 'love' – and her feelings were returned, their pleasure in each other's company being almost as intense as the physical pleasure they shared in her narrow bed above Lee's Garage.

In the midst of this happiness, one evening, now confident in their love for each other, Skennen asked Carson why porcelain jugs upset her as they did. Dismayed, she asked how he could not know the answer, knowing as he did that porcelain jugs *had* an effect on her. Had he only guessed 'porcelain jug'? Did he not know her at all? In answer, he lied.

– I've heard the story, he said, but I want to hear it from you, Carse.

– It's too hard to talk about, she said.

But she told him how much porcelain vessels reminded her of her father, a potter, and she reminisced about him. How strong he'd been! Handsome and tall, gentle and loving, but terrifying, too. He'd once put her mother in the hospital with a single, back-handed blow.

– Do all jugs make you cry? he asked. Or is it just the one?

A difficult question because what moved her, at the thought of porcelain jugs, was knowing that the one from her childhood still existed. But, in the end, she supposed it was the one jug that made her cry, really, the bone-white pitcher made by her father when he'd been a boy in Chatham, the one whose place had been on the night table beside her parents' bed, the one still in the house in Schomberg, where she and her siblings grew up, where her brother still lived.

Moved by thoughts of home, of her siblings, of her parents, Carson again began to weep, her tears falling on his chest, where her head lay.

There and then, with Carson in his arms, John Skennen felt a number of things. He felt guilt for having brought the pitcher to her mind. He felt a deepening love and pity for his beloved. He longed for a world in which Carson would never cry again. But these emotions brought a host of assumptions and misinterpretations. To begin with, he took Carson's tears for painful, because he himself did not cry, except when in pain. And then, knowing Lee had been a close friend of her father's, he imagined Carson's father had been as hulking and violent as Lee, just the kind to put a woman in hospital with the back of his hand. He thought: no wonder memories of childhood brought her to tears. He reasoned: he could not wipe out her childhood, but he could eradicate its symbol, an act that would liberate Carson and her siblings. He resolved: to decimate the jug and surprise Carson with its fragments.

His chance to 'put things right' came shortly. Over months of pillow talk, Skennen had learned much about Carson's siblings, including the fact that her brother and his family still lived in Schomberg, not far from the Scruffy Dog Tavern. The house, which faced the road, was mostly hidden by trees. That in itself helped to identify it, as did the faded oranges painted on its post box by Carson herself when she was twelve. He found the house easily. Not only that but he found what he assumed was *the* porcelain jug at once. He could not have missed it. It was displayed in the home's front window, as if it were a statue of the Virgin or a painting of Jesus with his finger pointing to his own bleeding heart. And though he knew it was an offence to Carson's brother, he stole the jug, breaking into the house when no one was home.

Even while smashing the jug to pieces, taking pure pleasure in destroying an object that caused Carson pain, Skennen had an inkling that something was wrong. The pleasure itself was too intense for such a small act. He broke the jug first with stones, then used a crowbar to reduce it to fragments, keeping one small piece to show Carson. All the while, he imagined he was obliterating a living pest, not smashing a delicate thing that had spent most of its life on a bedside table. But thoughts of its delicacy did creep in, along with fleeting doubts. For instance, why would Carson's brother keep a thing that caused his family pain in the front window of his house?

When he told Carson what he'd done — what he'd done for *her* — she laughed.

— As if, she said.

— No, sweetie, I did! he answered.

And showed her the oddly shaped fragment he'd kept: a small trident, its middle tine a stump.

Recognizing the whole from a fragment, as one might recognize a loved one from a mole or a finger, Carson Michaels fainted, losing consciousness so quickly she'd have fallen straight to the ground if he hadn't caught her. It took some time to revive her, too. When he did, he found that the woman he revived was not the woman who'd fainted. Carson could not hate him. It was too late for that. She'd taken him into her soul, and though love has any number of bad habits, leaving without notice is not one of them. But the fact was ineradicable: John had destroyed one of the most precious things she and her family had: the last true memento of their father, a man they'd all adored. And the destruction was her fault.

— But you said he was violent, said Skennen.

— To protect his children, yes.

— But he sent your mother to the hospital.

— My mother was an alcoholic, John. He came home and caught her whipping my brother with a telephone cord. He hit her to protect him!

— But the jug makes you cry!

— Of course it does! I miss my father terribly. Not a day goes by that I don't remember how much he loved us. If you knew me well enough to know the thing that made me cry, how could you not know its meaning?

And so, it finally came to her that she'd fallen in love with a man who'd known nothing about her, the very thing she'd tried to avoid!

But don't we usually fall in love with strangers?

Not always, but often enough that her wish to be known before letting herself love had been naive. The thought of her own naïveté mitigated her devastation. But only slightly, because now she blamed herself for the destruction of the jug her father had made when he was a boy. The thing was irreplaceable. Thoughts of John now brought thoughts of irreparable loss.

In the weeks that followed, Skennen hoped that Carson would see that he'd meant well, that he'd done everything for her. He hoped she would forgive him his mistake. But forgiveness was not the problem. She did forgive him. She even chose not to tell her siblings what she knew about the jug's disappearance. And yet, it was as if an invisible worm had made its way to the inner folds of their love, feeding on it till there was not enough left to sustain them. About a month after Skennen had broken the porcelain jug, they parted – both humiliated, both banished from the garden only two in love can reach.

Is it any wonder John's life fell apart after that? Any wonder that, drunk out of his mind, he helped Bob Grenville burn down the post office in Coulson's Hill, hoping he himself would die in the conflagration? Any wonder that he spread rumours of his own death – himself starting the story that he had died in the post office – and wandered around the province like a madman?

Answering his own questions, Mr. Henderson said

– It's no wonder at all.

And then there was a long pause, during which I listened to the cicadas humming like a hydro tower outside the window. Mr. Henderson had finished his story.

The professor and I were caught off guard, waiting as we were for the rest of the story, wanting to know about John Skennen's fate. But no, the story was through. Mr. Henderson wiped tears from his face and wordlessly got up to make tea.

– What a story, said Professor Bruno.

– Yes, said Mr. Henderson. And it has so many ins and outs. Every time I tell it, I'm struck by something new. Just the other day we were talking about this, John and me, and he says, 'Don't you think it's strange Baillie didn't know what "Ego domini fata tui" meant?' I said, 'What do you mean, strange? Who understands Latin these days?' And he said, 'Yes, but who remembers words they don't understand? I'm telling you, Henny, "I'm the master of your fate" was meant for me. I'm sure this Madame Madeg was telling me that she was the master of *my* fate, not just Baillie's. But I didn't think about that till too late.'

— Oh, said Professor Bruno, what a touching detail! If Skennen's right about 'Ego domini,' then this is a most wonderful
love story you've told us. Just think, this Madame Madeg not
only cursed her beloved but she also cursed the man who took
her beloved's first love. She punished Skennen out of love for
Mr. Baillie!

— But what if she was just angry in general? I asked.

Both men looked at me with pity.

— That's possible, said Professor Bruno. But it doesn't feel
right, Alfie. If Skennen ruined Baillie's chances with Carson
Michaels, then he did Madame Madeg a favour, didn't he? He
helped her make Baillie feel what she'd felt. So, why punish Skennen? She might have been angry in general, as you say, but her
anger was directed at Skennen, a stranger, someone she'd never
meet. And for no apparent reason! I say she punished him because
deep in her heart she couldn't stand to have anyone hurt her
beloved. If I had to guess, I'd say Madame Madeg must still have
loved this Baillie fellow completely.

— It's a love story, said Mr. Henderson. It's a hell of a love story.

Mr. Henderson and Professor Bruno were quiet. They were,
no doubt, contemplating some aspect of life brought out by the
story. I was grateful that neither was in tears. As for me, I'd found
the whole story disturbing. What remains of our feelings for
those we've loved when they've left us? Of the four people in the
story – Madame Madeg, Baillie, Skennen, Michaels – I had most
sympathy for Madame Madeg. In fact, I was comforted by Professor Bruno's idea that her love for Baillie persisted, even as she
sought revenge. But what a terrible thought: that you can wish
harm on someone you've loved. Was there something in me that
wanted Anne to suffer? Yes, of course, but not exactly. Even
though she'd left me, I wanted to know that my absence hurt her
at least as much as hers hurt me. I wasn't after revenge or even
justice. I wanted to know that the feelings I'd had for her had
been reciprocal, that our despair was mutual.

At the thought that our intimacy might have meant nothing to Anne, that it had been barren, the tears that were welling up in me fell. I tried to hide my emotion, but, seeing my tears, Mr. Henderson, too, began to cry. And seeing Mr. Henderson's tears, Professor Bruno also began to cry. Seeing Professor Bruno cry, I was overcome by another wave of tears. All of us then tried, I think, to hide our emotions. Mr. Henderson turned away from me as he wiped his face, and I turned away from Professor Bruno, who turned away from Mr. Henderson. Unfortunately, in turning away from Mr. Henderson, Professor Bruno saw me and was again moved to tears. In turning away from me, Mr. Henderson had turned to Professor Bruno and, seeing his tears, was again overwhelmed, sniffling as he wiped his nose. And I, having turned away from Professor Bruno, was overcome by emotion at the sight of Mr. Henderson brusquely wiping the tears from his face. I began again to weep, my body shuddering as tears fell. I don't know about the others, how they got hold of themselves, but I put a hand over my face and held it there until – after what seemed a long time – all my thoughts of Anne faded and I was calm again.

The stories and breakfast had set us back a few hours, the professor and me. I was afraid that we would not get to Feversham in time to meet with Reverend Crosbie, the woman to whom John Skennen had dedicated his final collection of poetry, the very collection I had with me.

– She's the one to talk to, said Mr. Henderson. They had a deep relationship. They still might. For all I know, you'll see him there.

Just before we left him, Professor Bruno asked if Carson Michaels still worked at Lee's Garage. Mr. Henderson, his hair back to its previous unruly state, assured us that she did. She had married one of Lee's sons and raised a family in Coulson's Hill.

– Do you think she'd mind if we introduced ourselves?

– I don't see why, said Mr. Henderson. She's as down-to-earth as you get.

The two men hugged. Then Mr. Henderson put his hand on my shoulder, the weight of it like a small bag of potatoes.

– You're a good man, he said. You'll make sure Morgan gets back home in one piece, won't you?

– I will, I said. I'll do my best.

I thought the visit to Lee's Garage might hold us back, but it turned out to be a brief encounter. Carson Michaels was now in her sixties. Her face was one that, in daylight, was surprisingly variable. It refused to settle into one fixed face. If he noticed this, Professor Bruno was not the least put off by it. He clearly thought Carson Michaels fascinating. He was transfixed. If this had been the old days, Ms. Michaels would no doubt have asked him to name the object that made her sad.

– Excuse me, said Professor Bruno, but are you Carson Michaels?

– Yes, she answered. Can I help you?

– I'm writing a book about John Skennen, he said. I wonder if I could ask you a few questions.

She looked up at us, then. Her eyes were brown and lively and, for a unnerving moment, it was as if I were looking into my mother's eyes, the loving face I remember from when I was a child.

– John is someone I knew a long time ago, she said.

– Yes, said Professor Bruno. I wonder if you'd share any memories you have of him with me.

– I'm sorry, said Carson, but I can't help you.

Nor did she give him a chance to change her mind. She walked away from the till and left the store. After a moment, she was replaced by a young man who politely asked if we meant to buy anything.

I could see the professor was disappointed, but he was too much the gentleman to say anything. He bought a litre of water and we left. I'd have been happy to go on to New Tecumseth, but Professor Bruno, still under Carson Michaels's spell, suggested we stop in Schomberg, the town where she'd grown up, where her family still lived, where Skennen had stolen the porcelain jug.

– Don't you think we should go to New Tecumseth? I asked. Mr. Henderson said Reverend Crosbie was the right person to talk to.

– Very true, he said. But it's almost noon, Alfie. We have to eat sometime. We can eat at the Scruffy Dog in Schomberg. I've heard it's good.

I thought it was unlikely that anyone had said anything about the Scruffy Dog. But that isn't what struck me. What struck me was that it sounded as if Professor Bruno was no longer interested in John Skennen. From the moment Mr. Henderson told us that Skennen might be around, the professor seemed less and less charmed by the idea of meeting him. I began to wonder if he dreaded the possibility.

– No, no, he said. I don't dread anything, Alfie. Besides, we're going to Schomberg for research!

I wasn't convinced by his answer.

The Scruffy Dog was no different from taverns all around the province, except that it was in Schomberg. Of course, that, in itself, was noteworthy. Schomberg is different. I knew the town. I'd known it since I was a child, having spent summers there as a boy, between the ages of seven and fourteen. Even so, I find it an unsettling place. My unease has nothing to do with Schomberg's Black population. Being Black, I'm comforted by the thought of a town of Black people. My problem is more practical: when I'm in Schomberg, I'm often unsure of what's being said to me.

Given that he'd grown up in the region, I was surprised the professor knew so little about Schomberg. But then, Professor Bruno is Caucasian and Schomberg is difficult for white Canadians to understand. This is partly because the town is reflexively cool toward white Canadians and partly because it is traditional for the Black people of Schomberg to hide meaning from white Canadians.

This had to do with the town's history. In the early 1800s, Schomberg was a bastion of abolitionists. Most of them had come to Canada from Britain and the United States and were against slavery for emotional, religious, or other theoretical reasons. They did not know anything about actual Black people. Few of them had dealt with any. In fact, it's often said that if – in the 1800s – the abolitionists of Schomberg had lived with actual Black people, they might have discovered sooner that 'Black people' are human beings and, so, unlikely to meet the idealized – and often primitive – versions Canadians had of them.

In any case, delegations of abolitionists shepherded into town numerous freed slaves who'd come to Canada by way of the Underground Railroad. The freed men and women were collected in such numbers that they quickly became a significant part of the community. Now Schomberg was forced to deal with real Black people and, for the most part, the townsfolk did well. Black people were more or less accepted. What was not accepted was the way Black people spoke. It was disconcerting for Schombergians to hear their town become foreign. So, with overwhelming public support, Schomberg's lawmakers made it illegal for Black people to speak on the streets of Schomberg during the day. Black people were free to live their lives to the fullest: they could own property, send their children to schools outside of Schomberg, attend churches, work wherever they were needed. But there were fines for Blacks who spoke during the day. The fines were heavy and could, if unpaid, lead to time in jail.

For the first generation of freed slaves, the injunction against public speech was bewildering. But it was also a reasonable bargain. As they'd recently come from places where they could be sold like chattel and whipped like animals, the idea of remaining silent on the streets of Schomberg was lightly borne. They kept quiet but developed a culture of silence, communicating with each other by hand signals and movements of the head. Moreover, as time passed, they came to take pride in their command of quietness and passed 'day speak' on to their offspring.

As the decades passed, the white population gradually moved away to Toronto or Newmarket, Markham or Quinte, leaving Schomberg to its largely Black citizenry. And so, 150 years after the first freed slaves were introduced to the town, Black people owned all of the companies in Schomberg, ran its institutions, and, to help maintain the daily quiet, sent their children to school in Newmarket. When, in 1998, the town council voted on whether to take the old, racist bylaws off the books, they decided instead to keep them, arguing that their ancestors had put racism to good use, creating a unique language and culture. By the year 2015, Schomberg, Ontario, was 90 per cent Black and, during the day, it was the quietest town in the country.

None of this history meant much to me when my parents first took me to Schomberg. Nor was I upset at being forbidden to speak in public. I accepted the reasons and felt proud to be in a town filled with people like me. What unnerved me was the way people moved. Though the town was quiet, save for the noises of traffic, the people in it were constantly 'speaking' – hands and heads in peculiar but specific motion. Naturally, my parents had told me that people in Schomberg 'spoke' with their whole bodies, but I discovered that there were also times when heads and hands moved without signifying. And I found it embarrassing not to know when a movement meant something and when it did not. For years after my first visit, I had bad dreams in which trembling willows and billowing drapes said nasty things to me.

As always when I'm in Schomberg, my first reaction to the town was pleasure at the sight of so many Black people. I feel an immediate connection to the place, a sense of belonging. This time, with Professor Bruno accompanying me, the feeling did not last long. Professor Bruno was enchanted by everything. It was as if he'd never seen hardware stores or bank machines. But what he hadn't seen was a Canadian town in which it was mostly Black people who used these things. He knew, or was familiar with, the idea that there are places in Ontario where he, though white, would be in the minority. But an idea is not a thing. It's the thing behind a thing and it's always at least a little odd (or exhilarating) to feel an idea come into the world, like a phantom become solid.

As we walked, he couldn't help pointing to objects and saying
– This is wonderful!
or
– How delightful!
when they were neither wonderful nor much cause for delight.

But the professor's words were, in the quiet town, a kind of pollution. We were noticed, and, after his sixth or seventh 'Wonderful!' a woman walking toward us stopped, looked at the professor, and put a finger to her lips. She then looked at me and raised the middle finger of her right hand. I nodded. But I could see the professor was taken aback. He held up both his hands, palms out as in surrender. At this, the woman slapped him across the face and, furious, walked away.

This was just the type of situation I'd worried about. I'd warned the professor to keep his hands by his side and to say as little as possible. The woman had, while looking at Professor Bruno, asked him to keep quiet. She'd asked politely, using a universally understood sign for 'silence' – finger up before the lips. Showing me the middle finger of her right hand, she'd asked – just as politely – if I was from out of town. As I answered, Professor Bruno had – in lifting his hands palms up – inadvertently communicated his desire for sexual contact.

The woman must have known Professor Bruno was a stranger. She'd have approached him differently, otherwise. So, she must also have known that he'd not intended anything inappropriate. But the professor's gesture had been so rude and so unexpected, it must have been impossible for her to quell her indignation. To be fair to the professor, misunderstandings of this sort between residents and strangers are common in Schomberg.

The professor, his face red – a deeper shade where hand had met cheek – stood where he was for a while, speechless. Though I'd have liked to spare him the humiliation, and though I'd worried about this kind of encounter, this confrontation was the best thing that could have happened to us. It showed the professor that I hadn't exaggerated the problems strangers face in Schomberg. It dampened his enthusiasm for the place, so we were able to leave it sooner. From the moment he was slapped, he kept his arms at his side as if he were in a crush of people, afraid of signifying. And, as it turned out, the only other contretemps we had in Schomberg was entirely my fault.

Though he was upset after his encounter with the woman, Professor Bruno decided we should at least stop at the Scruffy Dog. He was still curious about the town Carson Michaels had come from and, besides, he wanted a cup of tea – camomile, if possible – to calm him.

The Scruffy Dog was very like the Rebarbative Moose, the pub in Coulson's Hill. It offered pub grub, inexpensive beer, cheap Scotch, reasonable rum, and economical vodka. In other towns, the music playing in places like the Dog is almost always older, nostalgic, comforting (if you're old enough), or irritating (otherwise): Beatles, Stones, Eagles, or country and western if you're near farmland. In the Scruffy Dog, the music was from the same era but Black and resolutely American: James Brown, Motown, Philly soul, rhythm and blues.

Feeling that the Dog was a safe place – there being only one other patron in it besides the two of us – I encouraged Professor Bruno to order the tea for himself. The sign for 'tea' in Schomberg is one I've always found funny. It resembles someone milking a cow. So, wittily, 'teats' stand for 'tea.' I showed the professor how it's done: hands making circles (like monoculars) and then one up, one down, imitating milking or pistons moving.

– But what do I do for camomile? he asked.

There was no sign for 'camomile' as far as I knew. What there was was a sign for 'herbal.' For this, one moved one's fingers as if playing the piano. That is, fingers moving up and down while hands moved from side to side – an imitation of plants moving in a field serving to suggest herbs.

Once I was sure he could do the signs clearly – and, after all, they were not difficult – I sent Professor Bruno to the bar for his order, there being no wait staff around to serve us. From where I sat, I could see if the professor was speaking correctly. He approached the bar, nodded at the bartender, imitated the milking of a cow, as I'd told him, and followed that with an imitation of a field in motion (or of piano playing). As far as I could tell, it was done properly, so I don't know which of us – Professor Bruno, me, the bartender – was more surprised by what followed.

Without taking his eyes off the professor, the bartender backed away immediately, as if the professor had shown him something dangerous. I could see Professor Bruno was puzzled but determined to maintain quiet. He again imitated the milking of a cow and the playing of a piano. Now the bartender put a grease bucket before the professor and gave him a glass of water. More puzzled than ever – his face red – Professor Bruno persisted, moving his hands up and down, then fluttering his fingers back and forth. The bartender pushed the bucket toward him and held up a bar towel, as if to ward him off.

It was only then that I saw the problem. It was, in a way, a question of accent. Instead of keeping his fingers in the shape of a circle, Professor Bruno held his fingers (pinky, ring, and middle) out like crab legs – (((– so that when he moved them up and down he was making the sign for 'vomit.' Nor was he moving his hands back and forth when he imitated a field. He was holding them in place, which is the sign for water. So, in effect, he'd been telling the bartender that he was about to vomit and needed a glass of water.

I caught the bartender's attention and corrected the professor. He nodded and brought a pot of orange pekoe tea and another glass of water. I made what I thought was the sign for 'herbal' again and this time the bartender shrugged and pointed to the glass of water. A light must have switched on in his mind, though. He looked at me and, questioning, made the proper sign for 'herbal,' which was like piano playing but with the palms upward. I nodded, and only then did he bring a selection of tisanes from which to choose.

Professor Bruno seemed happy to sit and drink his camomile. But I was uncomfortable. Schomberg had defeated me or taught me again – as if I needed the lesson – the gulf between blood and culture. I felt humiliated that I'd mistaken the signs for 'water' and 'herbal.' But why should my mistake be humiliating? I don't live in Schomberg and I'm not all that familiar with its 'day speak.' Really, there was no reason for my humiliation, except that not knowing the language of Black people created a kind of doubt in me that I was myself Black. I brooded on the idea that the remaining white people of Schomberg who knew 'day speak' were, in some way, more 'Black' than I was. Was I, then, more Canadian than Black? This was an even stranger thought, since Schomberg and its inhabitants were all proudly Canadian. It was proof that I unconsciously excluded the people of Schomberg from 'the Canadian.' Which is to say that, to some extent, I excluded myself, too. In Schomberg, I ended up feeling inadequate, shamed, cancelled out, as if I only precariously belonged anywhere. So, it was a relief when Professor Bruno finished his camomile and we left the Scruffy Dog, heading (at last) for Feversham.

As if Schomberg itself were pleased by our departure, I discovered a wide patch of silk locket (*Carcere Canadensis*) as the professor and I walked back to the car. And I was reminded of how rich in small wonders Canada is, how rich *my* country is.

It's true that silk lockets are common – and classified as a weed – but I've always thought they were a fascinating variant of the 'flytrap' plants that exist around the world. To begin with, the locket's appearance when open is like a circular clump of reddish-blond hair, in the middle of which there is a circular depression, in the middle of which there is a circular blue speck that smells of butter in the morning and of rotten chicken in the afternoon. The blue is attractive to flies. But when a fly – or any insect – touches the speck, the strands of hair knit themselves into what, when the plant is closed, looks like a small locket. The remarkable thing is that it takes silk locket .227 of a second to close the trap, about the same time as it takes someone to blink, so it's virtually impossible for the human eye to see the plant in action.

As with any carnivorous plant, there is something terribly cruel about silk locket. But when I was a child, it was considered good luck to find one that had just closed. You could hear the fly inside the plant, buzzing for some time before it died. And though I hadn't done this in years, I searched among the lockets to see if I could find a noisy one, wasting a few minutes before giving up.

Having lost the morning, we should have headed straight to Feversham, but the day seemed intent on driving us off course. As we got into the car and fastened our seat belts, there was a knock on the passenger-side window. A short, stocky Black man, his Afro greying in a small circle on his head, repeatedly made

the sign for 'hitchhike' – fist held sideways, thumb out and pointing in the direction of the road. No sooner was he in the back of
car than he began to talk.

– Malky Jenkins, he said. Good to meet you.

– Oh, said Professor Bruno. You're talking!

– Course I'm talking, said Malky. I can't be Black twenty-four
hours a day. Besides, I like Schomberg but I love to talk. I'd croak
if I lived here. You guys going anywhere near New Tecumseth?

Malky's voice was pleasant and he himself was good company.

– What's a Caucasian individual like you doing in Schomberg?
he asked Professor Bruno.

– Well, said Professor Bruno, Alfred and I were curious about
the town Carson Michaels came from. Do you know her?

– Sure I know her, said Malky. What about it?

– We heard a story about her and ...

Malky interrupted him.

– You heard she's the most beautiful woman around here,
didn't you? But it's not true! Carson was okay in her day, but her
sister Kate's the one. That's a fine woman! Carson's one of those
who believes they're beautiful, and when a person believes themself strong enough, they get others to believe them, too. Without
trying! That's the kind of beautiful Carson was. I just don't believe
her, is what I'm saying. You can see for yourself, you know. She
works in Coulson's Hill.

– We were just in Coulson's Hill, said the professor. I found
her quite lovely.

– Man, I'm not arguing with you, said Malky. What a person
finds beautiful is their own business. I'll just say, we don't go to
the same church. But I am observant, where beauty's concerned.

In the half-hour it took to reach New Tecumseth, Malky must
have talked about a hundred things, but what stuck with me,
distracted as I was with the driving, were his words about Carson
Michaels's beauty and his talk about the Museum of Canadian
Sexuality in New Tecumseth. The two things were related. At

least, they were for Malky, physical beauty being a hidden aspect of the museum, as far as he was concerned.

Had we been to the Museum of Canadian Sexuality? No? Neither of us? How wonderful that we could see it for the first time today! He highly recommended the place. And, it just so happened, he worked at the museum. He was a ticket taker and it would be his pleasure to give us each an employee discount on the entrance fee.

The thought of visiting a museum devoted to sexuality didn't appeal to me at all. I'm not prudish, but I've begun to think my father was right about the 'publicizing' of sex.

– What's the point, he'd ask, of surrendering the most wonderful thing humans have to businessmen and carnies? I just don't understand this need to abase the sacred.

The older I am, the more I understand my father's scruples. But Professor Bruno's curiosity was piqued. He couldn't imagine what a museum devoted to 'Canadian sexuality' would look like. And, to be fair, neither could I. So, when we got to New Tecumseth, the professor decided we should see the place for ourselves.

The Museum of Canadian Sexuality was in an old-style theatre. It looked like the Victoria playhouse in Petrolia but without the clock tower. The building was brick, but it had been recently painted white, with black trim around the windows and doors. It looked elegant and compact, almost Quaker-built. Inside, it was more colourful. Once you got beyond the box office, some of the walls had brightly coloured images projected on them. For instance, in the antechamber where we waited for our guide, a single scarlet tanager feather was projected on our left: bright red and imposing, about four feet long from tip to crown. On the wall to our right, directly opposite the feather, there was a green maple tree in leaf, also about four feet tall.

For five minutes or so, we were alone in the antechamber, the professor and me. The only sound was the drone of a distant fan.

We were eventually joined by a person in a royal-blue pantsuit, a necklace of thick, false pearls, and dark shoes whose soles were so high you could have said the person was perched when they weren't in motion.

– Is it just you two? the person asked.

– Dear madam, I think it is, answered the professor.

The person looked at him for a moment.

– Are you heterosexual? they asked.

Embarrassed, the professor said

– Well, in general, yes.

– Oh, no judgment, they said. Is your partner also heterosexual?

They both looked at me.

– Yes, I'm hetero, I said.

Though it felt strange having to admit it.

– I don't like to ask, said our guide. It's a bit of an invasion. And you may not feel comfortable in any of the usual categories. But I find it useful to know when I'm leading heterosexuals through the museum. You see, here we don't pretend heterosexuality is the only or most interesting approach to the movable feast that is sex. But neither do we judge. Your inclinations are your own affair. You should know, though, that Canadian sexuality includes any number of gratifications. So, if you think you're likely to be offended, you can get a full refund at this stage and we'll go no further. Are you both okay to proceed?

I nodded to show my assent, but Professor Bruno asked

– What kind of gratifications?

– I don't want to tell you before we see the exhibits, answered our guide. It would spoil your surprise. But all the acts depicted are within the norms of Canadian conduct, if not approval.

Which didn't exactly put the professor at ease.

– Well, he said, if they're within the norms ...

– Wonderful, said our guide. Now, if you'll just follow me.

We went through a door, from the quiet antechamber into a large, darkened room. The ceiling was some thirty feet up, satin-black with dozens of illuminated specks on it, as if fluorescent rice had been thrown at it and stuck. Around us were four brightly lit dioramas in glass showcases. But our guide, who introduced themself as Michael, first pointed to what I took to be a person standing in the centre of the room and looking up at the ceiling, as if up at a night sky.

– We're a country of erotic distances, said Michael. The statue you see over there represents this, and it stands for all Canadians.

On looking closer, I could see how it stood for many of us. It was like a sculpture done by Evan Penny, lifelike. But it represented neither man nor woman or it represented both. The figure was in a long coat that descended past its knees. The coat was navy blue and seemed heavy. Beneath the coat the statue, which had cleavage and notable breasts, was unclothed – or looked as though it were. It had silky blond hair that fell past its clavicles, and along its narrow back. But it also had a prominent Adam's apple and a tidy black moustache.

Taking me aside, Michael said in a low voice

– This is, of course, our Caucasian model. We have a number of others, different ages and races. If you'd come yesterday, we had the older Negro out. I hope you're not offended. I'm able to refund your entrance fee, if you are.

I assured Michael that I wasn't offended, and, reassured, Michael took us to the first of the dioramas.

I found the first diorama – maybe because it *was* first – the most disturbing. In a glass showcase was a hotel room, its walls light blue. At its centre was a queen-sized bed, well made, its bedclothes cream-coloured. The floor was a pale, grainy wood and, to the left of the bed, there was a door. Stencilled on the glass between the spectators and the diorama were some twenty columns of numerals and letters neatly organized and clearly legible.

As I was looking at the diorama, Michael gave Professor Bruno a square of paper and quietly spoke words that I didn't catch. The professor's face reddened and, as if food had gone

down his throat the wrong way, he coughed wildly. Making soothing sounds, Michael patted the professor's back until he recovered. Michael then came to where I was standing and said

— The most interesting thing about Canadian sexuality is the
theatre of it, don't you think?

Michael then gave me a square of paper like the one they'd
given the professor.

— These are the permutations, Michael said.

The paper was thick, the size of a playing card, and on it, in
fluorescent ink, were printed the meanings of the symbols and
numbers that were on the glass of the dioramas. I immediately
understood the professor's embarrassment. Most of the symbols
stood for 'protrusions' or 'declivities.' The rest of them stood for
types of motion. Equipped with this chart, it was possible to
translate the 'notations' on the glass, if you wished. So, I could
now see that a previously indecipherable string of symbols —
$\alpha \times 2$ non-m, $3 \times \chi$ non-m — represented what is called 'soixante-
neuf.' In this way — that is, by way of symbols and numbers — the
geometry of penetration and accommodation was dealt with as
exhaustively as possible. This desire for completion — which was
a desire for inclusion — accounted for the sheer number of 'notations' stencilled on the glass. Meanwhile, penetrations and accommodations accounted for, the theatre of the Canadian sexual
imagination could be given its due with the dioramas.

Knowing the meanings of the symbols did not ease my discomfort. If anything, it made things worse. From the moment Michael
gave me the 'chart of correspondences,' I wanted out of the
museum. I stayed for Professor Bruno's sake. Having overcome
his embarrassment, he seemed intrigued by the exhibits.

The second diorama in the room was a representation of a
historical scene, a botanical one. It was a faithfully rendered
field of fire-lions (*Taraxacum angustifolium*), among the most beautiful plants native to our country. The fire-lions seemed to go
on for miles in all directions with, in the distance facing the

spectator, a border of willows whose light green crest was like a small, kind idea.

– This field, said Michael, represents a field of fire-lions from the 1500s. It's here, not far from Saguenay, that Jacques Cartier and a handful of his men are rumoured to have engaged in a spontaneous orgy amongst themselves, under the influence of what we now know to be the aphrodisiac contained in fire-lions. After writing a discreet account of what happened, Cartier wrote in his diary: 'Nous ne sommes pas sortis indemnes'.

Michael here looked at Professor Bruno and, as if anticipating some learnèd reproach, said

– There are other accounts of this incident. One of Cartier's own men wrote that the Iroquois had warned them about the field and had told them in the plainest way what would happen.

I'd never heard of this orgy among Jacques Cartier and his men, but if they'd wandered into a field of fire-lions, they would not have been able to help themselves. And you'd have thought this episode would, at least among botanists, be known. It isn't. But the professor asked no questions about the *fact* of Cartier's predicament. Instead, he and our guide discussed Cartier's diary entry, its vagueness. As far as Professor Bruno was concerned, 'ne pas sortir indemne' – to *not* get away without consequences – could mean any number of things, not necessarily an orgy, as we in the twenty-first century understood the term. Michael's counter-argument was that, knowing what we do about the effects of fire-lions, it would be unusual if Jacques Cartier and his men had not engaged in some form of drastic sensuality. Besides, the explorers were young Europeans whose very idea of a 'new world' would have included the notion of unchecked sensuality. When you added to that the explorers' own accounts, however vague they sometimes were, it tilted the argument in the museum's favour, although, admittedly, there were historians who disagreed.

Professor Bruno seemed more interested than convinced.

– Well, I suppose that's a viable argument, he said.

I was not interested in either side of the argument, not interested in the historical record, not interested in the sexual activity of men who'd been dead for centuries. My thoughts were uniquely – maybe desperately – about the fire-lions. I was grateful for them. They were, ironically, a distraction from the museum.

I'd never seen a field of fire-lions – I still haven't – but whoever did the diorama must have been something of a botanist, so accurately were the plants made.

Though I appreciate how unlikely and wonderful it is that a plant should be both an herbal ecstasy and a natural Viagra, what caught my imagination, where the fire-lions were concerned, was the fact that a plant should evolve to look as if it were on fire: its leaves flame-red and streaked with yellow, its floating tufts (like dandelion seeds) rising black and grey from hidden seed heads. It's with plants like this (fire-lion, royal candles, bee balm, butterfly weed ...) that I feel the land's desire for joy, its willingness to play with us, to frustrate, to fool, to delight, to leave perplexed. Professor Bruno and Michael had moved on to the next diorama, but I stood for some time before the field of fire-lions, admiring the plants themselves and the willows in the distance.

After that, I looked over at the third diorama – a white icefield with a jagged white cliff for background and a full-sized orange tent in the foreground – and decided I didn't want to see any more. Professor Bruno and Michael were waiting for me in front of the showcase. Each seemed pleased with the other's company. Not that the professor was happy per se. When I'd caught up to them, he looked pensive. And, as if answering a question, he said

– Well, after all, the soul has no gender.

– Oh, said Michael, we make no assumptions about the soul. This is a museum of sex, not religion. And it isn't the soul that copulates. Our various bodies do that.

Then, looking at me, Michael asked

– Are you all right?

– I'm feeling overwhelmed, I said. I'm going to go sit down for a while. You two go on. I'll catch up later.

And I left them on their own.

Unfortunately, I had to pass the fourth diorama on the way out. It was a scene in a forest – a thickening of birches and spruce like a wooded haven in the distance. There was a well-trod path that led from the front of the diorama – where the viewer stood – toward the trees at the back. To the sides of the path: trodden grasses, white-headed clover, and a smattering of purple-tufted thistles. Lying on the path in front of the viewer: a bloodied body, one of its arms struggling or instinctively pulling at the ground in order to escape the grizzly bear that had just mauled it. The grizzly – which was extremely realistic – was up on its hind legs facing the viewer. And as the viewer approached the diorama, the bear roared, its jaws agape so one could see its bloody teeth.

The effect was to put the looker suddenly and without warning *in loco praedae*: in the place of the grizzly's prey. So realistically was this done that one could not help backing away. On stepping back, however, the viewer tripped a mechanism and the bear in the diorama lunged forward, its growl pure nature – loud and ferocious, the thud of its paw against the glass powerful enough to shake the diorama.

When I'd recovered from my distress, Michael and Professor Bruno had caught up to me. Both were smiling, no doubt admiring the diorama and, maybe, amused by the effect it had had on me. Still stunned, I told Michael I couldn't see how this diorama had come to be in a museum devoted to sexuality. Nothing about being killed by a bear struck me as erotic.

– Many people say this, said Michael. But the connection between arousal and danger is well documented. We know for a fact that all sorts of animals, when facing death, become aroused. And humans regularly court danger while having intercourse. Couples mate on rooftops, while driving cars, on planes, in Ferris wheels. God knows where. For my money, this is the most sensual of the dioramas.

Professor Bruno nodded in agreement.

– This is very true, he said. And just think, Alfie, we live in a world where people dress up as wild animals to have pleasure. I find this diorama quite convincing.

I saw the professor's point, but I simply could not accept that an enraged and marauding grizzly could be taken as an adjunct to pleasure. I'd mistaken the realistic representation of a grizzly for a real one and I'd been frightened, but even knowing that there was no danger, I felt uncomfortable standing in front of the diorama. This and my discomfort with the museum itself was too much. I let the professor and Michael discuss the nature of sexual fantasy on their own. I left the room, looking for a way out of the museum.

Leaving the room with the dioramas, I followed a wall-painted arrow that pointed to my left. Above this arrow were the words 'The Instruments/Les Instruments.' Beneath the arrow it said, 'This Way Out.' Which is to say, I had to go through another gallery to get out of the place.

'The Instruments/Les Instruments' was in a space as large as the one I'd left, though it seemed smaller because there were no dioramas. I tried to avoid looking closely at anything as I passed through the room, but what I did see resembled a work of conceptual art more than it did a museum exhibit. Along all four walls, there was a latticework of white squares – hundreds of white squares, each of which held one object, each object lit by its own tiny light: bananas, melons, and dildos on the top shelves, followed by more modest 'dilators' and 'recipients' (false vaginas, plastic fish heads), which were in turn followed by smaller things. What those smaller things were, I can't say, because I kept my eyes on the door as I made my way to what I hoped was the last exit.

But it wasn't. The third exit was through the museum's bookstore, a well-lit space on whose walls hung posters from previous exhibits. Despite my desire to leave the museum, I couldn't help admiring the images. The least one could say was that most made you wonder about the exhibits they advertised. For instance, the professor and I had apparently just missed a show called

PIERRE TRUDEAU: ANGEL OF THE EROTIC

whose poster was a painting of Pierre Elliott Trudeau's face. The former prime minister looked out, smiling kindly. But his image gave nothing away about the show's content.

After leafing through a pricey book called *Custard, Twigs, and Berries*, I went to the foyer, sat on its marble bench, and, for the hour it took before Professor Bruno came out, I tried to make sense of my feelings: my unease. I assumed it had nothing to do with sex itself. Having been born in a time when it's increasingly difficult *not* to know that humans have peculiar ideas of what constitutes sexual pleasure, I wasn't offended by what I'd seen. It is simply a fact that some of my contemporaries find motorcycles arousing: motorcycles, monocles, the smell of bleach, rubber gloves, cheese graters, maple leaves, and so on, endlessly. I also assumed it had nothing to do with the way the information was presented. I love taxonomy and I take pleasure in small variations.

An extra leaf, an unusual shade of flower, stamens of improbable length, etc.: all these details move me.

And yet, the collision of sex and taxonomy was at the heart of my unease. The museum was disturbing in its institutional desire for inclusivity, a desire that had turned the sexual into a thing that could be dealt with alphanumerically. Seeing the notations on the glass of the dioramas, I'd felt the tyranny of the specific. If every instance of the sexual could be plotted, turned to symbols, catalogued, and boxed, could the emotions behind our couplings and caresses also be assigned a symbol? Could the museum place a 'Λ' beside certain notations, so that some were performed with love (Λ) and some without (-Λ)?

At the thought of this, it was as if Anne had left me again. Or, rather, it was as if she came back and *then* left. I had, as I sat there, a vivid memory of her. We'd been walking together along Kingston Road when she showed me the steps down to Glen Stewart Park, not far from where she lived. It was summer, my first time in that green place, and I was enchanted by everything: the broad wooden steps, the plank railing, the steep decline into the ravine, the sound of the stream running through it. We were happy then, and she turned to me, smiling, tucking a strand of light-brown hair behind her ear and then kissing me, for no reason but pleasure in the moment, knowing the pleasure was shared, taking pleasure in the knowing, before we walked through the park, past houses that were like modest mansions in some secret England.

As the memory overwhelmed me, I sat on the marble bench in the Museum of Sex, feeling as devastated as if she'd just told me – told me again – that she thought she loved someone else, that she was sorry but we couldn't go on, that it was her fault not mine, that our stars were misaligned, that I shouldn't call because it was no use talking until she knew what she wanted, until I knew how I felt, until we'd both had a chance to heal.

Painful as the moment was, however, release from my unhappiness came soon after. As I wondered about the connection between love and fleshy mechanics, I thought of the story Mr. Henderson had told us about John Skennen and Carson Michaels. Though the story sounded fanciful – more legend than fact – I found, as I sat in the foyer, that I preferred the story's invention (its dishonesty, even) to the catalogue of couplings and preferences housed in the museum. I preferred the myths of intimacy to the facts of it. Professor Bruno had speculated that Madame Madeg's love for Baillie was evident in her punishment of John Skennen. Long after Madeg's proximity to Baillie, her feelings for the man were still strong. That idea brought me peace. Love was not just a superfluous part of what bodies did, it was in the moments before and after the mechanics as well. We were in the Canadian Museum of Sex not the Canadian Museum of Love, after all. This simple and obvious realization brought with it a more complicated puzzle: if we find love with someone, as I had with Anne, was it possible to lose it when that person was gone? Or did it, rather, stay within us: a perpetual gift, an inexhaustible resource?

I was reminded of a poem by John Skennen:

> A blue heron rose this morning from White Lake –
> wings pulling at air, dangling feet encumbrances,
> until it caught an updraft and was still
> having found its daily elegance in flight.
> Restless predator gone the lake unrippled
> soothing the stump from which the bird had flown
> setting cattails and reeds quietly rocking
> shaking the birches and alders – their leaves.
>
> O Canada, O my country
> for whom am I meant to keep this love?

A list of things. But a list behind which there's something irreducible. On first reading the poem, I thought Skennen had been confused about which of his partners he was meant to love and I'd found it strange that he'd ask his country's help to decide. But when I thought about it in the museum, it struck me that Skennen's feelings were caught in the web of things he'd listed: herons, birches, cattails, alders, and leaves. The world – people and things – brings us to love but it is not love itself. I might have said those very words about my parents and Anne, that they had brought me to love, that they were not love itself. That they were gone from me could not spoil what they'd given.

Obvious though this idea might have been to others, it was a revelation to me. So much so, that I began to feel as if our journey – mine and the professor's – was not to help Professor Bruno but to help me, Alfred Homer. It briefly felt as if all were meant for me, as if I'd generated everything in order to tell myself this small thing. Then again, I suppose every traveller feels this, because, in the end, every journey has a special – not general – meaning, a meaning particular to each traveller. A strange idea: that the professor was there to help me, not the other way around.

Just as I was thinking about him, Professor Bruno came out of the museum. He was red-faced.

– My, my, my, he said. What an institution! I don't think I've ever seen anything like it. What did you think? I loved it! I'd say this is one place where our tax dollars are well spent! And I'm not ashamed to say I was quite aroused. At times, *quite* aroused. On an unrelated note, Alfie, we're going to Marsville.

Without meaning to challenge him, I said

– I thought we were going to Feversham.

He frowned, but only for a moment.

– Je te vois venir, Alfie! he said. Yes, all right, I *am* wary of meeting John Skennen, so I'm *wary* of Feversham, too. I admit it. But you've got to understand, my boy, that in my mind and in all the work I've done, John Skennen is an artist and a brilliant thinker. I'd hate to have that image of him destroyed by facts. You see? The real Skennen could just as easily kill my version of him as improve it! And I don't mind saying I think my version of the man and his work is better than any real version could be. I'm not a coward, Alfie. I can face reality. But we old people know the cost of that confrontation more than you youngsters! I didn't know I'd feel this way when we started out, but there you have it. I *do* feel this way. We'll go to Feversham, don't worry. But it'll be tomorrow. Not today. For today, I've made arrangements with Michael to visit Michael's home in Marsville. Such a pleasant person! And so witty! Like finding an ounce of gold. We couldn't *not* go! Anyway, I'm sure you don't mind. I'm very happy about it myself. Very happy.

– Are we going to spend the night in Marsville? I asked.

– I'm not sure where we'll spend the night. We'll see how it goes. Michael's invited us for supper, but we'll be eating after six, once Michael finishes work. And it would be good for us to take our time, get to know Michael and Michael's roommate.

– Michael's roommate?

– Oh, yes. Michael's roommate will let us in. We can wait at their house.

As we drove to Marsville, the professor was almost chatty.

– You should have stayed for the other exhibits, he said. I can't tell you how interesting it all was. Did you at least see the Canadian Construction? Now *that* was fascinating! It's a program that allows you to create a Canadian lover. Imagine that! You choose from a set of characteristics: mouths, eyes, accents, vocabularies, the works! But all the aspects on offer are typically Canadian, based on the population we have. There's a large percentage of European characteristics on offer, of course: brown hair, freckles, that sort of thing. So, if you want a Malaysian accent, you have to ask for it, and the program might refuse, based on how many Malaysian accents have been asked for that week. So, it's a surprise what you end up with. Very surprising. The program creates a hologram that can talk! I'm not ashamed to say I was pleased with my hologram. Very lifelike. But Michael pointed out that my hologram looked exactly like Michael. That was an embarrassing moment, Alfie, but ... I went with it, as young people say. And, after all, Michael is very attractive. I don't mind saying that if I were younger and if I could tell Michael's gender, I'd be fit for an adventure. I really would.

This was more information than I needed. But I didn't want him to think I disapproved.

– Why does Michael's gender matter? I asked. Couldn't you have an adventure, anyway?

– Now, *there*, Alfie, is where you're one up on me, he said. It's too late for the old professor! I've spent seventy years getting used to a certain kind of plumbing. I'm too old to take things as I find them. I need them as I'm used to them.

My question gave him something to reflect on, I think. He kept quiet for a while, looking out his window at the late summer fields – the land faded, the sky as if unwillingly blue, the bale-ready hay lying out like a yellowish carpet. I worried that I'd saddened him, but, when I looked over at him, the professor was smiling.

– Maybe I shouldn't make assumptions, he said.

A mysterious sentence. I couldn't tell if he was referring to assumptions about Michael, assumptions about himself, or assumptions about life in general. But I agreed with him, nodding in an understanding way, and we continued along the Orangeville-Fergus Road with nothing but flat fields, outcroppings of trees, and the occasional farmhouse to distract us.

The directions to Michael's home were vague – 'Turn right at 13th Line' – but they were enough. The house wasn't far from the main road and it was painted white – white and blue, rather, the window frames being indigo. To the left of the front door, there was a patch of bat's delight (*Asclepias onterica*) – dark green leaves, crimson 'bars' (transverse pistils), the plants at full height touching the aprons of the windows on the first floor.

(The first time I ever saw bat's delight was at the Musical Gardens in Toronto. There was a patch of it on a hillock facing the lake, its crimson pistils vivid. But the plant is best seen in early evening. *Asclepius onterica* is a natural calmative for bats, working on them the way Prozac is supposed to work on humans. In the evening, when bats awaken, they seek the plant out, flying over the lake in a cluster and feasting on *Asclepius's* pollen. When they're sated, some of the bats will hang from the pistils like grey fruit. Or like grey fruit that hisses at you, if you get too close.)

I thought, from the way Michael's house looked and from the *Asclepius* that surrounded it, that Michael and Michael's room-mate might be eccentric. But the woman who answered the door and let us in – Judith – was so unassuming and charming that our welcome was uncomplicated.

– Michael told me you were coming, she said. And here you are. Would you like something to drink?

She was in her late twenties, I thought. A few years younger than me. Her nose was crooked in an intriguing way. Her neck was elegant and her voice deep. She wore faded blue jeans and a white shirt under a pink sweater. I thought she resembled Carson Michaels, but, if so, the professor didn't notice.

– I'd love some tea, he said. Thank you very much.

What captured his interest were the many framed photographs on the walls of the house. There were some twenty or so, all eight by eleven, all black and white, all photographs of decaying fruit – their textures and parasites – looking like the sullen phases of a distant planet.

– These are remarkable, said Professor Bruno.

– Thank you, said Judith. They're from my last show. They're apples or pomegranates.

The kitchen was a pleasant room, its walls a kind of pastel yellow, its floor a white linoleum with black harlequin diamonds, its two windows looking over the bat's delight onto a green lawn. The room was large enough to accommodate a long wooden table. And at the table there was an older man – sixty or thereabouts – whose face looked familiar to me.

– Did I hear you talking about the photographs? he asked. Aren't they wonderful?

Judith blushed, covering her face while straightening her eyebrows.

– This is my father, she said. *Of course* he likes my work.

– It shows he has excellent taste, said Professor Bruno.

The professor and Judith's father made a show of shaking hands and bowing to each other in a courtly way. And it was while watching them that I realized why the father seemed familiar. He resembled Professor Bruno – same eyes and ears, same height. But Judith's father looked younger – more dark hair on his head – and his manner was completely different. You would not have taken him, at least not on first impression, for an academic. Professor Bruno must have seen the resemblance, too.

– Have we met? he asked. You look familiar.

– My name's John, he said. I don't think we've met. I'm sure I'd remember you.

Then, as if carrying on a long-running conversation with his daughter that we'd interrupted, he mentioned Ansel Adams, whose work he disdained, and Josef Sudek, whose work he adored.

— Daddy, stop it, Judith said. You know Ansel Adams is great.

— I do, he answered. I get it. But his work is arid. I prefer landscapes that are intimate, photos that makes you feel something strange is about to happen. Or something strange just happened and you're dealing with the ghost of it. The ghost of an event or a premonition of it. That's intimacy! And that's why I like your work, sweetie.

The conversation was, for me at least, instructive. I knew nothing at all about photography. In some ways, I dislike it, preferring the world as it's caught by pen and ink. (The truth is, I find looking directly at 'someone else's looking' disorienting.) But whenever her father mentioned a photographer — Geneviève Cadieux was one, Jeff Wall another — Judith, who could see I wasn't familiar with them, would show me their work and talk about their techniques and that would set her father and Professor Bruno going, so that, by the time Michael came home, the four of us were happily engaged in conversation.

After a while, I felt a kind of hesitancy from the professor. We'd come to Marsville to see Michael. When Michael came home, it would have been right to stop what we were doing and pay attention to Michael. But Michael wouldn't hear of it. Instead, Michael insisted that we carry on talking about photography and, while making supper, joined in on the conversation.

After we'd drunk wine with our asparagus risotto, then grappa with our olive cake, then Four Roses bourbon with our coffee, I gave up wondering where we'd sleep. I could not drive, so we were bound to sleep in Marsville. And if we were sleeping in Marsville, there was nowhere else but chez Judith and Michael. The nearest hotel was miles away.

To her father, Judith said

— You're not going anywhere tonight, Daddy. You can sleep in my room. Michael and I'll sleep together.

And that was it. We all relaxed and went on drinking and talking about Art.

It was Michael who changed the subject to poetry. Saying '*Ut pictura poesis*' – meaning: as goes painting, so goes poetry – Michael began talking about the way poets see versus the seeing of photographers. Here, John's knowledge seemed unusually vast. At one point, he mentioned Arnaut Daniel and Giotto. I had no idea who these people were, but Professor Bruno was almost speechless with pleasure. As Michael showed me reproductions of Giotto's paintings, the professor began a poem by Daniel:

– 'When I see leaves, flowers and fruit blooming on the boughs and hear the song frogs make in the stream ...'

Which was then finished by John himself.

– 'Go to her, song, go to my beloved's heart and tell her that Arnaut forsakes all other loves and turns to her alone.'

Again, Professor Bruno seemed delighted. After days spent with me – someone who knows so little about literature – it must have been like an oasis in the desert to find a fellow devotee, one who could recite the end of such a little-known poem. But it was clear John did not feel relief or gratitude. He seemed unhappy, as if reciting a poem were like hearing bad news. He poured himself more bourbon and drank it down. Just as surprising were the reactions of Judith and Michael. Both seemed stunned that Judith's father had recited anything at all.

– Dad, are you all right? Judith asked.

– I'm fine, he said. The bourbon's a little strong, that's all.

Michael tried to change the subject. But Professor Bruno asked John how'd he'd come to know of Arnaut Daniel. It's not everyone, after all, who knows the poetry – the *music* – of the twelfth century.

Though the subject obviously made him uncomfortable, John answered.

– I've translated the poems myself, he said. I used to know the language well.

– Do you write poetry?

– In the past, a long time ago, when I was younger.

– Ah, said Professor Bruno, and now you're through at last with all kinds of knowing!

As if reluctant to acknowledge it, John took a moment before he said

– Yes.

At which Professor Bruno, staring at him, said

– I wonder if you know the poet I'm researching? He came from these parts. I'm sure you've heard of him. His name is John Skennen.

And Judith's father – Mr. Stephens, as it turned out – resignedly said

– I'm John Skennen.

– You're who? asked Professor Bruno.

– Well, I was, he said. I *was* John Skennen.

And he looked at his watch.

4

A VISION IN FEVERSHAM

— A breakfast with bards!

Those were Professor Bruno's first words to me the following morning. Though the two of us had slept on a narrow, spine-jangly couch, he woke early, excited by the possibility of talking to a John Skennen he could admire. And to Skennen's daughter — another poet, though her medium was photography.

I had barely slept. I'd had a recursive dream, one of those that comes back to the same incident and place, endlessly. In the dream, I could not escape from a charging white lion whose terrifying roar woke me time and again only for me to discover I was listening to Professor Bruno's snoring. By eight in the morning I was still sleepy, but I was caught up in the professor's excitement. Having heard so much about John Skennen, I wondered which of the versions of him was real, which of the tales true.

I'd eaten a slice of toast off a plate from which I'd brushed what had looked like insect legs. Then, when I was given a mug for tea, Judith warned me about finding pieces of ants at the bottom. The dishwasher worked well enough, it seemed, but a colony of ants had established itself within. Inevitably, some were trapped in the machine while it was on. The poor things would be tossed about, broken, and then dried on cutlery, plates, pots, and pans. Michael said that, having been thoroughly washed, the insect parts were probably safe to consume. But it was dismaying to discover the ants' beadlike torsos, twiglike legs, or minute heads stuck to a plate or lying at the bottom of a cup.

Except for Professor Bruno, those around the table were more sombre than they'd been the night before, when the man who once was John Skennen had promised to tell us his story. Judith, in particular, seemed wary. She was, after all, meeting a new version of a man she loved, her father. Michael took quick, regular sips from a mug on which there was a picture of Measha Brueggergosman.

Then Mr. Stephens said

– Do you know? I haven't told anybody my story.

How to describe the devastation of a lost love? As Petrarch wrote: whoever can say the flame is painful is in a small fire. And as Montaigne said after him: the biggest emotions breed only silence.

It wasn't just the shock he felt at the loss of his beloved. It was the revelation that this disappearance could affect every atom of his being. For years, he couldn't speak of Carson Michaels.

(Yes, that much of the story was true. He'd loved Carson Michaels.

– A beautiful woman, said Professor Bruno.

– I wonder if you know her well enough to say, answered Mr. Stephens.)

That is, he couldn't speak of her unless he was out of his mind on drugs or alcohol. For years, all he did was wander and drink, poisoned by the humiliation that came from knowing he would do anything to be with Carson. There was no shame he could not imagine himself suffering for love of her. His soul was hers, what did it matter about the rest of him?

The thing that saved his life was his inheritance – not the inheritance itself but the fact that it was shared with his brother. The two of them received five hundred dollars a month, thanks to their great-grandfather's invention of a spring mechanism used to open and close umbrellas. His share was not quite enough to drink himself to death. It fed him on most days and kept him drunk. So, at his lowest, he spent his days drinking or passing out in bars, while at night he wandered between small towns. For a year and a half, he walked the province from Windsor to Owen Sound, Sarnia to Niagara-on-the-Lake; from Chatham to Barrie and Stratford to Peterborough.

It was strange to remember how far he'd travelled in that time. Stranger still to think how little of the province he'd seen: the insides of countless bars and taverns, most of them interchangeable. When he was woken and kicked out of these places, it was usually night and he would walk in the direction of the next town or the town after that, getting sober as dawn approached. What he saw of Southern Ontario he saw by aurora.

Mind you, if there was any beauty in his despair, it came from this sobering up as the world woke: the way a stealthy vein of light would come, gradually chasing shadows and creating silhouettes, silhouettes first seen against the indigo sky, then against the blue sky with dark clouds, then against the light-blue firmament with white clouds, until the dark silhouettes disappeared, the buildings and landscape reacquainted by sunlight.

He had memories of walking into Glencoe and being startled by a rabbit hopping out of a cornfield beside him. How massive they sound – like deer! – moving in the undergrowth. The Glencoe rabbit looked at him, watching him approach and watching him pass, each aware of the other, because both happened to be awake at dawn.

Or hurrying out of Dresden, over by the racetrack. He had no sentimental attachment to racing or horses. He remembered Dresden because he was being chased by dogs.

Or sleeping in a barren field near Listowel (cold, tired, and hungry) and waking because the rain was suddenly torrential and the sky was like a black door through which cracks of light came, the land around him flat and endless and unpeopled.

– How old were you? asked Professor Bruno.

– Early thirties, answered Mr. Stephens.

– Ah, said Professor Bruno. That is the age when love desolates, isn't it?

Mr. Stephens didn't mean to suggest, though, that these memories of the province at dawn were his deepest or most significant. Though they were less visually striking, his memories of the world by night were more profound. For one thing, he usually entered night while drunk, open to the suggestions of night itself and vulnerable to the creatures who made it their home.

One night, after closing time at a bar in Ingersoll, he was walking along a county road, the nth Line somewhere, when he was startled by a pig walking not far from him along the border of a field. In the moonlight, he could clearly see the pig to the right of him. And though he was drunk, he crossed to the other side of road, it being strange to walk with the animal. Moments later, there was another pig – or was it the same one? – again on his side of the road, to his left. When he looked to see where the 'first' pig had gone, there was only darkness. He was suddenly sober, frightened by the grunting and flatulent creature beside him. It was as if the pig were playing a game. It moved toward him. And when it began to trot, John Stephens began to run.

The pig kept up with him. Stephens ran faster and faster until, nearly spent, he turned to see where the pig had gone and found himself alone and unfollowed, still on the nth Line, somewhere between Ingersoll and Woodstock, the sky filled with stars and a platinum moon whose light bathed the stalks of whatever it was in the fields. He could laugh then, having left the pig behind. At least, he tried to see the amusing side of things. He'd been chased by a pig on a moonlit night. A good story. Something to dine out on, even.

But then he looked up and the pig was in front of him, now in the middle of the road. And it was difficult for Mr. Stephens to describe the texture of his fear or the reason for it. It wasn't as if he was afraid of death. And he wasn't afraid of pigs, but he was afraid of the thing in front of him. He was afraid the thing in front of him was not a pig, though he had no idea what it was if it wasn't. Was he afraid of the unknown? Yes, but what a strange thing to say when he was surrounded by the familiar. He had been on countless country roads on nights exactly like this. His fear entirely transcended reason. It was a feeling he ever after associated with the land, as the land was the only thing that had ever provoked it.

All very odd, but the important thing was the creature in the road. It began to run at him and, exhausted, he could not decide what to do: run, dodge, kick. He imagined pushing his fingers through the pig's eyes. It was huge, though. It looked even more ferocious as it came close, and it was mesmerizing. He thought he recognized his death as it approached and he was almost amused that this was his fate, that all the years of a life led to this creature on this night.

Would anyone find his body?

Or would he be eaten where he stood?

The pig grunted lasciviously as it came. It was steps away when he heard a car backfire – once, twice –and felt drops of warm rain on his face and neck. It was then that he realized his eyes were closed. Opening them, he saw that he wasn't quite where he thought he was. He was on his knees in the middle of the road. Before him was a tall figure, a man who said

– Do you mind if I slap you?

Before he could answer, the man slapped his face hard enough to make his back teeth hurt.

— Did you feel that? the man asked.

— You're damn right, I felt it! That hurt!

— I'm sorry, said the man.

It was then that Stephens saw the pig. It lay dead on the ground, its feet pawing at the air. The man who'd just slapped him had shot it.

— The name's Kit, said the man. I was in the pub?

Mr. Stephens didn't recognize him.

— Why did you slap me? he asked.

They walked on then, leaving the pig in the middle of the road. Kit, a Methodist from Manitoba, was tall and broad, his dark hair gathered in a ponytail. John Stephens couldn't see much of his face in the dark, but he recognized the man's voice and remembered that they'd spoken while waiting for their drinks at the bar. The man was Scottish on his father's side and Jamaican on his mother's.

— I slapped you because I wasn't sure if you're possessed.

— What would you have done if I was possessed?

— I'd have shot you, said Kit. But just in the leg so you couldn't walk. I couldn't kill you after drinking with you like that.

Kit hadn't followed him from the pub. He'd chosen the road they were on because he was walking to Feversham. A coincidence. He'd been surprised to see someone else out at this time of night. More surprised still to find a man kneeling in the middle of the road with a pig in front of him. The pig had seemed like a breathing, white marble figure. You didn't even have to believe in demons to feel the malevolence. It was palpable. The thing he couldn't tell was who, of pig or man, was host to the demon and who was not. Because the pig was unnaturally still, he shot it. Twice. He was sorry to have killed a fellow being, but his almost instinctive concern had been for the kneeling man.

Given that Kit had almost shot him in the leg, it's surprising how untroubled their relationship was. That first night, John Stephens was preoccupied by what had happened. Had he really been possessed by a pig possessed by a demon? The idea wasn't easy for an atheist to accept. He preferred to think that the earth was a being of many aspects, some of which were malign, that people and animals could be overcome by 'evil' the way an early-morning traveller is shrouded by fog in a valley. The land had a 'dark side,' and he'd touched it. Or had it touched him? As dawn came, he and Kit finally saw that he'd been spattered by pig's blood: his clothes, his face and neck, his hands.

Naturally, John Stephens wondered about his companion. Why was an imposing, intimidating Manitoban walking the back roads of Ontario with a gun? And was it better or worse, for him, that Kit could tell – or thought he could tell – if a man was possessed by slapping him? Mr. Stephens felt both anxious and curious. He and Kit walked easily together, though, neither of them saying much until Woodstock, where Mr. Stephens cleaned up and they had a coffee in a place near the Ingersoll Road.

In total, the two travelled together for five days. They slept where they could: in hotel lobbies, taverns, restaurants, and McDonald's. They were close, in the way that road acquaintances sometimes are. But Ùisdean Ross who preferred being called 'Kit' to having his name mangled – was not a man to waste words. He seemed happier to keep quiet rather than talk about trivial things.

Then again, Kit was always ready to talk about the spiritual. He allowed it to influence his life. He was walking from Winnipeg to Feversham, for instance, as penance. He wouldn't say what he'd done to require penance. It was a family matter. Kit was convinced, though, that his soul would be healed by walking – as opposed to wandering, which is what John Stephens had been doing. Kit had been a month on the road when they met, and he felt almost whole. More than that, he believed that rescuing John Stephens from a demon was a sign that his penance was near its end. This did not free him from actually going to Feversham, however. Feversham was inescapable.

But who in their right mind would journey all that way – almost 1,250 kilometres – to Feversham? Feversham was what the French called 'un bled,' a place with no appeal, a village you leave as soon as you're able, a place where it rains five days a week, even when it doesn't rain at all. Stephens had never heard anyone say anything about it – good or bad – and that included the one time he'd walked through it.

That, said Kit, was because he'd judged Feversham with his eyes. He had taken its unpaved roads, the modesty of its houses, stores, and institutions as the basis for his judgment. But did he realize that Feversham had the highest percentage in the world of priests and holy people living in it? Well, it did. Surpassing even Vatican City. Ninety-five per cent of those who live in Feversham are spiritual masters, men and women of all denominations. If Stephens had looked in the general store on River Road, for instance, he'd have seen a bewildering variety of food, foods to accommodate Jews, Hindus, Buddhists, Muslims, Shintoists, Neo-Pagans, Wiccans, and so on. The choice of fruit and vegetables alone was stunning. You could buy everything from yuzu to custard apples, from jicama to marrow-stem kale.

Was Kit himself a holy man?

No. Holy men don't walk around with guns. But Feversham wasn't a place to be trifled with. Kit was going because he wasn't sure whether he wanted to live or die, and this was the kind of question that could be answered in Feversham. The gun, its bullets, had been meant for himself. Until, that is, he'd shot the pig.

As if all that wasn't enough spiritual matter to think about, somewhere around the town of Arthur, where they shared a bed at an inn, Kit suggested that, given how they'd met and where they were going, it was likely that Feversham was Stephens's destiny too. Kit recognized in John Stephens a man suffering from the same hesitation to live that he himself suffered from. The difference, said Kit, was that he could admit to a longing for death. But Stephens seemed not to have admitted this – not even to himself.

This was true and obvious, and John Stephens at last admitted it to himself. He *did* want to die, but he didn't know how. So, he'd chosen a way that reflected his irresolution: death by drink.

– You can speak to God with me, said Kit. I really think you should, John.

Feversham's sanctity had first been described to Kit by a Christian monk from Neepawa, in metaphorical terms. Think of it this way, the monk had said: God needs sleep as much as mortals do. We were made in God's image. We share God's habits. So, God obviously sleeps. No surprise, then, that there are places God prefers to rest. These places are little known. They're northern – Feversham, Pangnirtung, Sarqaq, Ny-Ålesund, Chatanga – and modest and quiet and, evidently, suited to divine repose. Those in distress, those teetering between life and death who manage to stay with God as God sleeps, those who manage to share God's dreams, are granted grace if they choose it.

Two strange ideas: that God would choose to sleep in Feversham, Ontario, and that Stephens's journey with Kit Ross was now a pilgrimage.

– What happens when a god dreams? John Stephens asked.

This no one could say, said Kit, because, according to his monk, we all exist only within a divine dream. When God awakens, we will vanish. Not knowing the awakened God, we cannot know the one who dreams, either, having nothing to compare the dreamer with. We can say, though, that, as with any dream, the dreamer is all and all is the dreamer. Trees, gourds, people, clouds, dresses, ants, boots ... all are part of the same wonderful dream. And to be where the dreamer dreams – in Feversham – is to be closer to the source, as when one lies beside a dreaming beloved and feels a dream pass through them as if it were a current. To be in Feversham is to be next to the dreamer and to experience something deeper: intimations of the self.

As far as Stephens was concerned, the monk from Neepawa's ideas were pure contradiction. God was either asleep in some real place – in which case He could be approached while He slept – or we were all (including God Himself) part of a dream and, so, equidistant from the dreamer wherever we might be. To be beside the dreamer's dream of himself would, in that case, mean nothing, with Feversham no more significant than anywhere else..

Kit, who believed the monk from Neepawa, saw no contradiction at all. To him, it was obvious that the dreamer would dream himself, and that, to know the dreamer, even in the dream, was to be blessed. More: it was the definition of grace to find the dreamer in the dream. Which is why Feversham, one of the places where God dreams Himself into our 'reality,' is sacred.

Knowing Feversham as Stephens did, it was hard for him to imagine where exactly the Lord's bed might be. But it was questions like that that convinced him to travel on with Kit. Atheist or not – and unsure though he was of Kit's sanity – Stephens's curiosity got the better of him. So, days after being attacked by a pig, John Stephens walked into the sacred town of Feversham.

What is it you see when you enter a legendary place? Not the place itself, surely, not the place in and of itself. Rather, you see it through a curtain of ghosts, expectations, and legend. So it was for John Stephens. Feversham was more or less as he remembered it: bland and unremarkable. But now its blandness had an ascetic feel to it. Its small houses, identical to small houses all over the province, now seemed falsely normal, hiding as they did the priests and holy people Kit had told him about. The tar on its roads seemed like a stratagem. The river was like a river in a vision of small towns. Stephens accepted that Feversham might be sacred to him because he could no longer see it as profane. But he couldn't tell if profane Feversham was real or if sacred Feversham was. Which Feversham was the illusion, which the real? Or, to put it another way: between illusion and reality, which was least untrue?

(Of course, if the monk from Neepawa was right, the question was pointless, there being no such division as illusion/reality, all being dream-stuff. Then again, Stephens did not believe the monk knew any more about the world than we do. And, without denying the influence of illusion on reality, it was important to remember that, for those of us who are not mystics, the distinction between 'real' and 'unreal' is crucial.)

The Methodist home was a white A-frame on River Road. Its driveway sloped toward the street, and a white Ford Fusion was parked on the slope. From outside, nothing gave the house away as anything other than a modest family home. Even the spring mechanism on its screen door was slightly flawed, so that the door pulled quickly open and had to be pulled shut, rattling like a sheet of tin behind you.

Once inside, though, the story was different. Past the entrance alcove, the living room was white with no furniture, save two lacquered wooden pews, both ten feet long. Beyond the pews, suspended from the ceiling, was a gold-painted crucifix, four feet tall with a two-foot crossbar. The living room wasn't hushed, as a church might be, but it felt like a place of worship. On the front pew, the pastor – Rev. Sara Crosbie – was speaking to a Coptic monk, her next-door neighbour, a man dressed in black save for his bonnet, which had white crosses on it.

Seeing Kit, Reverend Crosbie got up.

– You're Kit, she said, extending a hand. Welcome!

John Stephens knew, at that moment, that everything Kit Ross had told him about the town was true. It wasn't only the fact that they'd found a Methodist church in a fixer-upper by the river. It was the look on the monk's face: serene but engaged. Stephens would meet a number of the holy men and holy women over the following days, their homes like spiritual Tardises – plain on the outside, temples within. But he believed Kit Ross the moment he saw the monk's face. The business here was clearly spiritual.

On the other hand, Kit's version of what would happen – communion with a dreaming God – was (perhaps) off the mark.

According to Reverend Crosbie, whose guest room served as a place for pilgrims, the only certain thing, the only thing all the holy people gathered in Feversham believed, was that God, however defined, was often close to Feversham, and even in those times when God's presence was less pronounced, God's absence was a warm one. Now, here, the analogy of beds and sleep actually worked. You could say, and Reverend Crosbie did, that God's absence from Feversham was very like the warmth on one side of the bed when your beloved has gotten up in the middle of the night and you reach over to touch the place where they've been.

A point of contention among the spiritual leaders was whether God communed with anyone who came to Feversham or only with those who'd prepared for communion with God. This was a particularly lively debate. There had been a number of cases in which 'common people,' wandering near the sacred clearing, had been touched by God, coming away with prophecies or scriptural interpretations or predictions about the future. Some believed that those who had been in the company of God were holy, whether 'spiritual' or not. Others believed that those claiming to have been in God's company were not to be trusted unless they were spiritual leaders. Still others believed that common people should not be allowed in Feversham at all, as they might intercept messages meant for the reverend.

It seemed to Reverend Crosbie that there were good argu-ments for many of the positions. She herself did not like the idea of people trampling on sacred ground looking for God to solve their problems, as if the Lord were running a garage for the soul.

And yet, who knew the will of God? In one baffling case, it seems the Lord provided a poor supplicant with the names of all the winners at Dresden Raceway. That is, every winning horse in every race for thirty days. A miracle, surely. None doubted it was the work of a divinity. And the poor supplicant used the entirety of his winnings to build a church beside the racetrack, a church that burned to the ground the day it was finished. This incident alone brought up a thousand questions. To begin with, there was the question of whether or not God sent 'mixed signals.' Some felt that, in burning the church to the ground, God had changed Their mind. Others felt it was too soon to tell what God meant. Some felt God was condemning gambling, though why, having used gambling to build a church, would God then burn the church, not the racetrack? None of Feversham's spiritual leaders was prepared to admit that God had made a mistake but, after the incident, all of them wrestled even more intensely with the meaning of God's actions in the world.

Reverend Crosbie was wrestling with the idea still, which is why she was sympathetic to Kit's situation. She didn't entirely approve of petitioning God for earthly advice, but neither did she feel she had the right to decide who should be encouraged or who discouraged from communing with the Lord.

Having listened to Reverend Crosbie, the atheist in John Stephens got the better of him. After admitting he did not believe in God, he suggested he was an atheist precisely because 'God' – as described by theists – was always mysterious or vague or difficult to interpret. The whole notion of God was vague from beginning to end, and this vagueness was a sign, at least to him, that God was a human creation, that God was nothing more than a sheet of gossamer placed over an abyss.

Stephens imagined Reverend Crosbie would be offended by his words. But she was not.

– I've often felt the same way, she said.

– But you have your faith, said Stephens, and that keeps you from needing anything real.

– My faith doesn't always help me, said the reverend, but my reason sometimes does. I think of us as creatures who are fated to interpret. We question everything. I believe it's our fundamental nature to question. As such, how could our Lord be anything but unknowable? If we were suddenly certain God existed, if we ceased to question God's existence, God would cease to exist for us. Do you see what I mean?

Stephens did *not* see what she meant. It was sophistry, as far as he could tell. But he was amused. For this reason – such a small thing! – he accompanied Kit and Reverend Crosbie to the 'sacred clearing,' as the reverend called it, the following morning.

Each denomination or sect had its own procedure and its own days of the week when they could go to the place of the Lord. All agreed, though, that those who approached the clearing should be clean – no makeup or cologne, watches or jewellery – and should, as well, wear white robes, so none of the denominations could distinguish its supplicants from the supplicants of other sects. The practice of wearing standard white robes was a sad necessity, as different sects sometimes responded violently to the presence of members of rival religions. This passion, said Reverend Crosbie, was to be expected from those who truly loved God. But it was good to remember that faith, too, could lead you astray.

To support Kit, whom he agreed to accompany, Stephens washed his clothes for the first time in months, showered for the first time in weeks, and wore a white robe as if he, too, were a supplicant. As well, Reverend Crosbie had him read an issue of *The Lancet* that contained an article – 'The pathophysiology of religious trance: implications for clinical management' – that she felt would warn him about the potential dangers of what he might experience.

It was early morning and, with the sound of Hindu chants behind them, they walked into Feversham gorge along an immaculately kept road made of carefully placed fragments of different-coloured stones: black, white, red, green, blue. This road went on for a quarter mile, after which there was only grass and a beaten path. At the end of the road, almost half the supplicants stopped and got down on their knees, praying, chanting, singing.

This is where Reverend Crosbie stopped and where Stephens would have liked to stop as well. It was already wonderful to see the road and hear the plaintive singing. But the place for those who sought communion was farther on. After having a thick rope tied to his right ankle, Kit walked to the clearing, and Stephens – also roped at the ankle – dutifully followed.

Around a curve in the beaten path, a row of willows stood like a shivering wall. Beyond the willows was a clearing, an unremarkable clearing, save for the bodies lying face down within it. At the far end of the clearing: water of some sort, a pond maybe, something that reflected the sky. In front of that: a patch of what looked like human hands – greyish, severed from bodies, some lying palms up, some fingers down. Stephens was about to mention how spooky the hands were when he realized that Kit was no longer beside him. Kit was gone and there was only silence.

There was silence for a long time. Or so it seemed. He hadn't lost consciousness – or didn't remember losing consciousness – but after a while he was, somehow, sitting on a chair facing a red wall. He felt someone touch the back of his head.

– You're an atheist, a woman's voice said.

– Yes, he answered.

He turned to look at her, but she would not let him.

– It's better if you don't see me, she said.

– Because I'm an atheist?

– No, no. Because you're a man of a certain type. It wouldn't help you to see me. Isn't the wall beautiful?

And it *was* beautiful, suggestive of scarlet tanagers and holly berries.

– You've come to this place to help someone who can't use your help, she said. Your own soul is in as much pain as his.

Hearing these words, Stephens was suddenly angry.

– What do you know about it? he asked.

– You are in love and love is my domain. Ask me what you've come to ask.

It was a surprise to him that he'd come to ask anything. He was about to deny it when he felt in his soul how true it was. From the moment Kit had told him about Feversham, he'd been nourishing a question: was there a way for the woman he loved – the woman who'd once loved him – to love him again?

– There is a way, said the one behind him, but it would be a violation of your beloved.

– How could love be a violation? Stephens asked.

– You know the answer to that already. You would be coercing her to love. But if you're willing to proceed and if you accept that the violation of the one who's left you would have to be met by a drastic sacrifice on your part, then I will help you.

Without hesitation, he agreed. To be with Carson again, there were no terms he would not accept, however brief the reunion, whatever the consequences.

– The consequences, said the one behind him, are these: in exchange for one day with your beloved, a day during which she will love you as deeply as she ever did, you will lose the ability to write poetry and you will take care of the path to this place – four hours a day, for twenty-one years.

This was an unexpectedly vicious choice. He'd been writing poetry since childhood. It was his one solace, his way of understanding the world or, failing that, himself. It was asking him to give up not just his identity but an aspect of his being. It would have been kinder to offer him death. At least, so he felt at that moment. And he was offended.

– But this is just a transaction, he said. How is any of this divine?

– I understand, said the one behind him, but you have come for a transaction. You are willing to have a woman coerced into loving you. You won't give up anything in return?

– I choose poetry then, he said. The price of this love is too high.

And with that, he came out of a trance that had lasted three days.

The ramifications of this moment were difficult for John Stephens to describe, to explain. Its tendrils made their way into every aspect of his life.

Why had he come out of his trance?

Methodist supplicants who are unresponsive for three days are taken from the clearing or pulled from it by the rope attached to their right legs, if there's no one who dares to go into the clearing to get them. (Some people are, after all, wary of visions.) Other sects allowed supplicants to remain in the clearing longer – up to seven days – on the understanding that communion with God ought not to be interrupted unless it became a clear danger to the supplicant. Having come with the Methodists, John Stephens was pulled out after three days. Kit Ross, who'd gone with him, never lost consciousness and did not commune with God, though he was a believer and Stephens was not. In fact, Kit had walked out of the clearing on his own steam on the first day, as soon as it had gotten dark, after praying for hours.

Did John Stephens now accept that there is a God?

No, not at all. He believed even less than he had before. The being he'd spoken with had not been godlike at all. If he believed anything, it was that he'd been drugged. Not by Reverend Crosbie. That was inconceivable. Besides, he'd fasted before entering the field. But something *had* put him under, and his hallucination had been as vivid as if he'd done good blotter acid. What he'd communed with, as far as he was concerned, was himself. He had searched in his own soul and discovered both his desire and its resolution.

So, he wasn't affected by what he'd gone through?

No, that wasn't true. On coming to consciousness, Stephens had felt as if the burden of love had been taken from him. He no longer yearned for Carson Michaels. Knowing that, back against the wall, he could choose poetry over love, it seemed hollow to go on mourning the one he'd lost. He still longed for Carson, but the pain her memory brought dissipated. It was bearable. Unlike poor Kit – who remained in Feversham for weeks, waiting for a communion that never came – John Stephens's question, a question he hadn't known he harboured, had been answered at once.

So, fortune was with him?

Yes. Beginning with this encounter in Feversham, Stephens's life seemed to find its brightest way. He moved to a small town called Barrow, found part-time work, and – for ten years, under the name John Skennen – wrote all of the poems for which he would be known. It was also in Barrow that he fell in love again. He married Judith's mother and, at his daughter's birth, stayed home to mind their child.

– But then why did you stop writing poetry? Judith asked.

– Poetry stopped writing me, said John Stephens.

The moment that had saved him, the moment that sent him on to Barrow, was also the moment he was chased from paradise. Aside from being a man born to write poetry, he had always been one in need of grandeur. Some poets, like Eliot or Pound, took enormous pride in belonging to a noble tradition. Take the glorious past away from Eliot and you'd have poems too dry to read. The same if you took God from Blake, Nature from Wordsworth, or Death from Emily Dickinson. Every poet has a fount from which their work springs. And his, like Arnaut Daniel's, had been Love. The belief in Love's omnipotence and grandeur was what had fed his writing, even when he wasn't writing about love.

Yet, in that moment at the core of himself, he had chosen Art, not Love. He had chosen poetry, as if it were enough in and of itself. And from the moment he'd chosen, his soul had begun a bricking up, cutting his work off from its source. Choosing poetry over love began the slow death of poetry within him.

– But, Daddy, that doesn't make sense, said Judith. If you'd have chosen love, you'd have had to give up poetry on the spot. And, anyway, it would have been wrong to choose love if it meant this woman would've been forced to love you.

– I know that, sweetie, said John Stephens, but I wasn't thinking about Carson. I didn't think about how it would affect her. All I thought about was me, how unfair it was for me to have to choose. If there'd been no consequences, if I could've had Carson's love, even for an hour, without paying, I'd have gone for it. But in the end, I couldn't even be faithful to the selfishness I called 'love'. If I'd really loved Carson, instead of loving the way she made me feel, I'd have chosen neither love nor poetry. I'd have chosen to go on grieving but knowing I'd chosen grief. At least that would have been a way of honouring what I'd lost.'

When he wrote his final poem, he knew it was the last, knew that part of him had closed up shop. He didn't even resent it. He told his friends that John Skennen had died and asked them to help him spread the fact. Which they did, though, admittedly, some of their stories had got out of hand.

– So, said Professor Bruno, you're ... ambivalent about a biography?

– I look back on Skennen's poetry and I'm curious about it. But it's got nothing to do with me and I've got nothing to do with it. You might as well ask me to help with a bio of one of the younger poets, like Karen Solie. I don't know a thing about her, either.

– Dad, I wish you'd help Morgan, said Judith. People should know about your work.

– It's not *my* work anymore, sweetie. And there's no reason for me to go back there.

He hadn't quite broken with the past, however. Though John Stephens did not believe he'd communed with any god, there *was* something sacred about his moment in front of the red wall. Never before or since had he had such clear contact with what he took to be his own mind. And in commemoration of that irreducible encounter, he spent four hours a day, every day, cleaning the path to the clearing in Feversham, a path for those who wished to commune with a god he did not believe in. He'd been doing this for twenty-one years. Since Judith's birth. On her twenty-second birthday, in December, he would be released. He didn't like to think of it this way, but, really, his punishment had been decided just moments before he committed the infraction that called for it.

— That does feel spiritual, said Michael.

— But how strange, said Professor Bruno, that you made it so you couldn't have escaped punishment one way or the other. Whatever you'd chosen, you'd have been punished. If you really were talking to yourself in front of that red wall, you're a hard judge, sir, a very hard judge of yourself.

— I know what you mean, said John Stephens, but I sometimes think this task is my reward, not my punishment. It's liberating to have a task, one that reminds you how insignificant you are. People are too touchy about submission. The gardener submits to the garden, too, no? Anyhow, I like to be in Feversham early in the morning and it's getting late. Nice meeting you.

— Do you mind if we come to Feversham with you? asked Professor Bruno.

— Well, I can't stop you, said Mr. Stephens.

Though Mr. Stephens was not enthusiastic about our accompanying him, I was thrilled that we were going. During Mr. Stephens's telling of his story, I worried that Professor Bruno would forego Feversham, having met the person who'd known John Skennen best: John Stephens. But from the moment I heard Mr. Stephens's description of things on the ground that looked like hands, I knew he was describing *Oniaten grandiflora*, or five fingers, the plant I'd wanted so badly to see.

— Do you think I could visit the clearing you talked about? I asked.

— I wouldn't advise you to do it, said Mr. Stephens. But you can talk to Reverend Crosbie.

— Why do you want to commune with God? asked Michael. Are you so troubled?

When I explained that I was interested in *Oniaten grandiflora*, Michael said

– I don't know if that makes you more interesting than you look, or less.

– Oh, he's more interesting, said Professor Bruno. He's full of unplumbed depths.

Michael touched my arm and smiled, then volunteered to drive the professor and me to Feversham while Mr. Stephens and his daughter went in Mr. Stephens's car. More: Michael would drive us back when we wished because Michael was not working that day and was grateful for a reason to drive in lovely weather, the faintly blue sky full of clouds, the fields green, the trees in full leaf, though here and there patches of leaves had already changed colour.

'Sneaky season' is what my father used to call late summer – a chlorophyll conspiracy, as if one tree hoarded its share, and then other trees, suddenly aware of putting out more chlorophyll than they had to, began to hoard theirs as well, one by one until all the trees in the province were yellow, orange, or red. I felt such joy whenever I was first to find the tree in our neighbourhood whose leaves had first begun to change.

I don't remember much about the drive to Feversham, but somewhere along the Orangeville-Fergus Road, I remembered my father's voice and I was happy. Then, too, it was along the same road that I began to wonder if the 'sacred clearing' held some revelation for me, suffering as I was from the same thing that had afflicted John Stephens before his vision: grief.

Reverend Crosbie was not as I expected her to be. For one thing, she looked young, though she couldn't have been, having been in Feversham when Mr. Stephens was there with Kit. She was slim, red-haired with green eyes, and her presence was light, not at all dark. She was dressed plainly: blue jeans and a white shirt over a T-shirt with an image of Christ on it. Mr. Stephens, for whom she clearly had affection, had told her about my wanting to see the plants he'd described. But this was a more complicated matter than it seemed. For one thing, it wasn't clear to her that the plants Mr. Stephens had described really existed.

– You should know, Alfred, that pilgrims have different experiences. I've lived in Feversham for over thirty years and I've never had a vision or communed with God. I believe others have because I've seen lives changed by what people have gone through. But ...

Most who stood in the clearing came away with nothing: no visions, no strange plants, no red walls. A small number experienced communion or visions that lasted minutes, hours, or days. And, of that number, it didn't seem to matter how long this communion with God was. All lives were changed, however vivid or dull the vision, however brief or prolonged the communion. As to the content of these visions: that varied wildly from person to person. One man spent days entranced, though all he saw was a centipede whose body rotted before him. Another walked through an endless, shallow pond to touch a golden lily. The most interesting vision, to Reverend Crosbie's mind, was of a woman whose menses stained her own legs and feet red before turning the whole of Feversham white as dandelion fluff. The woman who had this vision – a wonderful person! – left her children and family to help the poor and unfortunate in Scotland.

As to the *Oniaten grandiflora* ... very few people had ever seen it. That in itself was no big deal because so few people notice plants. John Stephens had seen it, as had a handful of Buddhists, apparently. But the only other person Reverend Crosbie had spoken to who'd seen it was an Ojibwe man from Kettle Point and he hadn't been delighted by it at all. For him, it was like seeing what he called the 'dry hand,' and he'd turned away from it in fear.

– So, there you are, said Reverend Crosbie. I don't want to discourage you, but you should know what you're facing.

After having me read an article about Feversham – 'Feversham Syndrome: A Sceptic's Glance' – the reverend made sure I had a white robe that fit over my shirt and pants, and we walked – myself, Michael, Professor Bruno, and Reverend Crosbie – to the clearing.

I'd naturally formed an idea of what the way to the clearing might look like. But my imagination did not touch reality. It looked as if a road – ten feet wide, a quarter mile long – had been chiselled into the earth, so precise were its borders. On either side of the road, there were shallow runnels – three inches deep, rounded gutters as smooth as pearl. The surface of the road looked to be shards of polished jewellery – thousands and thousands of shards – carefully placed and wiped, not swept. It was like a mosaic in five colours: black stones for the first 330 feet, then white shards, then red ones, then green, and then blue fragments for the last three hundred feet. Where the colours ended and vegetation took over, the grass was almost as precise as the road itself. It was all so well-tended, you could immediately tell where the hours and hours of care had gone.

And then, as Mr. Stephens had said, there was a curtain of willows.

And then, as luck would have it, the first things I saw – looking exactly as Mr. Stephens had described them – were the *Oniaten grandiflora*.

A young woman walking beside me said
– Aren't they lovely?

To be polite, I agreed with her, but *lovely* isn't the word I'd have chosen. They were remarkable. The plants' gourds looked exactly like severed human hands: same bloodless, grey tinge and bluish veins. The plant had managed to imitate human skin so well that those lying 'palms up' had the kinds of markings palms generally do. And the *Oniaten* were so realistic that until I picked one up I thought they really might be severed hands. They were plants, though. Their roots held them to the ground and the places where they looked severed – their wrists, had they been real hands – were smooth and shiny with a sort of grey gelatin that wobbled slightly when the hands were moved.

My fellow pilgrim — dark hair, brown eyes, low voice, the bottom of her white robe dirty — touched my shoulder and pointed out just how many *Oniaten* were on the ground. There were hundreds.

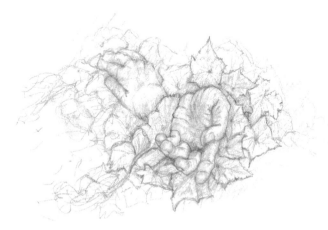

— Do you think anyone would mind if I took one? I asked.

— I don't see why, she said.

But they weren't easy to pick. They resisted. Their roots ran deep and I had no knife with which to cut them from the earth. Then, when I managed to pick one, its fingers curled up as if it were suddenly arthritic or suddenly holding an invisible golf ball. I put it (along with two of its leaves) in my pants pocket and for some time I could feel its fingers moving.

— Is this the first time you've seen these? the woman asked.

— Yes, I said. I've been looking for them. I hear they have medicinal qualities.

— I don't know about that, she said, but they make a good salad.

No sooner said than she had picked a dozen or so leaves — and a 'hand' — and we were at her cottage on the other side of the clearing, beyond the garden of five fingers. I wasn't sure about following her, but looking back at the pilgrims lying in the field and at the wall of willows beyond them, I didn't see how it could hurt spending a few minutes watching the woman make a salad and, if it came to that, eating a mouthful to see how the leaves tasted.

That said, the woman – whose name was Clare – lived in an eerie place. It was lovely enough from the outside, with its white stone walls and diamond pane windows and wind-ruffled cover of ivy. But the inside was dim even when the lights were turned on. There was little furniture or furnishings: an unsteady table surrounded by four stools, a darkly crimson sofa, a poker and shovel in front of a fireplace, a spinning wheel in a corner, and shelves of things above the kitchen sink. But what truly made the place eerie were the paintings on her walls. There were a number of them, all with lights beneath them to illuminate the images, each image depicting a man being torn apart by a wolf.

– I hope you don't think the paintings are morbid, she said. It's really just a coincidence they're so violent. I love their colours and their compositions. Don't you?

I studied them all again, looking for brilliant colours or striking composition. But they seemed even more ghastly on closer look. The artists had managed to capture men in various stages of abject terror, while the wolves' eyes shone brightly.

– Well, I guess they are interesting, I said.

As I spoke, I felt Clare's warm breath on the back of my neck. I jumped. But when I turned around, she was in the kitchen, some fifteen feet away, smiling.

– Why don't you sit at the table? she said. The salad's ready.

The tabletop was rough, unvarnished wood with splits in it, as if it had been an old barn door sawed in half and nailed to uneven legs. Clare put out two settings. Between us she set a red bowl in which the *Oniaten*'s leaves had been torn to manageable pieces. On top of the leaves, the *Oniaten*'s fingers were arranged around the greyish square that was the 'palm.'

– I like my salads plain, she said, but I've made a dressing if you want some.

She then showed me what looked to be a cup of mayonnaise over which she'd sprinkled paprika and scattered chives. Though I was sorry to waste the dressing, I ate the salad as she did: plain. To my surprise, the leaves were exquisite. They were somewhere between a mild coriander and the taste of clover. I was not at all interested in the fingers. I watched her bite one and it cracked like a chicken bone. But I'd have been ashamed to refuse the fingers after passing up the dressing. So, I bit into one. It, too, was delicious. How marvellous, I thought, that the plant had learned to imitate human anatomy so well that it had grown this hard, crackling cartilage that tasted like savoury rock candy: saffron and cinnamon.

Having finished the salad, Clare and I spoke, sitting at the dinner table. I was happy to talk and to listen, relieved as I was that five fingers were edible. I don't know what it was that turned the conversation to personal matters. But after hours of talking, as I was about to leave, Clare asked if I'd spend the night with her.

— It's not what you think, she said. I don't want to have sex. It's just ... I see that you're a good man, Alfred, and so few good men come here. And you being a good man, if you were to spend the night in my bed without feeling desire for me, I'd be set free.

I was, of course, surprised. I hadn't thought about sleeping with Clare. Not that it was the farthest thing from my mind. She was certainly attractive. And, having been propositioned, I was forcefully reminded of my heterosexual feelings.

— I shouldn't feel desire for you? I asked.

— I'm cursed, she answered. I'm a lycanthrope, but I turn into a wolf only when men desire me. That's why I live alone. I'm afraid of what I might do. But you've been so kind, Alfred, I'm certain you've been sent to help me.

— I'm flattered, I said. And I'd like to help, but I can't always control my desires. What would happen if I were aroused without meaning to be?

— Well, that would be unfortunate, she said.

— You'd attack me?

— If you felt desire for me, yes.

I considered Clare's proposition because I wanted to help. But, like most people, I respond to sexual provocation in instinctive ways. I didn't want to die for it.

— I'm very sorry, I said. I should really be going now. Maybe I can help you some other time.

If Clare was disappointed, she didn't show it. She took my hand and smiled.

— I understand, she said. I wish it could be different.

I was so relieved to be leaving, I almost thought to stay.

Outside it was darker than I have ever known night to be. The moon — high, full, and pale — seemed to cast no light. I couldn't see my hand in front of me, even when I put it up to my face. Darkness like that is frightening on its own. But what terrified me was the presence of beings around me. I wasn't alone. I knew it. And the first growls I heard were hard proof of the danger. Luckily, I'd kept my hand on the door to Clare's cottage. I'm not sure I'd have found it in time, otherwise. I went back inside and closed the door so quickly I heard a strangled growl and the thump of a creature's body on the door.

As if I hadn't left at all, Clare said

— I'm going to bed now. If you're staying, you'll have to stay in the bedroom. I leave my front door open at night.

I protested. I mentioned that there were fierce creatures outside. But I was deluded about her kindness. She opened the front door as if she hadn't heard me. Not wishing to face whatever it was I'd just escaped, I went straight to the bedroom.

In contrast to the rest of the cottage, Clare's bedroom was large, neat, and frilly. The bed was a dark wood four-poster with red tulle draping, its two mattresses making it uncomfortably high. The floor was pinewood with scratches — like dry rivulets — everywhere. What I thought were two windows looked onto the full, sky-poised moon. These turned out to be paintings of windows.

I got under the covers fully clothed, keeping my shoes on in case I had to run from the cottage and letting my feet hang over the edge of the bed so my shoes wouldn't get tangled in the bedclothes. I was uncomfortable, but my discomfort, I think, distracted me from Clare's entrance. Which was good because Clare had undressed and was — for one attracted to women, their bodies, their smells — desirable. I looked away at once and closed my eyes as she climbed onto her side of the bed.

— I'm sorry, she said. I have to sleep like this. If I turn into a wolf, I'll ruin my nightclothes.

How to describe my desire? It was like rain over the lake on a summer day — the rain cloud in the distance, dimpling the face of the lake, moving toward land, changing the way the world smells, the way the air feels, the coming rain like a remembered taste, like a word on the tip of your tongue, but the rain will come and you want it to, feeling it before it makes landfall.

In the darkness, I could hear Clare's breathing turn to growls.

The inevitable happened. I was aroused by all my efforts to think of things that would *not* lead to arousal. The moment I was fully erect was the moment I felt Clare transform, the weight on the bed beside me now suddenly that of something with four legs — unmistakable, as when a dog jumps up on your bed and walks over to smell your breath.

The strange part of all this — apart from a woman turning into a wolf — is that I'm a sensitive man and I often lose my erection when I'm distracted. This has sometimes been a cause of shame. Once, for instance, I was making love to Anne when a car horn sounded so loudly the car seemed to be outside Anne's bedroom window. It startled me and I couldn't stop wondering who was in the car and I lost my erection entirely. You would think, then, that the presence of a growling wolf would stifle desire. But my arousal persisted, despite the smell of the wolf's breath, despite its angry snarls, despite the weight of it — its front legs — on my chest. Desire persisted because, having been reminded of Anne, I felt the kind of longing that pervades body, mind, and spirit.

The wolf stood on my chest for a while but then it jumped down from the bed and prowled the bedroom, back and forth, howling as if it had lost its mate. Sometime later it seemed to me that there were other wolves. I could feel their several selves pacing. But none of them attacked me. I assume this is because my longing had nothing to do with Clare. All my desire was for Anne. In my imagination I was with her and happy to face death in her arms.

But these are only assumptions. I'm not sure why I was spared. After what felt like days of night, I heard the morning

– Cheep!

of a bird, like a call to something, and I woke in the clearing in front of the field of *Oniaten* or, more accurately, in front of the place where there'd been countless *Oniaten grandiflora* but where, now, there was only grass, the *Oniaten* shrouded by mist or, maybe, eaten by wild animals.

I felt overwhelming gratitude. I'd been given another chance. I was alive – still alive, despite the wolves – and this feeling, this gratitude, was the first of my exhilarations.

Before me, there was the row of willows I'd passed on the way in, green branches unmoving. There were no pilgrims around. The clearing seemed to have been abandoned. The place was misty and so quiet that it felt wrong to move about. When I looked up, the sky was pale, as if clouds had wiped much of the colour away as they passed, leaving only the idea of blue.

How strange, I thought, that only hours before, wild beasts had chased me to Clare's cottage. It didn't seem possible that I'd almost been torn to shreds in what now felt like a sacred grove. As if the world agreed with me, when I looked back toward Clare's cottage, it was gone – shrouded by mist, my dangerous night erased.

As I passed the willows and left the clearing, I finally saw another being, someone in the distance. Between us was the well-kept road. Above us the blue of the sky had returned. The sunlight was brighter. The leaves of the trees were exactly the green of the grass. The morning had a limited palette – blue, yellow, green, brown – but this limitation corresponded to my own. My mind was as limited as the morning's. I could take in the physical world, but when, for instance, I was reminded of a poem by John Skennen, it came back to me in only vaguely meaningful form.

> When I was six, crick-side fields swayed on windless
> days, even. Johnson Grass, top heavy, bowing
> while white culms let birds go in panthuls, like grain,
> and moths sewed their pure up in pitches –
> the fields and I, summer-long we shared our secrets.
> When I was eighteen, grasses stood up after
> hard rain – stern and dark from bunches in the mud.
> Not like grass at all – defiant, unbending –
> as sheaves rose, wet and confused after the flood.
> I kept my own counsel, then. Fields did not matter.
> Now, I am sixty. I have nothing to hide.
> I've worn out the wishes sung in pitches
> and don't long for paradises to profane.
> I'm through at last with all kinds of knowing.
> The fields, close again, think of me less and less.

As I approached the path, I saw that the person I'd seen was a man and he was wiping the stones on the ground. I greeted him but he didn't even look up. He was intent on what he was doing, all of his labour given to the task he believed in. I remember being impressed by his devotion. More: I could feel the depth of his devotion, as if I myself were a believer keeping the path clean for others. Feeling this, there came such a flood of emotion that the rest of the way to Reverend Crosbie's was like a deepening revelation, the approach of something undeniable, something beyond interpretation. I finally felt, I think, the love that my father used to speak of, a love for creation itself, whether you believed in God or not. That is, as I walked into Feversham I felt increasing joy until I was overwhelmed, the love within me meeting the love I felt from the world around me. I was accounted for and taken in, taken in so completely that there was no longer any need for me to be a self. The boundary between Alfred Homer and the world was erased. There was no revelation or communion. There was, instead, a blissful fading away of my self as I walked.

And when this feeling had lasted for what seemed an eternity, I woke in Reverend Crosbie's guest room with the reverend herself in a chair beside me, her hand on my shoulder.

– You're back, she said. Are you hungry?

Hearing the word *hungry*, I was fully awake and I was Alfred Homer again, and I was famished.

– I'm not surprised, said Reverend Crosbie. You haven't eaten in three days.

Before this journey to Feversham, I'd have said I had no religious impulses. The religious was my father's domain. All my life, until he died, Pastor Homer tried to teach me about the things that meant most to him: God, Love, the sacredness of fidelity, the near insignificance of the human in the great scheme of things. I'd listened, of course, because my father was a kind man and I loved him. But I never felt as if his language ('gospels,' 'saints,' 'Jesus of Nazareth,' etc.) belonged to me.

After what happened in the clearing, I was still (mostly) irreligious. But I felt irreligious in a different way. Having experienced what I did, it seemed to me that religion – its language, biblical advice, sacred ritual, and so on – was insignificant to the universe. I now felt that the universe *is* and that one *is* and that sermons, prayers, and vows were all an outdated way of pointing to depths you could not reach. Whereas previously I'd accepted that what my father did was necessary, I was now unsure. Pastor Homer's church seemed to me like an abandoned train station, weeds growing up through the sunken platform, tiles from the station roof scattered about, a haven for rats and garter snakes.

Also: I wasn't sure that the vision I'd had and the dissolving I'd felt weren't purely personal things, the products of my own brain and chemistry. If that were the case, what was the point of bringing God into it? Better to treat it as a private matter. Better to try, like John Stephens had, to understand what I'd meant to tell myself. It couldn't be that the whole episode was random, could it? Yes, maybe. But even if the vision of a woman and wolves had been a spasm of the mind, there was still the oneness I'd felt, the dissolution. I'd never felt anything like it. I'd never felt anything so true. And, as I lay in Reverend Crosbie's guest room, I came to think that maybe, after all, I had had an inkling of the divine, an inkling of the thing my father had spent his life pointing to.

In light of my dumbfounding, I was glad Professor Bruno and I stayed in Feversham until the following day, the day after I was pulled from the clearing. We decided to stay because Reverend Crosbie wanted to know all the details of my experience. And, hearing about her interest, Professor Bruno decided that he, too, had questions for me. I'd gone through something similar to what John Skennen had gone through. Maybe there was some insight to be gained from my experience.

So, I became Professor Bruno's subject.

I found it difficult to talk about what I'd been through because I found it impossible to say when my hallucinations had begun. One minute I was a certain Alfred Homer and the next I was eating *Oniaten* with a lycanthrope. In fact, immediately following my return to consciousness, I had more questions for Reverend Crosbie and the professor than they had for me.

What, I wondered, had my experience looked like from the outside?

– Well, said Reverend Crosbie, you walked into the clearing with thirty pilgrims and you passed out.

– Yes, said Professor Bruno, you fell right into the apples, as the French say. You barely got past the willows.

— It wasn't just you, said Reverend Crosbie. A number of pilgrims fell where you did.

— How many? I asked.

— Two or three, said Reverend Crosbie.

— Four or five, said Professor Bruno.

The rest of the pilgrims walked on and prayed, leaving those who'd passed out where they were.

— You know, said Reverend Crosbie, I've been to the clearing most days I've been here. I've wished for what happened to you to happen to me. I've even wondered if there's something wrong with me. But in your case, Alfred, I'd say there's something *right* with you. God found you fit to commune with.

— But that depends, said Professor Bruno, on whether this vision has anything at all to do with this god of yours, dear lady. It's possible that young Alfie here was influenced by all the talk about Feversham. It's no surprise people are always having visions at Lourdes, because they're always talking about visions in Lourdes. It's auto-suggestion. Alfie had a vision, of course he did, but there's no need to turn him into a prophet, you know.

— Yes, said Reverend Crosbie, I agree. But the reason for a vision is less important than the vision itself, eh? And its consequences. Isaac Newton was as loopy as a crazy man, but we take his vision of a mechanistic universe seriously, don't we?

Professor Bruno looked at her as if seeing an old friend for the first time in a while. I could almost feel his admiration and surprise.

— Dear Reverend Crosbie, he said, we're in complete agreement.

If they were in complete agreement, that must have been the only time they were, at least while Professor Bruno and I were in Feversham. It wasn't a matter of discord or dislike. I'm sure the professor admired Reverend Crosbie as much as I did. She reminded us both of my father. But although Professor Bruno and Reverend Crosbie were people who loved ideas, they used them very differently. I feel a little guilty saying this, but I do think that ideas mattered more to Reverend Crosbie. She did

not want to mislead anyone, so she was careful with her arguments. For Professor Bruno, on the other hand, the whole business – ideas and arguments – was part of a game in which we
humans can't help being misled, because thought itself is mislead-
ing. Truth, for him, was like a miracle that happened despite us.
It's no surprise, then, that the only time one of them got angry, it
was Reverend Crosbie getting angry at the professor.

A further *un*-surprise: the point over which they argued most
was the meaning of my vision.

For Professor Bruno, it was all a psychological matter. As far
as he was concerned, the episode with Clare – the terror and
distress – was a way of punishing myself for my earthy desires.
But then, having proved myself faithful to a woman I love (Anne),
I allowed myself to experience an ecstasy greater than the physical
pleasure I might have had with Clare.

– I don't want to embarrass you, my boy, but this vision you
had is obviously psychosexual. Just think about the hand you
ate! You and this Clare woman sitting at a table – just you and
Clare – and what are you doing? You're eating a hand. You're
symbolically depriving yourselves of one of the means we all
have of giving ourselves sexual pleasure: manustupration.

Although Professor Bruno found the 'arena' of my visions
'obvious' – the arena being the psychosexual – he had kind
words to say about my use of symbols. Wolves, hands, salad,
shoes, painted moons. He found the whole array of symbols
wonderful. He was especially taken by the moons, which, he said,
likely pointed to a hidden, mysterious aspect of myself. The
professor wondered if the point of my vision wasn't to tell myself
that I was homosexual.

– But I don't think I am homosexual, I said.

– Really? he asked. Don't you think it's significant that you
denied yourself any desire for Clare, the woman, but then had
your most ecstatic moment after seeing a man wiping moisture
off the road?

To be polite, I told him that I saw his point. But my feelings on awakening in the clearing hadn't been sexual. And the sexual feelings I had experienced had been for Anne, with whom I had actually made love, in real life.

– Oh, he said, the real world has no place here. What you experienced wasn't real. It was symbolic.

– You mean I'm symbolically homosexual? I asked.

– I think all the signs point to it, he answered.

– But what does that mean? asked Reverend Crosbie.

– I think it means, said Professor Bruno, that on some deep level, Alfie here is ashamed of the desire he feels for women, and this entire episode may be his way of admitting to himself his longing for men.

Reverend Crosbie said

– Do you really think that's likely?

– I'm not sure, said Professor Bruno. Maybe I'm being too aggressively Freudian. It's part of my training. But you can't deny the element of shame in there. Then again, it could be more of a class-based shame, a Marxist vision. That was part of my training, too. I wrote my master's on Louis Althusser. So ... the way Alfie, in this vision, manages not to exploit Clare and the way he finds pleasure in being one with the collective. There are certainly Marxist avenues we could explore. But what's your take on this, my dear Reverend Crosbie?

Reverend Crosbie expressed sympathy for a Marxist inter-pretation. She wasn't Marxist herself, but she believed in absolute equality before the Lord. So, some version of the 'human collective' had always appealed to her, whether it was Marxist or Christian, Buddhist or Keynesian. But, as concerned my vision, she was hesitant to contradict Professor Bruno. She agreed that, of course, some degree of shame had played a part. But the detail that mattered to her most was the fact that, in my vision, I *hadn't* been attacked by the wolves.

– I think it's because I didn't desire Clare, I said.

— Yes, she answered, and that's an interesting point. But what if the reason they didn't attack you is that you were filled with desire, one of the purest feelings, and the wolves took you for one of their own? There are religions where wolves are sacred, you know. In Norse mythology, the wolf Fenrir is a god. And the Egyptians painted Anubis, god of the underworld, as a wolf ...

— Your bible doesn't much care for wolves, though, does it? Professor Bruno said.

— I know that, said Reverend Crosbie, but we're talking about symbols, aren't we? And wolves sometimes do represent God.

— They represent the devil, too, said the professor.

— Yes, said Reverend Crosbie. And the Devil is a fallen angel. In mythology, gods and devils are often taken for each other. It's an important distinction, but, as people say, it's a wise man who can tell God from Satan. To me it simply makes sense that once Alfred is accepted by the wolves — and even finds himself sleeping outdoors like a wolf — he experiences the oneness that erases the line between the human and the divine.

— But what about the hands, then? asked the professor. What do the hands mean?

— Well, said Reverend Crosbie, I don't think everything has to have a meaning, do you? It's important to know what has meaning and what doesn't. But hands are a symbol of God, you know. It could be that when Alfred was eating a hand, he was taking in a divine characteristic. Catholics eat the body of Christ, don't they?

Professor Bruno scratched his chin.

— I'm not sure there's ever respite from meaning, he said. All things tend to mean something.

— There must be respite from meaning, eventually, said Reverend Crosbie. I can't imagine an afterworld of calculus.

— My dear lady, said the professor, if you can imagine an afterworld at all, you're imagining pure calculus.

I hadn't been any more or less convinced by Reverend Crosbie's interpretation of my vision than I had been by Professor

Bruno's. I thought about it, though. I looked up at the sky through the guest room window. There was a sinuous column of smoke, like a pokey cobra ascending from a barbecue down the road.

— Reverend Crosbie, I said, do you think God is a civilizing influence or does God call us to wilderness?

Professor Bruno jumped in.

— Ah, he said, now there's a good question! God is an unimpeachable call to wilderness, Alfie. As soon as you hear the word *God*, you should think forest!

— I really don't think that's true, said Reverend Crosbie. When you're in the wilderness, a person might think about God, so as not to despair. I believe civilization is one of the gifts we get from the Lord.

— Well, there I think you're wrong, my dear Reverend Crosbie. Of all the ideas humans have come up with, civilization is one of frailest. All is illusion *except* wilderness!

— I don't think I'm wrong and it's rude of you to say so. You have no more idea than I do about God.

— My dear Reverend Crosbie, you've winged me! You've shot me down! I didn't mean to be rude! I shouldn't have said you were wrong but I couldn't help myself. Before there were civilizations, there was wilderness. When civilizations crumble, there'll be wilderness. If there's a God and if you're going to associate this God with something, it should be with the wild, not with civilization.

— But that's not the question! God is in the wild and the civilized. The question was whether God is a civilizing influence or a call to wilderness. At the very least, God gives humans a sense of order, a sense that we are not the centre of the universe. With order comes civilization. It may be a frail idea, but when you think of God, you don't think of going into the wild and killing things, do you?

— You said yourself, dear lady, that Fenrir was a god. When I think about Fenrir, I certainly think about going into the wild and killing things.

– Please don't call me 'dear lady,' said Reverend Crosbie. It's condescending. Fenrir is an aspect of God. Fenrir is a version of God the destroyer because God is also a destroyer.

– And because you're a Methodist, you reconcile these opposites with love, don't you?

– As a matter of fact, I do. Wilderness and civilization meet in God like lust and courtly love meet in desire.

– Well, there you have it! It's always love with you people, isn't it?

I thought for a moment that Reverend Crosbie was going to slap him. There was something inadmissible about his smirk. But, instead, she got up from her chair and said

– By 'you people' I assume you mean those of my faith as opposed to those of my gender. But yes, I'm afraid it's about God's love for us. And since I don't want to quarrel with you, I'll leave you and Alfred on your own. You should try to relax, Alfred. You've been through a lot.

Professor Bruno, finally aware that he'd been too familiar, apologized. But when the reverend had gone, he again made a case for my vision being of a sexual nature rather than a spiritual one. His arguments seemed to be the same as those he'd already made, so, as politely as I could, I tuned them out. I thought, instead, of how bittersweet it was that, in my vision, I should be saved by my feelings for a woman who no longer loved me. I had, in effect, saved myself by loving.

Yes, but that wasn't the whole story. Reverend Crosbie had been right to point out that the wolves may not have attacked me because they felt I was one of them. Despite my love for Anne and the purity of my longing – or, maybe, because of these things – I rarely admitted my part in the death of our relationship. I had ignored her needs, preferring my own concerns, preferring my drawings and botany, my rereadings of Wodehouse, my friendships at the lab. I had not been wronged. I was no innocent. I'd been as selfish as John Stephens in my evocations of love.

I, too, was self-interested, a kind of predator, however prissily I hid my claws from myself.

That night, in the Methodist guest room, I couldn't sleep. I went over my vision again and again, trying to understand what I'd seen and why I'd seen it.

Professor Bruno was in a bed on the other side of the room. His clothes were neatly folded on a wooden chair beside him. His snoring was constant but low and comforting. The night light at the foot of his bed was in the shape of a crucifix. It was a dim yellow glow.

My bed was beneath the window. Just above me as I lay down, there were curtains that I pulled aside to look up at the night sky. Far above me, Ursa Major, the great bear, had begun her nightly search for her cub while, just beyond her, her child was almost encircled by the sinuous curve of the dragon, Draco. I stared at the constellations for the longest while, until it suddenly struck me that they were beautiful, that each was a story in itself, that beauty is both order and story. I'd never thought of it that way, and I wondered if this is what Professor Bruno meant when he used the word *beauty*. More: it occurred to me, as Ursa Minor, the cub, came to life in my imagination and fled from the dragon, that there is beauty because God or the universe or my own psyche is merciful, that beauty is compensation for the oneness I remembered but could no longer feel.

Not much compensation, though.

Not enough.

I let the curtain go then, with the hope that, at the end of my days, I might feel the dissolution again. And I fell asleep thinking of a field of wheat – stems bowing, leaves rustling – that I'd run through, long ago, as a child, while my father delivered a sermon at a church in Alma, Ontario.

5

DAWN APPROACHES:
BARROW, TORONTO

We woke to the smell of fresh bread, its yeasty tang in the air. The professor and I had visited all the towns we'd meant to and then some. We'd interviewed the people we'd planned to interview and, on top of that, Professor Bruno had spoken to the man who'd been John Skennen. Given all this and my ongoing wonder about what I'd experienced, I was ready to go home. When, over breakfast, the professor and Reverend Crosbie spoke about my case, I listened but I kept out of it. I needed time to understand my situation for myself, and the best place to do that, I thought, was at home.

But as we were getting ready to go, the professor said

— I know it's out of the way, Alfie, and we really should be getting home, but I'd like to visit John in Barrow. He's here now, cleaning the way to the clearing. But he won't talk to anyone while he works. He'll be in Barrow by two in the afternoon. Reverend Crosbie says he really wants to speak to us. I'm hoping he's changed his mind about my manuscript. I might want to stay in Barrow tonight but I promise we can leave for home early tomorrow morning. Do you mind?

I minded, but I said

– No, Professor.

It would be an hour and a half to Barrow, and the drive itself would allow me time for reflection. Besides, I thought it might be good to speak to John Stephens, helpful to talk to someone who'd gone through what I had. So, after eating breakfast – soft-boiled eggs from chickens that ruled the reverend's yard, bread fresh from the oven, grapefruit marmalade made by the Benedictine monks from down the road, and back bacon from Mennonites two streets over – I packed the car: our car, brought back (by Michael) and left for us (with an open invitation to supper in Marsville taped to the dashboard) when I was in the 'sacred grove.' And we got ready for the drive to Barrow.

Before he got into the car, Professor Bruno thanked Reverend Crosbie for her hospitality and again apologized for his 'reckless debating style.' The reverend shook his hand, bid him safe travels, and closed the car door for him. But she held me back a moment.

– You're not religious, she said, but do you believe in God?

– I don't know what to believe about God, I answered.

– Well, despite what Professor Bruno said, I think you've had a religious experience, not a sexual one or a Marxist one. The kinds of people who have these experiences sometimes lead complicated lives afterwards, Alfred. I don't want to alarm you but things may be different for you from now on. I want you to know that you can come back to Feversham any time. You'd be welcomed by any of the congregations. I know it won't mean much to you, but, as far as I'm concerned, you've been blessed by our Lord and if you have it in your heart, please pray for me so I might one day know the Lord as you do.

She then kissed my right hand so earnestly, I was embarrassed.

– Thank you, I said. I'll be sure to come back if I need advice.

When I got into the car, Professor Bruno put his hand on my arm.

– Listen, Alfie, he said, I hope the reverend didn't try to sell you any more mumbo-jumbo. I don't like to bad-talk people, but, my goodness, these sinister ministers practically squitter their garbage at you. It's God this and God that, Love this and Love that. What a load of stinking socks! If I were you, I'd take this whole Feversham business for what it was: a brain fart that made you think of edible hands and sexy wolves. No need to give it a second thought.

I could see that he was worried about me, and that made me wonder if I was behaving strangely.

– I'm sure you're right, Professor. I'll put it out of my mind.

But I was constantly reminded of Feversham. The world itself seemed to be pointing at it. Not at the town but at the experience I'd had there. As I drove along Highway 4, the beauty of the land – my country as much as it was John Skennen's – overwhelmed me. Driving into Priceville was wonderful: a grey-tar, two-lane highway, a dip in the land so that we looked down onto a handful of houses encroaching on the wilds. To one side of the road, a row of firs, windbreak for a rough green field lying fallow, beyond the field a low-lying, plain brown farm house, beyond the farmhouse a forest of maples, oaks, and pines. To the other side of the road: a field of dried grasses – grey green, pale yellow – with a row of maples, perpendicular to the highway, stretching on for miles. Above us, the late-summer sky trafficked in clouds with, here and there, an opening for the infinite blue. The world smelled of gravel, dried-out grasses, pine, old wood, and various scents carried on the wind but gone too quickly to be identified.

I'd seen fields like these all my life and I'd driven past similar towns. Most had left little impression, only vague memories of gas stations and telephone poles. But now, as we drove to Barrow, the land folded itself into me. I experienced a milder version of the oneness I'd felt in Feversham — a ceasing-to-be — as we passed Orchardville, Minto, Gorrie, and Wroxeter.

— Are you feeling okay? Professor Bruno asked.

— Yes, I'm fine, I answered.

— Oh, he said. I wondered if you were thinking about Priceville. Wretched, awful place. They drove Black people from their homes so white people could take the land. For years, they even used a Black person's gravestone for home plate on a baseball diamond. Idiots. Fervent racists. Sometimes I wonder if there isn't some foul spirit that haunts the province. The land is beautiful, though.

It came to me then that those possessed by a spirit might not know who or what it was that possessed them, possession itself being so ecstatic. Was the spirit behind my own ecstasy sacred or malign? How was I to know? As Reverend Crosbie had said, it's a wise soul that knows God from Satan.

We stopped for coffee at the Tim Hortons in Seaforth. I'd have preferred the drive-through, but Professor Bruno wanted to drink his double-double in 'civilized fashion' — which was the first time in my life I'd heard Tims referred to as 'civilized.' It made me wonder what an alien species would make of our civilization if Tims were the only thing left of us.

— That's a fascinating question, said Professor Bruno. Do all the Tims survive or just one?

— Do you think it makes a difference, Professor?

— Of course it makes a difference, Alfie. If your alien species comes upon a single Timmy's in the middle of a wasteland, they won't know what to make of it or us. This lone Tim Hortons would be a mysterious artifact. But if all the Tims survived, like Canadian industrial cockroaches, they'd think we were insanely fond of plastic and bad coffee.

— But if that's how you feel, Professor, why did you want to stop at Tims?

— I'm Canadian, son. I *am* fond of bad coffee and plastic!

For some reason, I found this joke of the professor's moving. I thought of the places we'd been, of house burnings and Indigenous parades, of good intentions and savage politeness, of stories and dreams. Were these, too, what was meant by 'country'? It was easy to be at one with a world of autumnal trees and washed-out skies. It was something else to be one with a people's worst impulses, ideas, and behaviour. And yet, the Tim Hortons in Seaforth was where I first felt that when all is accepted, all is transcended. Though I said nothing about this feeling, I think something in me gave it away, as if I were covertly broadcasting transcendence.

An old man, his hands knobby and cramped with arthritis – so much so that he could barely hold his paper cup – looked over at our table. He looked over at me, his white eyebrows bushy, his face pink.

– Young man, he said, are you the healer?

– A healer? You mean a doctor?

– If I meant a doctor, I'd have said a doctor! I mean a healer. Someone that's got the touch.

– My young companion has no idea what you're talking about, said Professor Bruno. He's not from an age of healers.

At a table behind the old man, there were a number of the old man's contemporaries. They were casually dressed, the men wearing baseball caps, jeans, and T-shirts, the women in blouses, slacks, and comfortable shoes. One of them spoke up.

– Maury's right, she said. There *is* a healer in town.

– A Black one? said someone.

– You don't see too many Black healers, said someone else.

– Or men healers, said a woman.

– I hope you're not PC, said a man named Bill, but I just don't think Black people are sensitive enough.

– Now come on, Bill. You know it's hard to be poor and sensitive.

– I didn't say there's no reason. I just said they're not sensitive.

Professor Bruno, a man with no time for racism, was immediately annoyed.

— You're wrong about Black healers, he said. There are more of them than any other! Most of the Black people I know have healing powers, and Alfie here is no exception. It's too bad you spent your time insulting him, instead of asking for his help.

— Who insulted him? No one meant any harm.

— I didn't insult him, said Maury. I just want him to help with my arthritis.

— Well, I won't let him, said the professor. You hicks have shown him no respect, and, besides, why should he work without money?

— How much does he cost? Maury asked.

— A hundred dollars a session, said Professor Bruno.

— A hundred bucks? someone said. You got to be kidding!

Things escalated from there. At the mention of money, it seemed all the patrons came to our table or leaned in to hear clearly. Most thought I was a fraud, a quiet fraud, and weren't afraid to say so. Not to me, exactly, but loud enough so I could hear. Particularly interested were two barrel-chested men with long salt-and-pepper hair. They were, or had been, members of a local motorcycle club, and dressed the part: leather vests, blue jeans, black T-shirts, and, in one case, a blue-and-white bandana around his head. They were portly and I was sure I could outrun them, but I was almost certain Professor Bruno could not.

As for the professor: he was spooked. It wasn't like him to call anyone 'hick' and I don't know how he'd settled on a price. But Maury, the man who had first asked if I were a healer, agreed to pay me a hundred dollars.

— What are you going to pay *him* for? asked one of the beefy men. Give me the money and I'll touch your hands for you.

— Prob'ly get the same result, said the one in the bandana.

— Now listen, said Professor Bruno. This has gone far enough. Alfred August Homer does not go around touching everyone who's got a problem. You've got to make an appointment.

— Now that you named a price, said a woman, I think it's only fair you help him.

— That's right. Maury's got his money out. You can't turn him away.

Maury had, with some difficulty, extracted his wallet from a back pocket. He'd stood up, one hand using a tabletop for support, and then gently patted himself until he came to the square protuberance. His hands were so gnarled and his arthritis so obviously painful that the extraction was slow and it was followed by the equally slow pulling out of twenties from the black-leather billfold. Watching him try to maintain his dignity while doing this simple thing made me ashamed to take his money. But it would have been insulting to refuse it after all his effort.

— If it doesn't work, I said, I'll give you your money back.

— You better, said the man in the bandana.

Everybody else nodded, even Professor Bruno, who now chose to stay quiet. We were surrounded by a posse of excited or tense older people. The air was florid with perfumes and baked goods. And yet, despite it all, I was completely at ease: no shaking, no nerves, no fear.

Maury's hands were distressing to look at. They were pale. Each of the joints and the knuckles was so badly swollen it looked like his hands had suffered a disastrous pearling. Nor could he lay his hands out flat. They curled up as if they were perpetually clutching, while the hair between knuckles and joints was thick. Added to that, they shook uncontrolledly.

I had no idea what I was doing. I'd never seen a 'laying on of hands,' as Professor Bruno later called it. I took Maury's right hand between my own hands as if I were incubating it. Then, with his hand lying in the palm of mine, I made clockwise circles around his joints and knuckles with my thumb and index finger. I did the same with his left hand, but by the time I had his left hand in mine, the man was quietly crying, tears falling from his face while he sniffled.

When I was done, the swelling on both of his hands had gone down and he could make and unmake a fist with no pain.

Still in tears, he took my right hand, kissed it and held it to him, and croaked the words

— God bless you! God bless you!

over and over until I took my hand away.

— Well, that's extraordinary, said Professor Bruno.

After their initial enthusiasm, everyone else kept quiet. They moved away from me. Then, one of the men in ponytails spoke.

— What in the fuck did I just see? he said.

I imagine all of those in Tims were just as unnerved. And, finding the whole thing unbearably strange, I forcefully shepherded Professor Bruno out of the place while Maury talked about how like a sunny day it was not to feel pain.

We drove on across Southern Ontario — grey road, green or ungreening fields, woods bisected by grey roads — without much talk. For once, Professor Bruno seemed more confused by what had happened than I was. It looked as if he were desperately thinking Seaforth through. My own thoughts and feelings were too jumbled to share. I was both proud and horrified, doubtful and certain.

We were at Mitchell when Professor Bruno said

— What did you do to that man, Alfie?

— I think I cured his arthritis, I said.

— But you know that's unlikely, don't you? I've been thinking it over and I think it's more likely the power of suggestion. The man himself asked if you were a healer. He was desperate for one. And when I foolishly said you were a healer, he believed it wholeheartedly! He couldn't have believed it more. So, when you touched his hands — and let me just say that was a magnificent performance! as dramatic as if you'd really been a healer! — but when you touched his hands, Alfie, he did all the work. He cured himself. His brain manufactured its own analgesic and — voila! — he was cured. I feel for the poor man because by now he must be in terrible pain. Without the relief your presence gave him, he'll suffer like hell. But that's not your doing. Not your doing at all! Besides, you couldn't have been kinder. Your mother would be proud!

– I'm sure you're right, Professor. But I did feel a kind of current go between us.

– That just shows you were under your own spell, Alfie. And good for you! The more you believe a thing, the more others'll believe it. Now, who'd have thought young Alfred Homer, son of a pastor, would make a good confidence man? Not me! But I think you saved our skin back there. I don't know what those people would have done to us. Especially the two in ponytails. If that old man hadn't cured himself, we'd have been in real trouble.

I said nothing. I was still trying to work things out for myself. Despite my feeling that some kind of current had passed between Maury and me, I thought the professor's explanation was likely right. Maury had more or less cured himself. But the professor seemed to take my silence as a challenge to his idea. He sounded peeved when he said

– You don't really believe you can cure people, do you? Just like that?

– No, I said, I'm sure you're right.

After that, neither of us spoke until we got into Barrow, a while later. Our silence added to the strangeness of the day. I'd never seen – or is it heard? – Professor Bruno keep so deliberately quiet for so long. Under normal circumstances, I'd have prompted him for conversation. But the idea that I'd kept someone from pain – just the possibility of it – was overwhelming. I wanted to know for certain if what I'd done for Maury had been a fluke or if I'd been granted a new talent, some kind of enhanced sympathy – which is what it had felt like when I'd held Maury's hands in mine.

The little I knew about Barrow came from a novel I'd read called *Pastoral*. I don't remember much of the story. It was about women fighting over a man, and a priest struggling with himself.

I'd read it out of curiosity, mostly. It had been recommended to me for the way the author describes the countryside, the flora in particular. In fact, I'd enjoyed the book for that reason. And I thought of *Pastoral* when we drove into Barrow, because the first thing I noticed, just after the town sign, was a ditch overrun by thistles, a plant poignantly described in the novel – their bright purple tufts distracting from their thorns.

I've always thought thistles wonderful for the come-hither/go-away-ness of them, furiously flirting with bees while daring anything else to touch them. I've been stung by their thorns a dozen times in my life – mostly by accident, falling on them while playing in fields – but it never turned me against them. I've never found them anything but fascinating.

It was noon when I parked across the street from the main square, a village green with a statue, park benches, and a flower garden full of yellow tulips. Having time to kill before Mr. Stephens came home, we ate at Ari's Charred Grill, a diner that looked like diners everywhere: booths, tables at the back, a sit-down counter with swivelling stools. It also felt the way diners feel: homey, because the grill smelled of cooking hamburger, and homey because you could dress almost any way you liked and be welcome, but also strange, because you could never be sure how friendly the patrons actually were.

Ari's was run by a man whose name was – no surprise – Aristotle. He was short, dumpling-shaped, bald, and he seemed to dislike Professor Bruno on sight. But he seemed to like me, also on sight. He brought us a complimentary tomato soup with macaroni, suggested we try the pork souvlaki, and then asked if I happened to be a healer.

– Oh! You think Ari is genius! he said when he saw the look on my face.

It turned out, though, that his brother Dimos had been in Seaforth and had witnessed what I'd done at Tim's. Ari had guessed – a little wildly – that I was the 'Black healer,' but the fact that he'd rightly guessed pleased him no end.

– You have lots of money, he said, but you don't have to spend it here! You eat for free if you help with my dogs.

Whereas in previous towns, we'd been mistaken for other people, the professor and I, it now felt as if I'd been mistaken for myself. Professor Bruno came to my defence.

– He's not doing that healing thing now, he said. He's eating lunch.

– You I don't listen to, said Ari. You are manager.

He pretended to spit on the floor.

– Like vampire, he said. Only reason I let you stay is him. So, don't get nosy!

The diner was quiet. Anyone who wasn't already looking at us turned to get a look. Ari put up his hand.

– But you eat first, he said to me. First you eat!

I hadn't ordered much: a hamburger and a glass of water. The professor had, 'in a moment of nostalgia,' ordered a grilled cheese sandwich. But while he got what he'd asked for, I got a hamburger, pork souvlaki, orange juice, coffee, and a Greek salad – lettuce with feta crumbled on it, olive oil, olives, tomato slices. It would have been too much for me even at my hungriest, but I made an effort to finish all of it, believing as I do — as my parents taught me — that food is as much a privilege as it is a right.

When I'd eaten as much as I could, Ari himself cleared the dishes from our table and snapped his fingers. Almost immediately, his wife brought a box to our table. In the box were two small dogs that looked nearly dead, though one of them growled as if to prove me wrong. I suppose, at some point, they had both been beautiful animals: Italian Greyhounds.

— We had accidents, Ari said.

When he took the dogs out, I could see what he meant. One of them had been run over by a car. Its back legs were flattened. As he lifted it from the box, it cried out raised, its head slightly, too tired to do anything more, and lay on the tabletop, as still as if it meant to escape further detection. The other was in worse shape. No one knew what had happened — a fight of some sort, it seemed, and most likely with another dog. One of its ears was bitten almost off and it was still bleeding from the head. Ari put down a white towel before putting the dogs gently on the table.

Ari's wife said

— Patina's been in an accident and Pietra got into a fight. Please do something.

Now all the patrons were crowded around. I was even more intimidated than I'd been in Seaforth. Having taken the box off the table, Ari sat across from me and smiled. His wife sat beside him, Professor Bruno having been relegated to the sidelines. I could feel a collective desire for something.

— What do you want me to do? I asked.

— Make them better, said Ari's wife.

— I don't know if I can, I said.

— Oh, like my cousin says, he's modest. You touch dogs. See what happens.

Out of the blue. Those words came to me then, as I looked at the creatures before me. I felt a rush of sympathy for both of them. I also wondered if I *could* lessen their suffering, if I was capable of it. This was the moment to see what I could do, to see if Seaforth had been a lucky coincidence: me touching Maury's hands while Maury's belief in me eased his pain. If I helped these dogs, it would be proof that I'd changed in Feversham, changed in some fundamental way.

I started with Patina. Stroking her back with one hand, I touched the places where she'd been run over with the other. It was immediately as if a current passed through the back part of her body, the part that had been crushed. Her back legs kicked out. Then, no doubt as shocked as I was, she got up, bit me so that my hand bled, jumped down from the table, and, making her way among the legs of the spectators, ran out the back of the diner.

I barely noticed I'd been bitten. I concentrated on Pictra. I touched her head, stroked her neck, and – this was the uncanny moment – somehow healed her ear so that, if you didn't know it had been almost bitten through, you'd never have guessed it had been bitten at all. She got up in less of a state than Patina had. She licked my hand where I was bleeding, before Ari's wife took her and held her as if she were a child.

Everybody now looked at me. I looked at Professor Bruno.

– We've got to be going, said Professor Bruno. We've got an appointment.

A thin, older woman, alarmed and puzzled, said

– How did you do that?

But Ari, who'd been quietly watching, told her to be quiet.

– He has somewhere to go, he should go. But we wash hands first.

By which he meant that they would wash my hands. The woman asked again

– How did you do that?

Ari pushed her aside, not gently, and told her to shut her mouth. Evidently, he felt a similar dislike for her as he'd felt for the professor. He returned to our table with soap and warm water, clean towels and bandages. Nor would he let me clean my own hands. He took each one in turn, washed it, dried it. He dressed the one the dog had bitten with bandages. When this ritual was done, people began to talk, all of them all at once, it seemed. It was now that Professor Bruno proved his concern for me.

– That's enough! he said. My son's done everything you asked. Get out of the way and let us go!

I think it must have been his tone: loud, forceful, parental. It calmed people down. And when Ari looked as if he were going to interrupt, the professor said

– How dare you keep him here, sir! He's done enough for you. Get out of our way.

Taking me by the elbow, he moved me through the crowd. When we were at the door, Ari said

– What about grilled cheese?

– Your dogs paid for it, said Professor Bruno.

I have no idea what Ari's reaction was. I was amazed at what I'd done. A number of people followed us out of the diner, but the professor, who'd taken me by the arm, led me directly to the car, and, once I'd got behind the wheel, slammed the door after me. We drove off in the direction of John Stephens's home. But when we got there, the professor again put his hand on my arm – this time, to hold me back.

– All right, Alfred, he said. I want you to tell me what's going on. This isn't normal. What are you doing?

– I'm healing things, I said.

– I can see you're healing things, Alfie, but how? Those dogs were in horrible shape. How did you heal them?

I couldn't answer him, but that didn't stop the professor from trying to find an answer for himself.

– It's mass hypnosis, he said. It can't be anything else. Don't you think so, Alfie? Otherwise what we have is miracles and, to be honest, I don't believe in miracles.

– I don't know what you mean, Professor. Do you mean I *didn't* help those dogs?

– That's exactly what I mean! You've found a way to convince us all – even the dogs! – that you've healed them. But once the spell is broken, the dogs will discover that they're still horribly wounded and that'll be the end of that. Everything will go back to normal.

– But one of them ran out of the diner, I said. It couldn't have done that before.

– Such is the power of suggestion, said Professor Bruno. Our minds are our supplest instruments. Supplest and most powerful. Those dogs thought they were cured. So, they acted like it, at least for now. I bet you they'll be half-dead again before we leave town. That's the answer, Alfie. I'm sure of it! This was all suggestion! Very impressive, though. Very impressive.

Having reassured himself that the world was as he thought it, Professor Bruno stepped out of the car, leaving me to wonder what the extent of my capacities might be. I believed him – or wanted to believe him – when he said that the healing was done by suggestion. It was still strange that I'd suddenly learned how to convince a man his arthritis was cured, to convince dogs that they hadn't been run over or hadn't been bitten. But 'suggestion' was such a reasonable way around the unreasonable that it was difficult to dismiss. Then again, for Professor Bruno, almost everything had to do with mind, with thought. Even truth – which he didn't think humans could reach by argument – was a thing of the mind to him. So, of course, he'd reduce this healing to psychology. I wasn't ready to disbelieve him, but I wasn't convinced by his words.

We got to Mr. Stephens's house before two, but he was home already. He answered the door and invited us in.

– It's nice to see you again, Professor, he said as he shook Professor Bruno's hand.

He didn't shake my hand. He looked at my face and then hugged me. From that moment, it was clear we wouldn't be speaking of John Skennen. Mr. Stephens, too, had heard about the incident in Seaforth. Ari's wife, a friend of Mrs. Stephens, had called to tell her what had happened in Seaforth and at Ari's, and Mrs. Stephens had then told her own husband.

– It's amazing how quickly news travels through these small towns, said Professor Bruno.

– You're right about that, said Mr. Stephens. You can't fart in Bright's Grove without everyone for two counties knowing about it.

– I wonder, said the professor, if we could talk a little more about what Southern Ontario has meant for your work.

Mr. Stephens did not look away from me.

– I'd be happy to, he said. But could we do it later? I'd like to talk to Alfred for a little while. Do you mind?

– Not at all, said the professor. I'm most interested in what you two have to say.

– Yes, said Mr. Stephens, but for now I'd like a few minutes alone with Alfred. Just the two of us. I hope you understand. I feel like he and I have been through something similar, something I need to talk about with him. We'll talk about anything you like later, Professor.

– I understand perfectly, said Professor Bruno.

I'm not sure he did understand – nor could he hide his disappointment – but we left him in the living room, sitting on a couch whose side table held a bottle of Scotch, a pitcher of ice water, and a cup of coffee. Hanging on the wall behind the couch was a large framed painting of a black umbrella.

– That painting was commissioned by my father, Mr. Stephens said, in honour of *his* father, the inventor.

– It's marvellous, said Professor Bruno. A fitting tribute.

– Thank you, said Mr. Stephens. It's one of the few I like.

I wasn't sure what he meant by 'few,' until we went out to the coach house he'd built for himself. There, in what I first took to be a large garage, there were some twenty or thirty paintings of umbrellas. The walls were crowded with them and those that weren't hanging were stacked against a wall.

– My dad was a little OCD, said Mr. Stephens. He commissioned a painting of an umbrella every year from the time he inherited my granddad's wealth until he died. I think they're ugly, but I can't throw them away. My father cast no shadow in this life. You know what I mean? These are the only things I have of his.

The coach house was spacious. If it had been a garage, it could easily have accommodated three cars. There were windows in all four walls and stairs that led up to a loft. There were five bookcases filled with works of poetry.

– I don't write poetry anymore, said Mr. Stephens, but I still love to read it.

Against one wall, beneath the painting of a red umbrella, there was a wooden table on which a candle, a squat block of white, sat. Mr. Stephens used a match to light it, and the place soon smelled of vanilla. There were three more objects on the table: a square of writing paper, a square of white paper on which there was a grain of something, and a dead mouse. He asked me to sit in the chair facing the mouse and, though it made me uncomfortable to see the poor creature curled up as if sleeping, I sat down.

– I don't believe in miracles, said Mr. Stephens, but there are things I don't understand. And I want to tell you some of them, for your own protection.

The town of Feversham had been sacred ground for centuries. The Indigenous people who knew about it long before it was 'Feversham' left no written record. The clearing they'd made was rediscovered by settlers in the 1800s, but it didn't become an 'acknowledged secret' until sometime in 1957, when a man named Robert van den Bosch began carving a road to the clearing by himself. People thought him insane, but men and women have been coming to it since then.

– I'm sure Reverend Crosbie told you all you need to know about it, said Mr. Stephens. But there are things she doesn't know because she's never had a vision. The biggest thing she doesn't know is that there are two kinds of visionaries: some who receive visions and some who are given more. I know which kind you are already, but I'd like you to do me a favour. You see those three things in front of you? Touch them for me, would you? When you touch the paper, think of fire. When you touch the grain of sand, think of a beach. When you touch the mouse, do what you did in Seaforth. Once you've done that, I'll tell you my story.

I did what I was asked, but in reverse order. I put my hand on the mouse, and after a moment I could feel it moving. When I opened my hand, it climbed into my palm as if for protection, its heart beating so quickly it almost made my own heart race.

— I'll take that from you, said Mr. Stephens.

He cupped the little creature in his hands and let it loose in his yard.

— Go on, he said. Do the sand.

I put my hand over the grain of sand and waited. But nothing happened. I then put my hand on the piece of paper and, again, nothing happened.

— Isn't it strange? said Mr. Stephens. Look.

He put his hand over the grain of sand, then lifted it so I could see the sand had multiplied. There was now a clump of sand, its many grains indistinguishable from the first.

— I feel like I'm dreaming, I said.

— Don't we all, said Mr. Stephens.

— What about the piece of paper? I asked.

— Oh, he said, I can't do anything with that. The last man I saw set paper on fire lives in Toronto, like you. His name's Ray Stasiulis. Do you know him?

When I said I didn't, Mr. Stephens sat down on the other side of the table from me.

— It's not that I think you know everyone in Toronto, he said. It's that people with these gifts often find each other. I mean, without looking. I met Ray while I was dead drunk on the Danforth one night. I can't remember anything about the night, except I met Ray and that was *before* I went to Feversham. There must be some reason behind all this. There's got to be some reason I can do this and you can do that and some people can set things on fire. But if there is, I can't figure it out.

– It does seem like a miracle, I said.

– It does, I admit it. But to call it a miracle I'd have to believe in God and I don't. I believe the universe is beyond reason and I accept that. But if God were behind all this, I'd say God is less God than an agent of chaos. Like a randomizer. What else would you call these contraventions of the laws of physics?

– Are there many people who can do this? I asked.

– A handful, he said. But you're the first of your kind I've seen for twenty years. Most of the people who're changed are fire starters. Do you know, Alfred? That mouse was dead for two days. At least two days. I found it in one of our traps two days ago and I kept it because I'd heard you'd had a vision and I wondered if you'd been changed. And now that I see that you have been, I can't tell you this enough: keep this to yourself. I mean, from now on, keep it to yourself.

Mr. Stephens put his hand on the pile of sand and it grew.

– I suppose I should be grateful for this ability, he said. But I find it more complicated than anything else. I've had to hide my nature.

Much of what he'd told us at his daughter's house had been what you could call true. He had been devastated by the loss of Carson Michaels. And he'd spent a year or so in mourning, unconcerned with his mental or physical well-being. He had been rescued, if you could call it that, by a man named Kit who'd apparently snatched him from the clutches of evil. (On the night in question, he'd been drunk out of his mind. So, he couldn't vouch for the truth of the possessed pig, etc.) And, after venturing into the clearing in Feversham, he had hallucinated: a woman touching his shoulder, an offer to find his beloved, the prospect of abandoning poetry.

His life had changed after that vision in Feversham, yes, but not because of it, no.

Leaving Feversham, he'd decided to go to London, where his mother lived. Reverend Crosbie had driven him to Collingwood, given him bus fare, and made him a ham sandwich for the trip. It should have been a dull journey, five hours of country window-licking. But the man beside him – large, American, and diabetic – warned him that, because of his diabetes and the fact he'd left his food in his suitcase in the belly of the bus, he might begin to act irrationally. Not fifteen minutes after the warning, the man began to talk out loud about his aunt Patty and her big muff. The American seemed to find the word *muff* hilarious – his aunt was a guitarist in a Go-Go's cover band and the 'Big Muff π' was one of her effects pedals – but his hilarity seemed unnatural. Distress came through. It was like sitting beside someone who was losing his battle with sanity.

Mr. Stephens had been saving the ham sandwich for himself, but to refuse it to a diabetic would have been cruel. Reaching into the paper bag, Reverend Crosbie had given him, he found there were two sandwiches. Which was just as well because the man beside him snatched one of them and, hands shaking, bolted it down. His shaking stopped at once but he asked if he could have another sandwich. Not for right now but for somewhere between Barrie and Toronto when, he just knew, he'd be hungry again. Feeling sorry for the man, Stephens reached into the bag and found that, no, Reverend Crosbie had in fact left him *three* sandwiches. He gave one of these to his neighbour and, this time, counted the sandwiches left: one.

When, somewhere around Hamilton, he decided to eat, Stephens found he had two sandwiches left, the one he'd taken from the bag and one left in it. He took this second sandwich out and found there was another in the bag. He took out eleven sandwiches before he accepted that something was very strange.

– I've got to be honest, said Mr. Stephens, this thing frightened the hell out of me.

In other words, he was in the same state I'd been in at the Tims in Seaforth: convinced that there was something wrong with the universe or something wrong with him. For the hour it took him to reach London, he examined the paper sack Reverend Crosbie had given him, convinced there was some flaw in it that would explain what had happened. He didn't touch the sandwiches. He threw everything out at the bus depot in London.

– Do you know London? Mr. Stephens asked. It's the dullest city on earth, but it's home. I know my way around without having to think about it. Not that I was thinking when I got home. I was so hungry, I went to a Chinese food place across from the depot. A buffet with chicken balls and lemon sauce. That kind of thing. I'd filled my plate and sat down but there was no salt in the shaker. Almost no salt. I shook the shaker out in my palm, just to see how much there was. A few grains came out and then they multiplied and multiplied, and, in a few seconds, my palm was so full of salt that the grains were falling onto the table!

Mr. Stephens lost his appetite. The thing he felt wasn't joy or wonder. It was guilt, as if he'd committed a crime. Then, too, there was the torment of his search for logical explanations. As if reason would free him from guilt. He wondered if what he thought had happened – the multiplying of ham sandwiches and salt – had actually happened. Perhaps, he thought, he was still in Feversham hallucinating or, perhaps, on a hospital gurney somewhere, delusional.

Two days after the incident with the salt shaker, he was visited by a woman named Katerina Ranevsky-Bush. She was dressed in sackcloth so thick it made him itchy to see it. Nor did she seem to be wearing anything under it. But she had on expensive running shoes. Her dark hair was as clean and neat as if she'd recently had it permed and she had a black-metal lunch box, the kind construction workers carry. Mr. Stephens was not inclined to let her in, especially as he was still trying to understand what had happened to him.

She managed to put him at ease, though.

– I was in Feversham, she said. I spoke to Reverend Crosbie and she told me where you were. Do you mind if I come in? I might be able to help you.

And she did help him.

– She did almost the same thing for me that I've done for you, he said.

In her lunch box, she had a dead dove, a square of paper, an ashtray, and a grain of sand. His touch affected the sand, hers brought the dove to life. The paper persisted, unburnt in its ashtray. Naturally, he had questions. None of which she answered to his satisfaction because Katerina believed in both God and miracles and felt that the miraculous was as characteristic of life as were sunsets or hazel eyes. She was practical about it, too. It was her burden that she was a healer. She'd had to change her life to accommodate this ability, to accommodate God's will. He would have to do the same. To that end, he should avoid thinking of increase when touching things, unless he wanted to multiply them. The best way to do that was to learn how *not* to want. Whatever his spiritual beliefs, he'd have to live like a Buddhist.

Mr. Stephens said:

– Each of these gifts bring difficulties, Alfred. They all call for control and stealth. You don't want people to know about this thing you can do. You'll be tempted to use it to ease suffering. And so you should, when the moment and circumstances are right. I don't think you should deny your gift, Alfred. But just remember: as the story goes, people crucified the world's most famous healer.

– He brought people back from the dead, I said. Do you mean I can do that, too?

— Probably not, he answered. There are things I can't multiply. But think about it, Alfred. Do you really want to raise the dead? Katerina didn't want to tell me too much because she didn't want to interfere with God's will. Her God had given this gift to me. That's how she saw it, so whatever I was inclined to do was fine by her. But she did tell me a cautionary tale, and that's the thing I want to pass on, and you should think about it because someday you might want to pass it on, too.

Despite its placid exterior, Feversham is a hotbed of intrigue. Not simply because the different sects each feel they have a special claim to the clearing. But because the religious has a way of calling the irreligious to it. It isn't just that good and evil are related, of course. They're intertwined. Mr. Stephens thought of it this way: for every Reverend Crosbie who means to do good there is someone who means to do evil. Since 1957, when van den Bosch made a road to the clearing, there have been those who've sought to exploit it for their own good. And, really, it's almost difficult to blame the exploiters. Who wouldn't want to find someone to multiply food? Your catering service would be top of the block. And, then, fire starting. Throughout time, humans have had uses for fire.

— But your ability is the trickiest, Alfred. There are good people who'd exploit you, use you to help the suffering. And there are bad people who'd exploit you, to relieve their own suffering.

The worst case was of a healer named Geraint Jordan, who was kidnapped by a gang in Toronto. The man was a saint, devout before his vision in Feversham and tireless in helping others after it. The gang in question held him in their safe house, where he was expected to heal any gang members' injuries. Jordan was routinely beaten to keep him subservient. Naturally, this arrangement was a boon to the gang members. They became fearless, knowing their wounds, however severe, could be healed at a touch: no doctors, no hospitals, no official records. But their disdain for Jordan was almost pathological. They treated him like a pet with a useful talent, a pet they punished when it did not perform as quickly as they wanted. Finally, it occurred to one of the gang leaders that Jordan's hands were special, not Jordan. So, in a bold experiment, they cut off one of Jordan's hands to bring with them in their confrontation with a rival gang. This was, they thought, the way to a healing they could exploit as soon as they needed it. No surprise: this did not work out. Geraint Jordan died from blood loss, his left hand useless without the right, so that he could not even heal himself. And then, most of the gang members, used to a recklessness that came from knowing they would not die, were wiped out by their rivals.

– It's hard to imagine the callousness, said Mr. Stephens. The idea of taking a severed hand and rubbing it over your wounds in the hope it will heal you. Honestly, humans are strange. To make matters worse, Jordan was buried without his right hand, because – according to the rumours – the rival gang members kept it in a jar somewhere as a souvenir. So, you see ... I don't want to alarm you, Alfred, but you should be careful, from now on, about who you help and who knows you *can* help.

– You mean I should avoid helping people?

– No, Alfred, I think it's wrong *not* to do good when you can. But you've got to be stealthy with the irrational, stealthy the way artists and priests can be. You do the work so that the work eclipses you. When Geraint Jordan let everyone know what he could do, it became about him, even though he didn't mean it to. In the end, I think it's about learning where and how to do what you can.

Stephens himself taught himself to control his desires. He ate at deliberately specific times, training his body to crave food only at 6:52 a.m., 11:03 a.m., 2:36 p.m., and 7:49 p.m. Outside of those times, he allowed himself only water. He avoided restaurants and malls. And, after a while, he abandoned poetry or, rather, he gave up publication. He still wrote it. He had countless notebooks filled with poems. But he did not want to draw any attention to himself, even the meagre attention poetry gets. This was also why he'd had his family, friends, and colleagues tell stories about him: to throw anyone who might be interested off his trail.

– I had to learn not to want, said Mr. Stephens. You'll have to learn to avoid helplessly helping. You see what I mean? But until you learn that, try not to let people see what you can do. It could be dangerous.

– What about those who already know?

– Yes, well, there's nothing you can do about that. They can't un-know what they've seen. But if you're out of their lives for long enough and if you don't do anything to jog their memories, you should be okay in a few months. Tomorrow morning, why don't you leave early? Around five. That way no one's likely to see you go.

I thanked him then, for the wisdom in his and Ms. Ranevsky-Bush's stories. And I agreed it would be best if Professor Bruno and I left early the next morning.

– I wish you luck, he said. I was going to say it'll be a new world for you, but the world is always new. Something is always coming or going. When I was your age, I loved the idea that artists strive to make things new. But as I've grown, Alfred, the thing I want is for things to stay the same, at least till we've had time to see them for what they are. It's only with that kind of perspective that you can act for good in the world.

It occurred to me, as he spoke these last words, that there was something he hadn't mentioned, something we hadn't spoken about.

– If you don't mind my asking, I said, what happened to Carson Michaels? I mean, what happened to your love for her? Did you ever get over it?

Mr. Stephens looked at me then, and smiled.

– No, he said. I've never gotten over it. I'll love her till the day I die. But I don't need her with me anymore. I love my wife and my daughter. They're the most precious things to me on earth, but the feelings I had for Carson are within me and I keep them safe, if you know what I mean.

– You mean you don't feel pain when you think about her?

– The way you feel pain? No, I don't feel that kind of pain anymore. Carson made it clear that she wouldn't see me, and for years she wouldn't. But she'd loved me and when she was able to forgive me for what I'd done, we saw each other again. Ten years later. We'd changed. Her life had gone on without me and mine had gone on without her. It isn't that I got over anything. It's that there wasn't anything to get over anymore. I felt such grief when she left me. I could barely live with myself. But now I wonder if that grief wasn't the precious thing. It's because of that grieving – the trauma of it – that the Carson I love is part of who I've become. Do you know, I still think of her as she was when we first met. Sometimes I even feel the feelings I had for her. That's the thing about grief – it keeps its sources clean.

As he'd spoken about Carson, John Stephen had unwittingly multiplied the grains of sand before him. There was a small dune before him, four inches tall. He sighed as he rose from the table.

– It'll happen to you, too, Alfred. You'll see. Grief is a gift, if you survive it.

We returned to the living room, where Professor Bruno was slowly pacing the floor.

– Welcome back! said the professor. Welcome back! You must have had a fabulous confab, eh?

– I hope you weren't bored, said Mr. Stephens.

– Oh, there's no need to worry about that, sir. I'm never bored when I've got time to think. And I've been thinking about you two. What an extraordinary coincidence that you've both had visions. But I've been wondering if you noticed anything strange after your vision, John.

– Well, yes, said Mr. Stephens. I told you about it already, remember?

– No, no, said the professor. I mean, did you do strange things, like Alfie here? Did you make people better?

— No, Mr. Stephens answered. But I've spoken to others who thought they could. I wish I could say any of it was true. But in the cases I know, it was temporary delusion. Mind over matter for a while.

— Aha! said the professor. Just what I thought! I hope you told him about your delusion, Alfie!

— Yes, I did, I said. But I already thought you were right, Professor. I really did.

I could see, then, all the tension leave Professor Bruno's body. He embraced me.

— My dear boy, he said. I can't tell you how worried I was. Since your parents have gone, I've felt a responsibility for you. I asked you to come on this journey just to be sure you were all right. And I have to tell you ... for a moment there, I thought you'd lost it.

— He seems fine to me, said Mr. Stephens.

— It's a relief! said Professor Bruno. A great relief! We can turn our attention back to you and John Skennen, without guilt!

— I don't think there's anything else I can tell you, Mr. Stephens said. My friend, Father Penn, is coming for dinner tonight. We have a few hours before he gets here. Ask me anything you like.

But our journey's purpose — to learn about John Skennen — had been accomplished. The questions Professor Bruno asked Mr. Stephens were variants of those he'd asked him already, questions that served only to bolster the professor's ideas about John Skennen. After a while, it felt as if the professor's mind was wandering, and I felt guilty, thinking his worries about me were the distraction.

Finally, Mr. Stephens said:

— You know, Professor, I can honestly say that you know more about John Skennen than I do. You know his poems better, that's for sure.

It was at that moment that Professor Bruno accepted he'd got all that he wanted. I was happy for him, of course, but by then I was distracted, too. Mr. Stephens's story about Geraint Jordan had stuck in my imagination along with the thought that I might be able to raise people from the dead. The idea of raising the dead was repulsive, but the question of whether I could or couldn't do it was not.

The most surprising thing about Father Thomas Penn – for me, at least – was his Blackness. His skin was darker than mine. But Mr. Stephens had introduced him as the model for Father Christopher Pennant, a character in *Pastoral*. I did not remember Father Pennant being Black, a detail that would have stuck in my mind.

– I'm not surprised you're surprised, said Father Penn. The book wasn't faithful to reality.

– I don't know why it should have been, said Mr. Stephens. It was a novel.

– I know, said Father Penn. But there were things in it that were true to life, and that's what I find annoying. It's like the author couldn't choose between fantasy and reality.

– Now, there you're being unkind, said Professor Bruno. Whatever makes it into a book is fantasy, as far as I'm concerned. Or, at least, it has to be treated that way.

– I don't agree, said Father Penn. It makes no sense treating Isaac Newton's *Principia* as fantasy. Newton gets some things wrong, but it's a brilliant basis for thinking about the world and it's still useful as an example of how our predecessors thought. Anyway, Newton's not trying to muddy the waters. He believed what he wrote, and it's our job to understand what he's saying, why he's saying it, and why he believes it. With fiction though. Who knows what the writer believes? And it only makes it harder to know what the writer thinks when some parts of a novel are true and some parts false.

– Heavens! said Professor Bruno. You're the second religious type who's thrown Newton in my face lately. But, Father, no book is entirely true or entirely false. That's why I prefer fiction. It's open about being mixed. It encourages you to use your instincts and find your own way. So, let's say that anything that makes it into a book – any kind of book – is speculation. Some of it's useful. Some of it's entertaining. And some of it's too drab to be either.

– So, you don't care for truth? asked Father Penn.

– I do! I do! said Professor Bruno. But I'd prefer to call it the demonstrably useful.

– If that's the definition, said Mr. Stephens, then what we call lies are closer to what you call truth. They're more demonstrably useful than truth ever is.

– No, sir. You won't catch me out that way! said Professor Bruno. Lies are useful to a minority. Truth is indiscriminately useful!

– You know, said Mr. Stephens, these arguments always end at John Stuart Mill or Hitler. Useful in general or useful to one. It's tyranny either way.

The supper, made by Mr. Stephens, had been good: lamb, mint jelly, mashed potatoes, honeyed carrots, and string beans. Father Penn had brought dessert: a homemade, honey-vanilla ice cream. The meal was followed by Scotch. The Scotch was followed by more talk about literature, a subject I still knew nothing about, despite having spent the last few days listening to talk about it.

Mrs. Stephens – Darlene – taught English. She had as much to say about illusion and reality as the others. So, I was left to myself until she said

– What do you think, Alfred?

By that point I was so far out of the conversation that I admitted I wasn't listening.

– But I was wondering, I said, if Father Penn ever resolved his issues with God and Nature.

– My issues with God and Nature? said Father Penn. I don't have any issues with God and Nature.

— But in *Pastoral*, don't you struggle between God and Nature?

The three from Barrow — Mr. and Mrs. Stephens, Father Penn — were suddenly amused.

— You have to remember that the priest in that book is not me, said Father Penn. As far as I'm concerned, there's no contradiction between the word *God* and the word *Nature*. People forget that religion is a kind of language we use to express our sense of mystery. It's a way of giving coherence to thoughts and feelings that don't always cohere. It points to thoughts and feelings. You shouldn't take the word *God* literally. It doesn't refer to a grey-haired man sitting on a throne in the sky. It refers to metaphysical feelings we all have at one time or another about our place in the universe. Just like the word *Nature* refers to the thing scientists and philosophers endlessly try to describe. Nobody knows the why and wherefore of our universe, Alfred, but we have a variety of ways to talk about it. And these ways sometimes compete with each other.

— That's a lovely sentiment, said Professor Bruno, but people behave differently if they're interested in 'God' as opposed to 'Nature.' It's a very different thing if you say 'I don't believe in God' than if you say 'I don't believe in Nature.' People might kill you for one. They'd laugh at you for the other.

— That might be true, said Father Penn, but my point is that *I've* never been conflicted about these words. The author of the book described me as a nature-worshipping pagan because it suited his novel. Very little about me in that novel is true.

Teasing him, Mrs. Stephens said

— Now, now, Tom. Tell the truth.

— Darlene is referring to the fact, said Father Penn, that when the author knew me I *was* conflicted. But the conflict was between the love I felt for a woman and my duties as a priest.

— Was the woman named Elizabeth? I asked.

— That's exactly what her name is and everybody in town knew who it referred to, including her husband. So, that book caused me a great deal of embarrassment.

– I really must read this novel, said Professor Bruno.

– I was in love with a married woman, said Father Penn. There wasn't much to do but suffer. I can't think of *Pastoral* without remembering the feelings I had.

– I'm sorry for bringing it up, I said.

– You shouldn't be sorry, he answered. The pain's easier to bear, these days. But it's still strange to think that I and a woman I love are in a novel by someone from Ottawa. The least he could have done was give us a happy ending.

– But you've had a happy ending in real life, Tom, said Mr. Stephens. Everyone in Barrow loves you, even Liz's husband.

– My dear Father Penn, said Professor Bruno, how did you get over your feelings for the woman?

– I was helped by something I overheard, said Father Penn. I heard two people talking, and one of them happened to say something that felt like it was meant for me.

It was at a sheep shearing in Forest. Father Penn had been invited to bless the first shearing of the year – the flock vulnerable and confused, their fleeces in barrels. And he'd blessed the occasion, though the ceremony had felt frankly pagan, what with the maypole dances and the slaughter and barbecue of a young goat. It was while eating a plate of burnt goat and green mint jelly that he heard two men behind him speaking about meeting the loves of their lives. One of them had married his and, of course, considered himself lucky. His friend hadn't been so fortunate. He'd been in a long, close relationship with a woman. They decided to marry, and all was well until, at his own wedding reception, he met the love of his life.

– And there was no question about it?

– None whatsoever.

Both he and the woman – the friend of a bridesmaid – knew the moment they saw each other that it was more than a spark. They spoke for all of fifteen minutes and neither had any doubt. How his life might have turned out had he chosen to leave with his beloved, he would never know. Because, whatever his feelings, the woman he was marrying was his closest friend and, being the kind of man he was, there was no question he would cheat on her. He would be faithful to his wife until the day he died.

— Did he ever tell his wife he'd met the love of his life?

— Of course not.

— But didn't he suffer?

He told his friend:

— Yes, sometimes I do. But it is possible to do the right thing, you know. And I've never really regretted a moment. Why should I regret doing something that's allowed me to respect my wife and myself?

Hearing those words — 'it is possible to do the right thing' — Father Penn felt as if he'd been called back to himself, back to his vows. And at that moment in Forest, Ontario, after a shearing, he had chosen his vows over love.

— But what if Elizabeth's husband dies? said Professor Bruno. Could you choose your vows then?

— You mean if Robert died now? asked Father Penn. Liz and I are friends, but fidelity to my vows has become my anchor. I would choose my vows. That's the happy ending John was talking about.

I could see why Father Penn and Mr. Stephens had become close. They'd gone through something similar: love leading to a difficult moment. But Father Penn's decision and his reasoning resonated with me the way the unknown man's words had resonated with him. 'It is possible to do the right thing' struck me as immensely hopeful words. Hopeful not where my feelings of guilt and loss were concerned, but hopeful with respect to my new gift. In listening to Father Penn, I understood Skennen's words about stealth more clearly. The priest had chosen discretion and work. He'd eclipsed himself for the sake of others. And I wondered — not being an artist, not being a priest — how I might disappear behind the good, as opposed to behind my good intentions.

Professor Bruno and I left Barrow at five in the morning, as Mr. Stephens had suggested. I told the professor that I had business to do at home, business I'd suddenly remembered – something to do with banking. He didn't like to get up early, he said, because it was then that his joints – shoulders, elbows, knees – were at their worst. But he felt 'beholden' to me for accompanying him on his 'journey of discovery.' So, we both rose at four-thirty, dressed, ate breakfast with John Stephens, and were ready on the stroke of five.

Before we set out, Mr. Stephens thanked the professor for his interest in Skennen's poetry. But he asked that Professor Bruno respect his privacy. As far as he was concerned, John Skennen was no more and he didn't want to be troubled by readers or admirers or anyone. He considered himself retired and he would be upset if others came looking for him.

– But you wouldn't mind if I sent you a copy of my book on Skennen's work, would you? asked the professor. I think the book will please you.

– I'm sure it would if I read it, said Mr. Stephens, but it's about something I think of as over. After this, I won't be talking about John Skennen to anyone. But do send it to me, if you like. There might come a time when I can read it. You never know.

Turning to me, Mr. Stephens put a black-leather prayer book – supple, five by six inches, crimson-edged – in my hand.

– I hope I see you again, Alfred, he said. Use this when you need it. It's a *Book of Common Prayer*. I read from it every day to remind myself of my task.

I thanked him, and the professor and I drove off in darkness.

How different the return was to the setting out! All was dark, though in the east the first light of day showed the contours of the land: treetops, jagged cliffs, the roofs of faraway homes. We drove, first, past Lucan on our way to the 401, by which time

Professor Bruno was 'wide asleep,' as I think of it, snoring like nobody's business, while the occasional light in a farmhouse window winked at us as we passed. Save for the professor and the sound of the engine as I drove, the world was quiet, chastely dreaming of light.

And how different our journey had been to the one we'd planned. Professor Bruno had set out to confirm his ideas about John Skennen. And his doubts had been resolved, for the most part. I, on the other hand, had only wanted to help a close friend of my father's, to transcribe the professor's interviews, to learn a little about the land I've lived on all my life, and to look for *Oniaten grandiflora*. I was returning a changed man. It seemed to me as I drove that every atom of earth was miraculous, and every instant a parade of wonders. I was fascinated by questions that would have been inconceivable to me not eight days before.

Somewhere around the outskirts of Hamilton, dawn flooded the road. The landscape I knew so well, the dullest part of the ride home, was illuminated so that the Queensway – the highway itself, the industrial buildings, the glimpses of the lake's blue skirt – seemed new, as if no one before me had ever seen this stretch of road, though anyone who lived in Toronto would have seen it a thousand times at least. And, not for the first time, enchanted by a return, I wondered if home was home or only another part of the journey, and I remembered the words of the Romanian physicist Blavdak Vinomori: 'There is no home but in travel.'

Of course, this return really was a return to a new world. The lake – a constant in my imagination – was different, knowing that I might help the drowned or heal the sick. The boarded-up buildings made me think of the homeless and brought thoughts of duty to mind. Knowing that I could ease the suffering of others, I entered a city – my city – to which I had new obligations.

What saved me from messianic feelings – not that I had such feelings – was my sense of how difficult those obligations would be to fulfill, how difficult to know the difference between the just and the good, how difficult to act in such an uncertain and strange world.

In fact, my first experience of the difficulty came that very morning.

Professor Bruno had complained about his arthritis before we left Barrow, and I'd seen him wince as he sat down and got up from the Stephenses' table. When we arrived at his apartment near St. Clair and Bathurst, I thought about how I might help him without his knowing. I would have to touch his joints while he was still sleeping. But that meant I'd have to remove at least some of his clothing. This was not something I wanted to do while parked on Bathurst in what was now the full light of a busy day. Nor would I have wanted him to awaken while I was trying to undress him. It came to me, then, that the best way to go about it undetected would be to put my hand in his clothes, carefully, in such a way as to escape notice. I saw at once that his sleeves were too narrow to allow any kind of intrusion. He'd have awakened had I tried to insinuate my hand up his sleeve to touch his elbow. But his pant legs were wide enough and, if I could gently turn him so his legs were hanging out the car door, I'd have access to his knees.

Lying the professor down on the front seat and extracting his legs from the car was, surprisingly, easy. He didn't come close to waking – snored even louder, in fact – and I was pleased by the thought that I could, without further betraying my gift, ease the suffering his arthritis brought him. But while I was holding his shoe up so I could put my hand in his pant leg, an elderly woman stopped behind me.

– Is your friend all right? she asked.

– Yes, I whispered. Yes, he's fine. He's asleep.

– Then why are you holding his foot up like that?

There was nothing accusatory in her tone. She seemed kind but she was also, clearly, puzzled. Not knowing what to say, I said the only thing that came to mind.

– He's lost feeling in his legs, I said. Bad circulation.

– Oh, I know all about that, she said. You have to hold the leg higher.

Before I could thank her for her advice, she'd taken his leg from me and was holding it up so that it was at a forty-five-degree angle to his body. This was inadvertently helpful, because the professor's pant leg slid down and exposed his knee. I was even able to touch his knee with both hands, but it was then that I noticed he was awake and that he now looked as puzzled as the woman had before she'd taken his foot.

– Oh, you're awake, said the woman. Does that feel better?

– What are you doing? he asked.

For the *n*th time in eight days, Professor Bruno was bewildered. I thanked the woman and she walked away, pleased that she'd been able to help. When she'd gone, I explained what had happened. That is, I told the professor that the woman had tried to ease the inflammation in his joints. Strangely enough, he accepted this idea, but he wanted to know how she'd known about his inflammation in the first place.

– I told her about it, I said, when she asked why I was helping you out of the car.

– Ah, he said, you were helping me out. That was good of you, Alfie, but it was indiscreet of you, too.

He was curious as to why she'd wanted to start with his knee.

– We'd have had to undress you to get at your elbows, I answered.

– Well, there, at least, you're making sense, he said.

Though our travels had lasted only eight days, I began to miss his company as soon as I'd brought his suitcases up to his apartment. He must have guessed my mood. Before he closed the door, he hugged me, kissed the air in the vicinity of my cheeks and said

– You've been invaluable help, Alfie.

And I suddenly realized that Professor Bruno was one of the few witnesses – a partial witness – to my world's transformation. He'd gone through much of what I had. He was the only one with whom I could speak about John Stephens or Feversham. And these were things I wanted to talk about, even if I couldn't talk about certain things at all. Driving home, south on Bathurst, I felt a new loneliness.

Home again – key jiggling in the lock, apartment quiet – I was almost intimidated by solitude. I took my sketchbook and the prayer book Mr. Stephens had given me and walked down to the lake. I sat on a bench facing the water. How strange, I thought, that my ability to help others was partially to blame for my own bewilderment. As I was thinking this, I saw a stretch of Johnson grass growing through the pavement like a green scar. It immediately reminded me of John Stephens, a reminder I disliked, because I hated to think of the plant as representing anything but itself.

Still, it was then that I opened the prayer book and found Mr. Stephens's dedication to me. It was written in short sentences, as if it were a poem. But it was a simple reminder of my new state.

> *Let very few know what you can do.*
> *It's not safe.*
> *And remember always that silence abides.*

Well-meant words.

But, of course, I didn't yet know what I was capable of doing. If I was simply a healer – and one who could bring small animals back to life – I would live accordingly. If I could bring people back from the dead, I would have to deal with that, too. But what a complex moral equation! Though I accepted that it was, in principle, a bad idea to bring those who'd found peace back to this uncertain world, I would have to awaken someone dead to know what I could do, wouldn't I?

I looked out at the lake before me. The water nearest shore was greyish-green. In the mid-distance it was dark green, and far away it was dark blue. Above me a handful of clouds pretended they did not move, daring me to catch them at it as they made their way across the sky. Behind me was my city, Toronto, soothing for being a faithful presence, a boisterous Eurydice: cars passing on Lakeshore, people speaking, the occasional cries from the seagulls, the not-quite-autumn wind that was not quite cold.

I closed my eyes, the better to remember my parents' faces, the way they looked when they were young, just before they had me, which is the strongest visual impression I have of them, coming as it does from a photograph – taken before they were married – that hangs on a wall in my study.

– What a strange world you've left me, I said.

– Oh, Alfie, said my mother, you don't know the half of it.

– Marjory! said my father. No one knows anywhere near that much!

He was teasing her, as he always did when they were happy, and I was suddenly, deeply grateful for the love they'd had for each other. I wanted to tell them, but, of course, there was no need. Existing as they did within me, they knew everything I did.

When I opened my eyes, the daylight had dimmed and the water before me was an undulating grey, as a four-seat scull quietly passed, heading back to the Argonaut Boat Club at the end of the day.

Quincunx 5, Toronto–New York

A NOTE ON THE TEXT

Days by Moonlight is not a work of realism. It's not a work that uses the imagination to show the real, but one that uses the real to show the imagination. For instance, though most of the place names in the novel exist, the cities and towns they refer to are distortedly, exaggeratedly, or (even) perversely portrayed.

The novel was influenced by a handful of wonderful books about real or imagined travel, books read or remembered while writing:

> *Paradiso*, Dante Alighieri (1472)
> *Hypnerotomachia Poliphili*, Anonymous (1499)
> *Lazarillo de Tormes*, Anonymous (1554)
> *Bartram's Travels*, William Bartram (1791)
> *Don Quixote*, Miguel de Cervantes (1605, 1615)
> *Dead Souls*, Nikolai Gogol (1842) (Donald Rayfield, trans.)
> *The Golden Flower Pot*, E. T. A. Hoffman (1814)
> *The Unconsoled*, Kazuo Ishiguro (1995)
> *Voyage d'automne et d'hiver*, Gilbert Lascault (1979)
> *Manuscript Found in Saragossa*, Jan Potocki (1810)
> *Gulliver's Travels*, Jonathan Swift (1726)

But it was inspired by Pier Paolo Passolini's *Teorema* and *Ugetsu Monogatari*, a film by Kenji Mizoguchi.

John Skennen's poems were written by the author, except for 'Ticking Clocks,' which was written by Lea Crawford.

In Chapter 4, the dreamlike version of 'Johnson Grass' was created by Andy Patton.

The stanza quoted by John Skennen ('lovers by the score,' etc.) is from Dennis Lee's poem 'High Park, by Grenadier Pond.' The words 'a dense garden, a bed smooth as a wafer of sunlight' are from 'You Have the Lovers' by Leonard Cohen. The fragment of Arnaut Daniel's poem 'Lancan vei fuill'e flor e frug' was translated by the author.

All the poems of John Skennen were edited by Kim Maltman and Roo Borson. Kim also provided the repurposed graphs in Chapter Two.

Alfred Homer's drawings were by made by Linda Watson.